Pra

MW01193974

"Fans of romantic suspense, add Angela Carlisle to your must-read list!"

Lynn H Blackburn bestselling, award-winning author,
on *Secondary Target*

"A riveting debut novel guaranteed to intrigue you from page one to the very end. Fans of Lynette Eason will clamor for 'more, more, more' from this fabulous new suspense author. Make room on your shelves—this is a keeper!"

Jaime Jo Wright, bestselling and award-winning author, on *Secondary Target*

"Carlisle's debut is a fast-paced thrill ride that fans of Lynette Eason and Lynn H. Blackburn will devour. A real page-turner!"

Jessica R. Patch, award-winning author, on *Secondary Target*

"With a thrill a minute and myriad twists and turns, readers will devour this first novel in the Secrets of Kincaid series. Fans of Lynette Eason and Colleen Coble won't want to miss this enthralling debut."

Library Journal Starred Review on *Secondary Target*

SHADOWED
WITNESS

THE SECRETS OF KINCAID

SHADOWED WITNESS

ANGELA CARLISLE

BETHANYHOUSE

a division of Baker Publishing Group
Minneapolis, Minnesota

© 2025 by Angela Carlisle

Published by Bethany House Publishers
Minneapolis, Minnesota
BethanyHouse.com

Bethany House Publishers is a division of
Baker Publishing Group, Grand Rapids, Michigan

Printed in the United States of America

Library of Congress Cataloging-in-Publication Data
Name: Carlisle, Angela, author.
Title: Shadowed witness / Angela Carlisle.
Description: Minneapolis, Minnesota : Bethany House Publishers, a division
 of Baker Publishing Group, 2025. | Series: The Secrets of Kincaid
Identifiers: LCCN 2024052043 | ISBN 9780764242519 (paperback) | ISBN
 9780764244957 (casebound) | ISBN 9781493450725 (ebook)
Subjects: LCGFT: Christian fiction. | Detective and mystery fiction. |
 Novels.
Classification: LCC PS3603.A752574 S53 2025 | DDC 813/.6—dc23/eng/20241108
LC record available at https://lccn.loc.gov/2024052043

Scripture quotations are from The Holy Bible, English Standard Version® (ESV®), copyright © 2001 by Crossway, a publishing ministry of Good News Publishers. Used by permission. All rights reserved. ESV Text Edition: 2016

This book is a work of fiction. Names, characters, places, and incidents are the product of the author's imagination or are used fictitiously. Any resemblance to actual events, locales, or persons, living or dead, is coincidental.

Cover image by Nicole Matthews / Arcangel
Cover design by James Hall

Published in association with Books & Such Literary Management, BooksAndSuch.com.

Baker Publishing Group publications use paper produced from sustainable forestry practices and postconsumer waste whenever possible.

25 26 27 28 29 30 31   7 6 5 4 3 2 1

To Jonathan,
I promise I did not kill you off in book one—
but as they say, this is another story!
I love you and am so proud of you, little brother.

1

LIGHTS? CHECK.

Camera? Check.

Three bags and a purse? Check.

Allye Jessup looped all four sets of straps over her left shoulder and stepped out of her small second-story photography studio into a warm autumn evening. The sun had just set, but it was still light enough that the dusk-to-dawn light above the landing hadn't kicked on yet. That wouldn't last long, especially with the fog already beginning to move in.

Tightly gripping the rail, she started down the metal stairs. She didn't need another fall, and the way her equilibrium had been off lately, she wasn't taking any chances. When she was nearly at the bottom, a dull thud sounded from behind the building. Someone stifled a cry. Another thud.

What in the world?

Allye hurried down the last few stairs and toward the noise. She slowed before she reached the corner. Fished in her pocket for her phone. She groaned silently. Not there. No telling which bag she'd stuffed it into. Or if she'd left it in her studio. Wouldn't be the first time.

As she edged toward the back of the building, she heard a

louder ka-thump as if something heavy had fallen. The sounds changed to a muted, almost rhythmic thumping. She reached the corner and peered around.

Two men. One standing back in the shadows, watching.

The second man delivered another savage kick to something—no, someone—unmoving on the ground. The blow left the fallen man's head tilted at an unnatural angle. Allye sucked in a breath.

The attacker swung around, chest heaving. Looked her straight in the eyes.

No.

Allye pushed off the building and ran, bags flopping against her back and side. Pursuing footfalls pounded the gravel behind her. She didn't dare look back. She had to get out into the open. Had to—

A heavy weight plowed into her back. She screamed. Tried to catch herself as she went down in a tangle of bags. Pain shot through her knees and wrists, but she pushed herself up. Turned to fight.

Her attacker shoved her against the side of the building. The back of her head bounced against the wall.

She screamed again.

A rough hand closed around her throat, cutting off her cry and pinning her against the rough brick. Her hands flew to his, but his grip was like steel. Too tight for another scream. Just loose enough to allow her the slightest bit of oxygen.

"What do we have here?" He studied her, ignoring her struggles. He touched her hair, letting a curl wind around his finger, then slide off. His lips curved in a predatory grin. "Pretty little thing, aren't you?"

A new wave of fear skittered up her spine. She kicked, and the tip of her shoe connected solidly with his shin. He slapped her, then shifted his hold on her throat, lifting so her toes barely touched the ground. Rage glittered in his eyes.

And he started to squeeze.

She clawed at his fingers, his arm. He snatched both her hands in his free one with a grip that threatened to snap her wrists. Her vision darkened, punctuated by pinpricks of light. She tried to kick again, but he was too close and her strength was fading.

Someone shouted—the words garbled by the rushing in her ears. Hope flared.

Her attacker looked to the side, but the force of his grip didn't diminish.

Lungs feeling ready to burst, she jerked one last time against his hold. He didn't budge. The glimmer of hope faded.

Allye succumbed to the darkness.

"ALLYE. ALLYE!" A voice penetrated the smothering black hole of unconsciousness. Someone gripped her shoulders and gently shook her. "Are you okay?"

Allye groaned, and her throat rebelled against the sound. Pain. The attack. Panic flooded in.

She clawed her way to the light, ready to fight for her life. But rather than cooperating with her brain, her eyelids fluttered, and her body declined to move at all.

"Allye?" The voice came again, and this time she recognized it. Mayor Jennings. Not the attacker.

The edge of her panic eased. She concentrated her efforts on opening her eyes, and this time, they obeyed. Mayor Jennings leaned over her, his face a picture of concern.

"Oh, thank God, you're awake! Are you in pain?"

"Where . . . is he?" She forced the words out, her throat protesting every word.

Confusion etched new lines onto the mayor's forehead. "Who?"

"That man." Allye planted her elbows in the gravel and gathered her strength to rise. Her first attempt was pitiful, and she let her head fall back against the ground. Ouch. She waited a moment and tried again. She was partially successful, and Mayor Jennings assisted her into a full sitting position. She bit back another groan and straightened her glasses as she focused on regulating her breathing. Everything hurt. Especially her throat. She raised a shaky hand to her neck. "The man . . . choking me." She could hear the hoarseness in her voice, and every syllable scraped painfully across her damaged windpipe.

Mayor Jennings sat back on his heels. "There wasn't anyone else out here."

"A man came after me. Choked me because I saw—" The man on the ground. Could he still be alive?

She pushed to her feet. Dizziness washed over her, and her purse swung against her body. She clutched at the staircase railing. Instantly, she felt the mayor's strong hand cupping her elbow.

"Easy, Allye. You had a hard fall."

She shook her head, making the dizziness worse. She squeezed her eyes shut for a count of ten. "I didn't fall."

"You didn't?"

His gaze dropped to her knees, and she glanced down. Despite the harsh shadows cast by the light above the landing, she could make out the shredded mess of her leggings. She blinked and thought back.

"Well, I did fall when he was chasing me," she corrected.

"When who was chasing you?"

"The man." And she needed to see if the other person being beaten had survived—though she wasn't sure how he could have. She shook off the mayor's hold and stumbled toward the back of the building. He followed, hovering as if he expected her to collapse at any second.

"There was a man—men—back here," she explained. "One of them was beating another, and the one on the ground wasn't moving. I'm not sure he was even still alive." She rounded the corner and stopped short, nearly losing her balance. Mayor Jennings again reached out to steady her. No one was here now. No attacker. No victim.

She spun in a slow circle, even that motion increasing her dizziness. Had she confused the buildings? She crossed the space between structures and peered into the dimly lit area behind the newspaper office. Only an industrial-size dumpster and empty parking spaces met her gaze. That didn't match. Again she turned. What she'd seen had definitely been behind her building.

"I need to call 911. Maybe they'll be able to find trace evidence."

"Allye, you need to go home and rest." The mayor's voice was gentle, fatherly. "Or get a doctor to check you out. You fell down the steps."

"I don't need a doctor, and I didn't fall—"

"I heard your scream from my office." He took her arm and led her back the way they'd come. "I came outside immediately and found you at the bottom of the stairs. No one else was around."

"But—" They passed by the stairs, and her other bags lay as if she'd dropped them there. She slowed. "I need to get those."

"Let me get you to my car, then I'll collect them for you."

"My car's parked out front. I can drive."

"No." His tone brooked no debate. "You hit your head and passed out. I am not letting you on the road. It wouldn't be safe. Besides"—he winked at her—"your mother would never forgive me if something happened to you."

She tried to muster a smile, but the attempt fell flat. Mayor Jennings and her mom had been dating for the past three months, and Allye still hadn't quite gotten used to it. She had nothing against the man, who'd been Kincaid's mayor for well over a decade and a member of their church for much longer, or against her mom for exploring the possibility of finding love again. It was just new territory.

When they'd lost Allye's dad during what would have been his last active-duty tour in Afghanistan eighteen years ago, Julie Jessup had stepped into life as a single mom. In all these years, she'd shown little interest in dating—even after she abruptly entered the empty-nest stage when Allye's younger brother, Derryck, was killed in a car accident at fifteen. No, she'd just thrown herself more fully into her thriving realty career and spent her free time in volunteer work. Or hovering over her remaining two children as much as they let her.

As they reached the sidewalk, the mayor decisively steered them toward the parking lot on the other side of city hall—and away from her Jetta. Allye glanced over her shoulder. She didn't want to leave her car here and be stranded at home, but . . . the mayor was probably right about her driving. Regardless of how it came about, she *had* lost consciousness, and her brain still felt fuzzy. And truth be told, she didn't have the energy to argue any further.

She bit back a sigh and allowed him to lead her to his shiny black Mercedes. He insisted on helping her inside before heading back for her bags.

After hitting the locks, she slumped in the leather passenger seat and watched until he disappeared around the corner of the newspaper office. Could he be right? She replayed the moments before everything went dark. Though her memories weren't as crisp as normal—or what had been normal until the last couple of months—they were solid. Real.

She frowned. No matter what the mayor thought, she hadn't fallen down the steps. She'd seen someone getting attacked, and the attacker had chased her—choked her.

So where had everyone gone? And why was she still alive?

None of it made any sense.

But she knew what she'd seen. Felt. There was another victim out there, and the more she thought about it, the less she believed he'd be found alive. And if that was the case . . . she'd witnessed a murder tonight.

Her stomach flipped as the realization sank in. She needed to call the police, and the sooner the better. She dug in her purse for her phone but again failed to find it. She'd have to search her other bags once Mayor Jennings returned. Or just ask to borrow his phone.

When he rejoined her a moment later, she cleared her throat and grimaced at the pain. "I can't leave until I call the police. I'm almost positive that was a murder in progress, and at the very least, the man attempted to kill me." She saw the protest on Mayor Jennings's face, but before he could voice it, she plowed ahead. "I know you think I just fell, but what will it hurt to have them look?"

He sighed and rubbed the skin between his eyes. "How about this? I'll call the police and have them take a look around. But first let me take care of you. The last thing you need is to be stuck out here while we wait for an available officer to arrive and investigate."

"But they'll need my statement."

"If they find anything, yes. And they can follow up with you with any questions they have."

A wave of fatigue washed over her, making it hard to think. Would an extra ten or twenty minutes make a difference at this point? The men were gone, and she doubted they'd return anytime soon. And though she had no intention of admitting it, she needed to lie down. Holding herself upright was taking nearly all the energy she had left.

"Okay."

Satisfied with her one-word acquiescence, the mayor started the engine. "Am I taking you home or to the ER?"

"Home." The ER wouldn't do anything for bruises that she couldn't do just as well herself, and she had enough medical bills and doctor appointments as it was. She wasn't going to add one she didn't need.

They pulled onto the road, and the mayor aimed his car toward her house.

"Now, tell me what you think you saw, so I can give the police an accurate description."

Allye resisted the urge to correct his use of the word *think*. "I was coming down from my studio and heard what sounded like someone getting hit behind the building. I went to the corner and looked around and saw three men. One was on the ground like he'd fallen, and another was kicking him." She swallowed. "I think I made a noise because the attacker looked up and saw me. I tried to run, but . . ."

The mayor stopped at a light and turned to look at her. "And?"

"He pushed me down." She blinked. "Or I fell. I don't remember now. But when I got up, he grabbed me. Held me against the wall and started choking me. I blacked out. Then you were there."

The light changed, and the mayor returned his attention to the road. "You said you think you saw the attack behind the building. Right or left from the alley?"

"Right. And I *did* see it."

He didn't respond.

Tired as she was, Allye couldn't let the silence ride for long. "How did you find me?"

"I heard you scream and came looking."

"No, I mean how was I positioned? What did you see?"

His fingers tightened on the steering wheel. "When I came around the corner, I saw you face down at the base of the stairs. I turned you over and checked your pulse. Made sure you were breathing." He wiped his forehead. "You scared me, Allye."

His concern was comforting, but his statement didn't make sense. She'd been a couple of yards past the steps when the attacker caught up to her. He'd pinned her against the wall, choked her, and . . . what? She had no idea what had happened afterward, but much time couldn't have passed if the mayor had come looking for her when she screamed.

She realized she was holding her throat again. It still hurt, and her voice was becoming weaker the more she talked. Wasn't that proof of her being attacked?

"I didn't fall down the steps," she said quietly. "I passed out because he choked me."

"Allye"—the mayor sounded weary—"there wasn't anyone out there with you."

"Then why is my throat so sore?" Her raspy challenge was pitiful.

"You screamed pretty loud." He met her eyes for a brief second before returning his attention to the road. "And that purse you're carrying looks heavy. When you fell, it could have yanked against your neck."

She glanced down. She normally carried the bag slung over one shoulder, but the mayor was right. It hung cross-body. She couldn't remember doing that before leaving her studio. But with the brain fog she'd been fighting the last couple of months, that didn't mean much. She sighed and lapsed into silence, this time for the rest of the short drive to her duplex.

When they arrived, the mayor insisted on guiding her to the door. She reluctantly agreed, but only because she felt so awful. She unlocked her duplex and allowed him to set her bags just inside.

"Are you feeling up to staying by yourself? I could call your mother for you."

"No." Allye forced her aching body straighter. "I'm fine—just sore. Please don't tell my mom about tonight. I don't want her to worry."

The mayor frowned. "If your mom finds out you fell down the steps and I didn't let her know—"

"She won't." Allye forced a grin. "I'm sure not going to tell her, and if we were the only ones there . . ."

His expression didn't clear. "Okay." He took her hand. "But only if you promise me you'll go straight to bed and you'll be careful on those steps from now on."

"Deal." She hadn't fallen down the stairs, but she would continue to be careful when navigating them.

He patted her hand, then released it and headed for his car.

"And, Mayor Jennings?"

He turned back to her.

"Thank you."

He flashed the smile that had earned him nine-tenths of the vote last election cycle. "I'm always here when you need me."

Allye closed and locked her door, then limped to a nearby recliner. She hadn't lied to him exactly. But between the soreness and a renewed weight of fatigue, she didn't have it in her to make it to her bed tonight.

2

ANOTHER OVERDOSE.

The whole place reeked of cigarette smoke and weed, but neither of those had killed Ashley Harrison.

Detective Eric Thornton ignored the memories this scene called up. And the nausea. With gloved hands, he lifted a baggie from the home's scarred kitchen table. Remnants of a powdered substance coated the corners. He placed it in an evidence bag. The lab would verify what they were looking at. Meth, likely laced with fentanyl, if his suspicions were correct.

There'd been way too much of the stuff floating around Kincaid lately, judging by the uptick in ODs over the last couple of weeks. The medical examiner was still waiting for toxicology results on several of the victims, but the few finalized reports he'd sent Eric's way indicated fentanyl-laced methamphetamine was likely responsible for the deaths.

Where was it all coming from? Kincaid was a small town, a significant drive from any major cities or interstates. Weed was common enough—meth too, unfortunately. But fentanyl was relatively new to the area. And so much more dangerous.

Though it had been wreaking havoc on much of the country for years, Eric had held out hope that the synthetic opioid would skip over his hometown. So much for that.

He really should have known better. It had only been a matter of time until a greedy dealer succumbed to the lure of additional profit either through direct sales to willing customers or through cutting a more costly drug with the cheaper and more potent opioid—with or without the user's knowledge. But the consequences of using a drug with unknown or unexpected potency were often deadly.

Paramedics had been able to revive the last victim, but Ashley Harrison hadn't been so lucky. The thirty-four-year-old had been stone cold by the time someone claiming to be a concerned neighbor called in a wellness check.

He hated calls like this one. Too late to save the victim of an obvious overdose. Too little evidence to bring the dealers to justice—usually anyway. But he'd do his best.

Randi Owens, the patrol officer who'd found Ms. Harrison's body, leaned in the front door. "Medical examiner will be here in fifteen."

Good. The sooner the ME removed the body, the sooner Eric could finish evidence collection and get out of this place. Afterward, the family would have to be notified, if she had any.

Based on the contents of the small house, he'd guess she had a couple of kids, and he hurt for them. The neighbor who'd called in the well-check hadn't mentioned them, but it was possible the deceased shared custody with a father who lived elsewhere. He hoped that was the case—that her kids hadn't spent the night with their mom dead on the couch and just assumed she was passed out when they left to catch the school bus this morning. He couldn't make the call on time of death, but his guess was that she'd been gone for more than a few hours.

Something in another room crashed. He and Randi exchanged looks. They'd searched the house already and found no one. He slipped his gun from its holster and jerked his head toward the hallway. She nodded, her weapon already in hand too.

Eric led the way down the short hallway, breathing silently through his mouth to avoid the stench emanating from the bathroom. He quickly cleared it and the first bedroom while Randi covered him. They moved to the second and smaller of the bedrooms. A wooden chair now lay toppled under an open window where rain was beginning to blow inside. Something or someone had knocked the chair over. Considering they'd seen no sign of a pet and the window had barely been open an inch when they checked this room earlier, he'd put his money on a someone.

His eyes trailed to the closet door. Shut. It had been open before. He nodded at it. Randi's eyes hardened. Eric crept toward the closet, keeping himself positioned so that if someone was hiding inside, they wouldn't have a direct shot at him.

He leveled his gun and threw open the door.

"Police!"

A small boy—five, maybe six years old—crouched inside.

Eric caught his breath and quickly holstered his gun.

The kid had snot crusted below his nose, and his clothes smelled like they hadn't been washed in a while.

He crouched down to get on eye level with the boy. "Hey, I'm Eric. What's your name?"

The kid just stared at him.

"You hungry?"

He didn't respond for a moment, then gave an abrupt nod. Of course he was hungry. Eric knew what hunger looked like. Felt like.

"You like nuggets?"

Another nod.

"Okay." He slipped a mini chocolate bar from his pocket and handed it to the boy. The distrust in the kid's eyes didn't waver, but the tightness around his mouth eased.

And Eric recognized him. From church. The realization sucked the air from his lungs.

"Lucky?"

Lucky—Eric couldn't remember his real name—blinked and inclined his head.

"Where's Dion?"

At the mention of his brother's name, Lucky's defenses flew up. He pushed the candy bar back at Eric.

Eric raised his hands in a placating gesture. "No, you keep it. Dion's not in trouble. I just want to make sure he's okay." They stared at each other a moment before he decided to try again. "Is your brother okay?"

Lucky looked down at the candy bar and shrugged.

Eric traded glances with Randi. The officer nodded and joined them on the floor—crouching like Eric, rather than sitting, to avoid unnecessary scene contamination and whatever else was on this floor. She'd stay with Lucky and keep him away from his mother's body while Eric made the necessary calls.

While Randi pulled out her phone and started rambling about a litter of puppies in her brother's barn, Eric stood, barely resisting the urge to clap Lucky on the shoulder. The boy needed support, but he radiated defensiveness. An almost-stranger's touch wouldn't be welcome.

He backtracked through the house, refusing to look in the direction of Ms. Harrison's body as he passed through the living room. How could a mother care so little about her kid? Kids. Dion was out there somewhere too.

God, let him be okay.

He stepped outside, stripping off his gloves. Once in the fresh air, he dialed the station. "Darla, can you get somebody over here with a kid's meal?" He turned and stared at the chipped paint on the door. Rain dripped down his neck, but he ignored it. "Nuggets with extra fries. Boy's toy if there's an option. And we'll need a social worker."

Thirty minutes later, Eric watched the CPS caseworker's car pull away with Lucky. He shot up a prayer that he'd be placed with a good home—or, better yet, with a responsible family member.

Maybe he'd be able to reclaim some of his childhood before it was too late.

But Eric knew the boy would always bear a scar from losing his mom so early. And who knew what else he'd experienced before her death? Neglect? Probably. Deprivation? Almost certainly. Though neither of those were true in every case involving a parent with an addiction, it happened far too often. Eric knew that from personal experience. And the hunger he'd seen in Lucky's eyes had been more than one missed breakfast would account for.

Once the car disappeared from view, he pulled in a fortifying breath and headed back to the scene that would likely haunt him for days. But he'd gladly accept that for a chance to shut down even a tiny branch of this deadly industry. Illicit drugs had ruined far too many lives.

3

A COUPLE OF HOURS LATER, Eric logged the evidence he'd collected from Ashley Harrison's house and headed for his desk. Tucked into a corner of the Kincaid police station, his "office" space was small, but it served its purpose, and he was grateful to have it.

Somehow, Kincaid had found room in its budget to open a detective position earlier this year, and he'd managed to secure it. He'd needed the change after losing his mentor last fall. Maybe being able to focus on investigations would allow him to do more good than he'd been able to as a patrol officer. Especially on the drug front.

So many lives were being ruined. So many lost. He couldn't get Ashley Harrison's face out of his head. She'd been only a handful of years older than his twenty-nine, but she could have passed for fifty. And now she'd never reach that milestone. Drugs had cut her life short and left her boys without a mother.

He sank into his semi-comfortable chair and scrolled through his contacts until he found Dion's info. He had mentored Lucky's brother before Dion dropped out of youth group. They'd continued to text occasionally for about a year, but the teen had quit responding to his messages months ago. He could have simply gotten a new number. Maybe. But Eric suspected Dion's current group of friends wasn't the type to appreciate a cop's company. Still, he needed to try.

He clicked on Dion's number and lifted the phone to his ear. The call rang. And rang. Voice mail kicked in, but it was a generic recording. He left a message anyway, just in case. Once he ended the call, he dropped his head into his hands.

Eric had tried to locate him at school before heading to the station. Administration had informed him that Dion hadn't shown up today. Where would he be? At a friend's house?

The kid would have to return home at some point. But he'd be coming back to a missing mom and brother and a home recently processed as a crime scene. Eric would really like to intercept him before that point.

He scrubbed his forehead. Dion was only fourteen. Dad hadn't ever been in the picture as far as Eric knew, although Dion carried his last name—which was why Eric hadn't connected him with Ashley until he'd seen Lucky. Lucky's father, on the other hand, was in prison, and Eric was pretty sure his parental rights had been terminated years ago. And now with their mom gone . . .

If those boys didn't have family willing to take them in, there wasn't much chance the system would keep them together—not with such an age range between them. And teen boys like Dion were hard to place with foster families.

Could Eric take them?

As quickly as the thought came, he rejected it. He would absolutely love to provide a home for those boys, but the practicalities of his situation were far from ideal.

Though he had the necessary certification to foster—he'd completed the state-required training before his promotion to detective—his schedule was far too sporadic now. Perhaps he would have been able to make it work when he was on patrol, but his current position often ran him into overtime. Even off duty, he was still usually on call. There was no way he could be present enough to supply either the supervision or care the boys would need.

That was one of the few true downsides to his job. It wouldn't be such a barrier if he were married—or even if he had a family member nearby willing to offer respite care when he was called in to work a case. But he didn't have anyone.

He wanted so badly to be the home and security some kid needed—that *these* kids needed. But he had no clue how to make things work right now.

"Thornton, got something to run by you." Officer Stephen Moore approached his desk.

Eric pushed his phone aside. "Shoot."

"I got an odd call from Mayor Jennings at the beginning of my shift last night." He paused, but when Eric didn't respond, he continued. "He wanted to report a crime that he didn't believe happened."

Okay, that *was* odd. Eric leaned his chair back and crossed his arms.

"Allye Jessup told him she witnessed a beating."

An image of the spunky redhead popped into his mind.

"Why didn't she report it?"

"That's the thing. The mayor said she had fallen down her studio steps, and he found her unconscious. He's next to positive the beating never happened, but she was adamant that we check things out. He only convinced her to go home and rest by promising to call it in."

Eric almost winced. He knew exactly where Allye's studio was and how steep her stairs were. That had to have been a nasty fall. "She okay?"

"Far as I know."

"You check out her story?"

Moore spread his hands dramatically. "Of course. But there was no evidence anything had gone on, and the gravel at the bottom of her stairs was disturbed like someone had fallen there."

"Sounds like that's what happened, then."

"That was my conclusion."

"But?"

Moore swiped the back of his hand across his forehead. "She wants an update. She left a message with Darla a couple of hours ago, but I just had time to return her call. When I told her there wasn't anything to update her on, she got upset. She's on the way here now, and I'm supposed to be off"—he glanced at his watch—"in five minutes. I pulled a double to cover Kevin, and I'm bushed. I thought maybe since you two are friends . . ."

He sighed and waved Moore off. "Sure. Tell Darla to send her my way when she gets here."

"Thanks." The officer headed for the receptionist. "I owe you one."

Eric let his chair snap forward. Dealing with an agitated Allye Jessup would be fun, to use the term loosely. When that woman got something in her head, she was all in. Better get started on his notes while he had the chance.

Notes. "Hey, Moore!"

The officer turned back toward him.

"Shoot me a copy of your report before you go."

"Will do. Not much there, but I'll send it."

He nodded his thanks. Delusion or not, he preferred to be in the know before speaking to a potential witness.

As he reached for his laptop, his still-silent phone caught his eye. It had only been a few minutes since he'd left the voice mail, but he grabbed it anyway and tapped out a text.

Dion, I really need to talk to you. It's important.

Message sent, he powered on his laptop and began entering his handwritten notes into the system, adding to them as necessary. Taking his notes on a tablet or laptop in the first place would save time, but he'd found he processed better on paper, and sometimes things jumped out at him during the transcription process. It was worth the extra few minutes.

When Moore's report came through, he paused to read it. Not much there, and like Moore had said, nothing but Allye's word indicated that anything had actually happened.

Satisfied that he knew as much as he could, he returned to his own notes. Barely five minutes passed before the tap of fashion boots against tile announced Allye's arrival. He saved his progress and navigated back to Moore's email before rising to greet her.

"I hear you had a rough night."

"No kidding." Her voice was scratchy.

He pulled a chair from a nearby desk and offered it to her. "Officer Moore gave me a brief rundown of the situation. Why don't you tell me what happened?"

As Allye launched into her story, he grabbed a pen. But instead of taking notes, he studied the woman in front of him. Though naturally fair-skinned, Allye was more pale than usual, and she looked tired—no, weary. But her pupils appeared normal, and her voice was steady as she related what she believed happened the night before. Everything seemed to match the report. No inconsistencies.

". . . but he chased me."

Eric straightened. Neither Moore nor his notes had mentioned that part. He flipped to a blank page in his notebook. When she mentioned that she'd been choked, his pen stilled. He lifted his gaze to her neck, which was obscured by a bright, oversized scarf.

"Then I blacked out." Her voice cracked. "When I woke up, I was at the foot of the steps to my studio. Mayor Jennings was there, and everyone else was gone."

Eric clicked his pen as he digested the new information. Despite the mayor and Moore's opinion that Allye had imagined everything, her account was concerning. And it made him mad that someone might have put his hands on her.

He looked again at her scarf. "Do you mind showing me your neck?"

She grimaced but unwound the material. Ugly bruising consistent with attempted strangulation had formed on her fair skin.

The angry knot in his gut grew. Regardless of whether there'd been another victim, something had happened to her last night.

4

ALLYE PULLED DOWN HER VISOR to block the afternoon sunshine and tried to ignore the angry pulsing of yet another migraine on the short drive from the police station. She'd taken more meds before hitching a ride with a neighbor to retrieve her car from the studio, but the prescription didn't seem to do much anymore. Something else she'd need to follow up with her doctor on. She glanced in her rearview mirror to confirm Eric was still behind her. A flash of pain reprimanded her for the unnecessary eye movement. This was getting old.

Before agreeing to take another look at the crime scene, Eric had taken photos of her neck. She really should have thought to do that last night. Having them documented right away might have even been worth the ER trip she'd refused. But she hadn't thought of that. She sighed.

Eric had also taken the time to ask about the men—whether she'd seen them before and if she could identify them. She'd only gotten a good look at the one who'd come after her. He was a complete stranger to her. The man was muscular, but not in an attention-grabbing way. Average height. Average weight. Her impression was that he was tanned and had short dark hair. But the lighting had been horrible, the encounter short, and the terror . . .

She wasn't naïve enough to think that her memory couldn't be slightly skewed. But she would know him if she saw him again. She was sure of that.

But she was the only one who would. Her description hadn't been helpful. Eric's expression had remained impassive. They both knew those qualities could apply to any number of men. Maybe if she'd seen a tattoo or a scar. No such luck.

But his eyes. She shuddered. Felt her throat constrict. The look in those dark pools had haunted last night's dreams. He'd fully intended to kill her. Why hadn't he?

Hand shaking, she flipped her turn signal and pulled into a street-side parking spot in front of the building that housed her studio. A bump signaled she'd hit the curb again. She couldn't bring herself to care.

She exited the car and joined Eric on the sidewalk. "This way." She led him around the back of her building. "They were right about here."

"You're sure?"

"I am." Her heart sank. He didn't believe her either. She tried not to show her disappointment. "There were three of them. The attacker and victim were here, and the other one was leaning against the wall there." She pointed to the area a few feet away. "I didn't imagine it."

"Didn't say you did. But according to Moore's notes, Mayor Jennings reported that you said the attack occurred over there." He thumbed over his shoulder, indicating the back parking lot of the office building next door.

"No, I walked over there to double-check, but they were definitely over here."

He pulled something up on his phone. "It says that you told Jennings it happened behind the building to the right of the alley." He looked up at her.

She tried to remember exactly what she'd told the mayor, but that part of last night's events was blurry. Her headache wasn't helping. "I don't remember what I told him, but . . . I sometimes get my rights and lefts mixed up. I could have said the wrong direction." She could feel the heat rising in her cheeks at the admission.

Eric sighed and slipped his phone back into his pocket. "In that case, I can recheck for evidence, but there's a good chance this morning's rain washed things away already. I'll need you out of the area. Waiting in your car would be best."

Her shoulders drooped, and the pain in her head intensified. "I'm sorry. I should have just reported everything myself last night. If I'd been here, I could have cleared up the confusion."

Eric's expression didn't change before she turned away, but when she glanced over her shoulder, he was already examining the area. She retreated to her car and locked herself inside—something she wouldn't normally bother to do in Kincaid. But even in daylight and with Eric nearby, returning to the scene of last night's incident was giving her the creeps.

She angled to peer over her shoulder. Fire shot from her neck to her elbow, and she quickly returned to her previous position. Her muscles pulsed a reproach at her attempt to see down the alley. A fruitless attempt, considering she had pulled her car too far forward anyway. She leaned her head back and tried to ignore the pain.

Think of something else.

Last night. Evidence. Eric.

Although she couldn't see him, she had every confidence he'd be thorough. If there was evidence to find, he'd be the one to find it. Moore was a decent cop and meant well, but he had a tendency to jump to conclusions, especially if they provided an easy answer. Eric wasn't like that. She could trust him.

Some of her anxiety ebbed, and despite her pounding head and complaining muscles, she found herself relaxing into her seat.

OTHER THAN AT THE FOOT OF ALLYE'S STEPS, the gravel in the relevant areas behind the building and in the alley was smooth. A little too smooth. Almost as if someone had attempted to hide anything pointing to their presence. But he'd combed the area where she claimed the victim had been lying, had even turned over some of the gravel to check for bloodstains or vomit. Nothing.

He'd found a curly red hair caught in a crevice of the rough brick. Not conclusive evidence that Allye had been shoved against the wall, but it supported her story. Of course, she could have merely brushed against the wall on her way to the parking lot at some point. He bagged it anyway.

He stepped back and surveyed the area. He hated to tell Allye that there was practically no evidence to back up her claims, but he wasn't going to lie to her either.

He rubbed his forehead. This hadn't been handled well at any point. She should have made the report herself. When she didn't, Moore should have followed up with her last night. The man knew better, but considering the mayor's report, Eric could also see why he hadn't bothered. Nothing he could do about it now.

The memory of Allye's bruised neck and hoarse voice filled his mind, and he tightened his grip on his pen. *Something* had happened to her.

But her story didn't make sense. The beating she claimed to have witnessed sounded like the murder she suspected. But they had no body. Questions flew into his mind, one after another. If a would-be murderer had caught Allye—choked her badly enough to leave those marks—why hadn't he finished what he started? Had the mayor interrupted him? But then, why not just leave her where she was? Why take the time to move her to the foot of her stairs to make it appear as if she'd fallen?

Eric didn't know what to think. Allye sounded so sure of what she'd seen, but if it weren't for her injuries, he'd be inclined to side with Moore's conclusion—she'd fallen and hit her head, and everything she thought she'd seen had been imagined. But he couldn't deny that those bruises were obvious strangle marks. He'd seen enough of them to know. Didn't mean she'd gotten them at the hands of an interrupted killer though.

He'd need to contact Mayor Jennings for clarity on his side of the story. Maybe he could provide some detail that would help reconcile all this.

Unfortunately, most of the businesses in this part of town followed regular office hours. With Allye's alleged encounter taking place a little after 7:00 p.m., the area would have been essentially deserted. She was fortunate the mayor had been working late. If it weren't election season, he likely would have been gone too.

Which would have either left her dead at the hands of an unknown assailant . . . or waking up alone with a probable concussion.

The mayor should have allowed her to file a report and then insisted she go to the hospital. But Eric knew how stubborn Allye could be. The fact she'd allowed the mayor to drive her home was a miracle. Or a sign of how badly she'd been feeling. The woman was all about taking care of others, but try to convince her she needed taking care of herself . . .

Steeling himself, he returned to the street side of the building and approached Allye's car. She had her head leaned back against the headrest. He tapped lightly on her window, and she startled, a slightly confused look in her eyes as she turned them on him. She blinked, and the confusion cleared. She opened the door and joined him outside.

"Sorry. I must have dozed off." She adjusted her glasses and tucked a wayward curl behind her ear. Her fingers trembled slightly. "Did you find anything?"

"Nothing noteworthy." He watched her carefully, but it didn't take an expert to read Allye. Her face clearly broadcasted everything she thought. And right now, desperation and fear were vying for dominance.

She looked over his shoulder toward the alleyway. "I didn't

imagine this," she said again, but her voice lacked its earlier conviction.

He let silence linger for a few seconds before asking, "Could the bruises on your neck have come from another source?"

"Mayor Jennings thinks maybe my purse strap yanked against it when I *fell*." The emphasis she put on the last word was as clear as if she'd added finger quotes to it.

Eric shook his head. "Doubtful. The bruising would look very different. Those are strangulation marks." Hope rose in her eyes. He hated to squelch it, but he had to cover his bases, and since she wasn't getting the hint, he was going to have to be direct. "Has someone else hurt you? A boyfriend? Family member?"

Her mouth dropped open, but she didn't break eye contact when she answered. "Absolutely not. You know my family would never do anything like that."

He did—theoretically. He'd known them for a long time, and he and her brother had become good friends after Bryce's return to Kincaid from active military service. In Eric's opinion, her family would be the least likely suspects in something like this. But as an investigator, he'd had to ask. "What about a boyfriend?"

"I don't have one."

Good. Even as jaded as he was, the thought of Allye having an abusive boyfriend unsettled him. But the denial brought them back to square one. Someone had attempted to strangle her, and the only explanation she had was dubious at best. And while he only knew Allye to tell the truth—and to be terrible at hiding it on the rare occasions she tried to—she could still be protecting someone. That scenario happened more often than most people liked to consider. But if that was the case, there was little chance of determining the culprit without Allye's cooperation.

He stifled a sigh. "I'm sorry. I'll file the report, but there's not much I can do at this point."

"Do you . . . at least believe me?" Her voice was small.

"I believe something happened last night," he said as gently as he could. "And like I said, I believe those are strangulation marks on your neck. But the evidence indicates you fell down the stairs and hit your head."

She lowered her gaze, but not before he caught the sheen of tears. Great. Allye was the last person he wanted to make cry. But what could he say? He had to follow the evidence, which was severely lacking.

"Thanks for looking," she mumbled as she climbed back into her car. She sat there for a minute, then pulled onto the road without her customary exuberant wave.

He watched as she drove away—the brightness of her cherry red Jetta a stark contrast to the slump of her shoulders. He hated seeing her disappointment, but he couldn't lie to her. And there was little he could do without evidence to corroborate her story.

He put in a call to Mayor Jennings's office and requested a callback to schedule an interview. He owed Allye that much. But he couldn't spend much more time on this. There just wasn't enough evidence to warrant it, and he had other cases that needed his attention. Cases like Ashley Harrison's overdose.

He checked his phone. Nothing from Dion. The teen's absence was concerning. If he'd skipped school because he was sick, he should have been at home. But he could be at a friend's house. Overslept and decided not to show up late. Played hooky for some other reason. Not ideal, but at least he'd be okay.

Eric couldn't shake the feeling that wasn't the case though. Dion might be mixing with a bad crowd, but he was a good kid, a fairly responsible one. At least, he had been.

He tried calling him again. No answer, so he returned to his car and called the school again. Still no sign of him. Eric requested the names and numbers of his friends—especially any who had also missed school today—and was told they would get back to him. He pocketed his phone and stared through the windshield.

He'd check with Dion's friends. If he got nowhere, he'd return to the boy's home and see if he showed up. But if they still knew nothing by nightfall, he'd be adding a missing person investigation to the top of his caseload.

5

ALLYE WASN'T SURE WHERE SHE WAS HEADED, but she barely
made it around a bend in the road before the tears started falling. She knew what had happened last night—had the bruises to
prove it. Why wouldn't anyone listen to her? Eric obviously felt
bad about it, but he didn't believe her either. She didn't blame
him. He was a facts guy, and there wasn't much for him to go on.
Didn't mean it didn't hurt though.

She thought back to her conversation with the mayor, tried
to force herself to remember exactly what he'd said. He'd found
her face down at the bottom of the steps. But she had no abra-
sions on her face. No sore spots on her forehead or the sides of
her head—only a bit at the back where she remembered being
slammed against the brick wall. It didn't fit.

But she had to admit, her memories didn't fit either. She should
be dead. She was choked to the point of unconsciousness. Why
hadn't the attacker finished her off? How had he moved her to
the foot of the steps and gotten away before the mayor's arrival?
And why bother?

She snatched a tissue from the box on her passenger seat and
dried her tears. There had to be an explanation for last night's
events. Had to.

But what if the truth lay somewhere in the middle or in a third option? Her stomach tightened at the thought, but she forced herself to follow that line of reasoning. Could her recent health issues have progressed to include hallucinations? Over the past couple of months, she'd been experiencing severe brain fog in addition to a handful of other symptoms—including a persistent fatigue that no amount of sleep or caffeine could shake.

The threat of a cramp started in her right hand, and she shifted her hold on the steering wheel, using the thumb of her opposite hand to massage the offending area. Part of her wondered if dwelling on her condition had prompted the sensation—an anxiety response, as one specialist had suggested. But no. She pushed that thought aside. Again. She might harbor some anxiety about her health or lack thereof, but that had begun well *after* the symptoms appeared. And her other doctors had agreed with Allye that something more was going on.

That was some comfort, even if they hadn't yet pinpointed what that something was. So far all the tests had come back negative or inconclusive. Unfortunately, all that meant was she had a better idea of what she didn't have—and any of the things they'd checked for would be better than what she suspected. She hadn't shared her concerns with anyone but her doctors. But if she was correct, things were only going to get worse.

But hallucinations? That wasn't part of the disease, was it? Potential cognitive deficiency, yes, but hallucinations . . . that would be ten times worse.

And that possibility still didn't explain the bruising on her neck.

She needed to do more research. When she found the energy.

Her phone chimed a reminder tone. She snatched it from the center console. What had she forgotten this time? She glanced at the readout. *Senior Photos: Jayden Alexander, park, 4:00 p.m.*

She dropped her phone back into the console and redirected toward the park. She had time to get there and set up before

Jayden and his mom arrived, but it would be close. Good thing she kept her camera bag with her and wasn't still stuck at home without her car.

Resting her foot a bit heavily on the gas pedal, she grabbed another tissue and dabbed under her eyes again. Crying hadn't helped anything, and she'd probably have puffy eyes for the photo shoot. At least she'd be behind the camera, not in front of it. Still, she turned on the air conditioning and aimed the vents at her face.

Her thoughts returned to last night's incident. Maybe if she wrote out what happened, something would click. At the very least, she needed to have a written record of her own in case she started to forget. She'd work on that tonight—whether she felt like it or not.

That settled, she forced her brain into photography mode. She had an appointment to keep and a senior to celebrate. This was a special time in a teen's life, and she needed to make sure the photos reflected that. She'd do that even if she weren't being paid, but she did need the money.

After the last two weddings she shot had not only drained her but left her barely able to function for several days following, she'd been afraid to book more for the foreseeable future. That had seriously cut into her income as a freelance photographer. These less-demanding senior photo sessions for the local high schoolers, though not nearly as lucrative, were keeping her afloat right now. At least until more of the medical bills started coming in. But she'd cross that bridge when she came to it.

As she neared the turnoff for Kincaid Lake State Park, her phone went off. Her cousin Hailey. She hit the accept button on her steering wheel and waited for the call to connect through her car speakers.

"Hello."

"Hey, Allye. How are you feeling? Wesley told me you had a bad fall last night."

She let a beat of silence pass. "How did Wesley know?"

"Mayor Jennings told him. He seemed pretty concerned."

"Oh." Of course. Hailey's husband, Wesley, was on the city council and had been working closely with Mayor Jennings's campaign for state senator. If he won his race, she strongly suspected he intended to endorse Wesley as the new mayoral candidate to replace him.

"So . . . how are you?"

Allye shifted to ease a pinch in her right shoulder. "I'm okay, I guess. A few bruises and incredibly sore. I didn't fall though—at least, I don't think I did, but everyone else seems to."

Other than the clack-clack of a baby toy in the background, there was silence on the other end of the line. After a few seconds, Hailey said, "I'd think you'd be the first person to know if you fell."

"You'd think." She turned onto the road leading to the park. "At this point, I don't know what happened last night. Mayor Jennings thinks I fell, I thought I was attacked, none of it adds up."

"Hold up. You *thought* you were *attacked*? What happened?"

She drew in a deep breath, then let it out quickly, annoyed that it had made her a bit dizzy. What was she about to say? She blinked twice, then remembered Hailey's question. *Focus.* "When I left my studio last night, I thought I heard something behind the building." She pulled into the lot and parked as she gave Hailey the basics up to the point where the mayor dropped her off at home. "None of it adds up. No one thinks I actually saw anything last night, and I know it sounds crazy, but it's so clear in my mind. Well, as clear as anything is lately."

"What's that supposed to mean?"

She hadn't intended to let that last part slip. "Nothing."

"Not nothing, Allye Jessup."

"Really, Hailey—"

"Spill it. What's going on?"

"I don't know." She let the whispered words trail off, but Hailey remained quiet, waiting. "I've been . . . sick, I guess, for a couple months now. I've got awful brain fog, and I'm exhausted. All the time. The migraines are hitting more often, and I get dizzy . . ." She stopped herself before she said too much. "There's other symptoms too, but the doctors don't know what's going on yet."

"Allye, I'm so sorry."

"It's okay—I'm okay. Or I will be. Or I won't." She managed a nervous-sounding laugh. "But if I'm wrong about what happened last night . . ." She bit the side of her lip and blinked back tears.

"If you're wrong about last night, what?"

She squeezed her eyes shut. Did she really want to say it out loud?

"Allye."

The gentle way Hailey said her name broke down the wall, and she blurted out her fears. "My injuries from last night don't fit with me falling down the stairs, but my memory doesn't match the evidence. What if I'm starting to hallucinate? What if I imagined everything, then fainted at the foot of the steps? I've got bruises on my neck. Did I choke myself? My body's betraying me—maybe my mind is too." She sucked in a breath, then added softly, "I'm afraid."

"I'm so sorry." Her cousin didn't offer empty feel-good platitudes—wasn't her way. And Allye was thankful for that. "If there's anything I can do to help, drive you to appointments, anything—"

A thump followed by a loud cry from Hailey's end of the line made Allye jump.

"Oh, hold on." The sound muffled somewhat, but Allye could clearly hear the screams from Hailey's almost-one-year-old. After a moment, they settled to hiccuping sobs, then quieted. Finally, Hailey returned to the call. "Sorry. That had to be loud. I have you on speaker, and Jenna's baby walker got away from her. She crash-landed right by the coffee table where the phone was."

"She okay?"

"I think it scared her more than anything. You're okay, aren't you?" Hailey laughed softly, and Allye could picture her signing to her daughter as she spoke. "Yep, she's already squirming to get down." Her tone changed. "Hey, Wes? Could you grab milk on your way home tonight?"

"Sure thing, babe. Love you." Wesley's voice carried clearly across the line.

Heat surged to Allye's cheeks. She hadn't realized he was home. Hopefully, he hadn't heard too much of her side of the conversation.

"Love you too." A door closed, then Hailey's voice returned. "Sorry again, Allye. I had to catch Wesley before he left. He's been so busy lately that it's always a toss-up whether he'll see a text while he's out. I'll be so glad when this election season is over and things go back to normal."

"I'll bet." Allye checked the time. "Hey, I need to go. I've got to set up for a photo shoot. They're going to be here any minute."

"Keep me posted about the health stuff, okay?"

"All right. And please don't say anything to my mom or anyone."

"You haven't told her?"

"Not yet. I don't want to worry her about nothing."

"It doesn't sound like nothing."

I know. She blinked against more tears. "There will be plenty of time for that after I know something concrete." The MRI scheduled for next week should give them something definitive to work with. One way or the other. A car pulled into the lot and swung into the spot next to her.

"Allye, you really should—"

"My clients just arrived. I have to go, but we'll talk later, okay?"

"Later, for sure."

"Bye, Hailey. And thanks for listening."

"Anytime. Take care of yourself."

"Trying." Allye ended the call and climbed from the car, pushing through the dizziness at standing too quickly. She forced a smile at the Alexanders and gave them a wave. They'd have to wait for her to set up now, but it shouldn't take much time. And if they weren't in a hurry, she was glad to extend their time slot as needed. As long as her energy held out.

6

AN HOUR LATER, Jayden and his mom were pulling away, leaving Allye to pack up her equipment. Before she put her camera away, she leaned against the back of her car and scanned through a few of the photos. They'd gotten some really good shots, including some near the lake. And neither Jayden nor his mom had seemed to notice her slight shakiness or the few times she'd stumbled. Both were wins in Allye's book.

As she viewed some of the trail photos, a particularly pretty bush caught her eye. That would make a lovely postcard print for her table at the upcoming Wool Fest. The local festival showcasing much more than textiles was one of the highlights of her year.

She studied the photo. Could she find that bush again? She navigated back and forth through a few shots. Based on the surrounding photos, it shouldn't be too far from the beginning of Spicebush Trail. But did she have the energy to go back out there today?

She chewed on the side of her lip. It would be pushing it, but better to do it now while she was already out here than make a special trip later—if she even remembered to. With a sigh, she pulled a fresh memory card from her bag and swapped it for the one containing Jayden's photos. She placed the nearly full card into the small plastic casing and dropped it into her purse. After stashing most of her equipment in the trunk, she set out with just her camera and purse slung over her shoulder.

Her thoughts returned to her conversation with Hailey as she neared the trailhead. She hadn't told her everything, but she still cringed at having been so transparent. Still . . . it had felt good to tell someone. And if she had to choose someone to confide in, her cousin was a good option. She wouldn't rat her out to her mom, and unlike Allye's best friend, Hailey wasn't expecting a baby. Married to Allye's brother early this past spring, Corina was now expecting her first child while still running her own business. Allye didn't want to add to her stress levels. Of course, Hailey had her own stress with the unique challenges of an almost-one-year-old with hearing loss and a husband in local politics. . . .

Allye's shoulders slumped. She probably shouldn't have burdened her either. Couldn't be helped now though. She entered the shade of the trail and began looking for the bush or another that would do.

A bit farther in than she'd hoped, she found a good candidate for her still shot. She adjusted her settings to account for the difference in subject and lighting. She took a few photos, made more adjustments, then snapped a few more. That would probably be enough. But as long as she was here, she might as well grab plenty to be safe.

Careful not to disturb anything, she stepped off the trail and rounded the bush to see what it was like from the back. Nice. She lowered herself to a crouch and began to work that angle. As she was focusing for her third shot, a young, angry voice broke the silence.

"I didn't sign up to kill people!"

"These aren't tainted. You know that problem's been taken care of." The firm response sent Allye's heart into her throat. She recognized that voice. The attacker from last night.

"I don't care. I want out."

"Not an option."

"But—"

The sound of a hand cracking across someone's face rang through the air. "You'll do what you're told, or you and the kid will pay the same way Marco did. Got it?" A pause, then, "Good. Now, the money."

The voices quieted, but shuffling from around the nearby bend let Allye know they hadn't left. Her legs trembled beneath her, but she was afraid to rise. If he caught her out here alone . . .

Her purse began to slip from her shoulder. She tried to grab for it but only succeeded in knocking it further askew. The shift in weight pulled her off-balance. Both she and her oversized bag toppled to the ground. Twigs and leaves crunched, and the contents of her bag spilled out. She froze.

Footsteps sounded on the trail. Through a small break in the brush, she could see two sets of feet round the bend. Moderately worn tennis shoes, like a teen boy might own, and a pair of sturdy work boots. She held her breath. The brush was fairly thick here, but if they started looking off-trail, they'd spot her sunshine-yellow blouse in a heartbeat.

"Probably just an animal." The young voice again. The tennis-shoed feet shifted with the words.

Her attacker grunted. "Here."

Something dropped to the ground, and the other guy stooped to grab it. Allye caught a glimpse of an arm and hand, but not his face.

"Next meeting in two weeks. Location six."

"Who's my contact now?"

"Me. Until I tell you otherwise. Now get."

Without another word, the younger guy pounded up the trail toward where Allye had entered. Her attacker didn't move.

Allye was starting to feel lightheaded. She was going to have to breathe. Or faint. *God, please don't let me faint. Or make noise. Make him leave.* Desperate, she released her breath as quietly as she could. Drew in a shallow replacement. Wasn't going to be enough for long. *God—*

The booted feet of her attacker turned and disappeared back around the bend. Allye waited but allowed herself regular shallow breaths.

"What?"

Allye nearly jumped out of her skin at the barked word. He was still nearby. And close.

"You caused that problem. I had it under control." A pause—he must be on a phone call. "I'm not going to lie low because you messed up. . . . No, you fix it, or I will. . . . *I don't care* how. If I go down, you're coming with me, and your cops will turn on you quicker than . . ." Leaves crunched, and his words faded until he was completely out of earshot.

Was he actually gone this time? Or testing whether anyone was around?

She'd wait a bit longer, despite the spasms starting in her fingers and the sensation of losing circulation in the leg she'd fallen on. Willing herself to ignore the pain, she silently repeated what she'd overheard. The police would want a report.

If they believed her. She wished she had been able to take a picture. Staying hidden had been more important, but, oh, it would be nice to have something more than her word as proof.

When silence continued for several minutes and no boots reappeared in her line of sight, she eased herself to a more comfortable position and began scooping things back into her purse. Her calf burned and tingled as blood began to circulate freely again. Massaging it gently, she strained her ears for any hint of danger. She needed to get out of here, but no use forcing herself up before she could hold her weight.

Once full feeling had returned, she slowly rose, eyeing the direction the boots had disappeared. The opposite direction—where the younger guy had gone—was closer to her car. And given the choice, she'd rather meet him than the man who had attacked her.

She hurried back up the trail and to her Jetta, constantly looking around her and over her shoulder. Safely inside her car, she threw the locks and shoved her key into the ignition. Then and only then did she allow herself to slump against the seat back and catch her breath.

Need to call Eric. She grabbed her phone and managed to enter her PIN. She was shaking again. Badly. And there was no signal out here. She'd have to drive until she got a few bars.

She looked around once more as she started the car. This end of the park appeared deserted. And it creeped her out. If she'd been spotted out on the trail, there would have been no one around to help her.

But they hadn't seen her. And she needed to get out of here before that changed. With that thought in mind, she sped back toward town.

7

ERIC STOOD IN THE RECEPTION AREA outside Mayor Jennings's office. Before heading out for the night, the mayor's secretary had told him Jennings was in a meeting and offered him a seat, but he preferred to stand. The meeting must be going over. Eric's appointment was supposed to start five minutes ago, but the mayor was a busy man. He was just thankful he'd agreed to fit him in today.

A buzzing alerted him to an incoming call on his personal cell. He didn't recognize the number, but it had a local area code, so he answered.

"Thornton."

"Eric? It's Allye J-Jessup. I just saw the guy who attacked me last night."

He gripped his phone tighter. "Where are you? Did he see you?"

"No—at least, I don't think so. I was taking photos at Kincaid Lake, but I'm almost to town now."

"Tell me what happened."

Tucking his phone between his shoulder and his ear, he withdrew his notebook and took down the details she gave him about what she'd overheard.

"So you didn't actually see him?" he asked when she paused for a breath.

"Just his boots. But I *know* it was him. I recognized his voice."

"Okay. Were they still there when you left?"

"I don't know. I was afraid for them to see me, so I waited for them to leave the area before I returned to my car. And then I didn't have signal, so I had to drive a couple miles before calling."

So they were probably long gone or would be before someone could get out there. Unfortunate. "I'm about to conduct an interview. As soon as I'm finished, I'll head over there and check out the area. Where exactly did everything happen?"

Keeping an eye on the mayor's still-closed door, he jotted down the directions she gave him, then asked some clarifying questions. A few times during her responses, she paused awkwardly as if searching for the right word, but he didn't comment on it.

He scanned his notes. "I think I have what I need for now. Where are you headed?"

"I hadn't planned that far ahead. I was just trying to get out of there and get signal." Although calmer than when she'd first called, she still seemed rattled. Understandable.

"Do me a favor. Go home. Lock your doors. Get some rest. You've dealt with a lot today."

"You'll check things out?"

"I will."

Her relieved sigh came clearly across the line. "Okay."

He raised his brows at her quick agreement. "Okay? Really?"

"I trust you. Good-bye, Eric. And thanks." The line clicked softly in his ear before he had the chance to respond.

He lowered the phone but balanced it in his hand for a moment. He wasn't sure if that had been a hint of humor pushing through the exhaustion in Allye's voice, but her words warmed him. The feeling quickly faded. Whether she was right about her attacker or not, the conversation she'd just overheard clearly related to a drug deal.

Good news if he could use the information for a bust—which he doubted, based on the lack of many useful details. Very, very bad news if the men involved realized Allye had overheard and was a potential witness. And how had she gotten his number? Surely the station wouldn't have given it out. Maybe from Bryce? That was probably it.

He clicked his pen a few times before sliding everything back into their respective pockets. Like he'd told Allye, he'd head to the park after he was finished here. If the mayor ever got out of his current meeting.

The mission statement mounted in large print on the opposite wall caught his eye. He'd already read it twice, but the first lines drew his attention again: *To serve the citizens of Kincaid with excellence and integrity. To encourage job-creation and improve the average standard of living.*

Allye's report of the comment referencing the police force nagged at him. There was obviously another accomplice. Someone with connections? A dirty cop? Surely not.

The door to the office finally opened and local reporter Thomas Marshall stepped into the reception area, followed by Councilman Wesley Nieland.

"Eric! Or should I say Detective Thornton?" Wesley offered his hand as the reporter gave a quick wave and scurried outside. "Good to see you."

"Councilman." Eric returned the titled greeting and handshake with a smile.

"Everything going well?"

"Crime doesn't end, but we're doing our best."

"I wouldn't expect anything less from you. Sorry we cut into your time with Mayor Jennings." Wesley half turned to nod toward the mayor, who now stood in the doorway.

"No problem. It was a last-minute appointment."

"Well, you'd better get in there. Keep up the good work." Wesley clapped him on the shoulder and headed down the hall that led to the various council members' offices.

"Detective Thornton. Come on in." Jennings beckoned him

into the office, and Eric strode across the room to join him. He took the chair Jennings offered and readied his notebook and pen.

This was the first time he'd had reason to visit the mayor's office, and he scanned the tastefully decorated room as the mayor filled two cups of water from a dispenser. Framed newspaper clippings and certificates of achievement hung on the wall behind Jennings's desk and on the wall to his right—all declaring ways the mayor had fulfilled his mission statement over the years he'd been in office. Even Eric was impressed.

"Sorry you had to wait." The mayor handed Eric one of the cups, then settled into his chair. He leaned forward, resting his elbows on the desk between them and steepling his fingers. "Now, what can I help you with, Detective? Something about Allye Jessup's fall, you said? I'm surprised they put a detective on it."

Eric set the cup on the edge of the desk. "Thank you for taking the time to meet with me, Mayor Jennings. I won't keep you long. I took the report from Officer Moore on last night's incident and followed up with Allye Jessup today. There are a few details I'm hoping you can clear up. Can I get your account of the events?"

"Of course. I was working late—campaign season, you know. About seven thirty, I heard a scream. I rushed outside and tried to determine the source. No one was immediately visible, so I glanced between the nearby buildings and spotted Allye at the foot of the steps leading to her studio. She was unconscious, which truly scared me. I realize I shouldn't have moved her in case she'd been seriously injured, but I didn't think of that in the moment—I just wanted to make sure she was okay. I turned her over to check for obvious injury and confirm she had a pulse, then I tried to wake her up. She came to quickly, but she was very upset, thinking someone was hurt and someone else had tried to kill her. She must have hit her head pretty hard.

I suggested she go to the emergency room, but she refused. I barely convinced her to let me drive her home."

"You didn't see anyone else around?"

"No. And I got out there pretty quickly. I think I would have at least heard someone running away if they'd been there."

"Ms. Jessup is certain she was attacked."

The mayor sat back and spread his hands. "I don't see how that could be the case. But like I said, she apparently had a traumatic fall."

"She also has bruising on her neck."

"She mentioned her throat was sore," Jennings admitted. "But I assumed it was either from her scream or perhaps from her purse strap. It was a large bag, and she was wearing it cross-body, so it could have twisted around when she fell."

Eric shook his head. "I saw the bruises myself this morning. A purse strap alone couldn't have made those marks. They're consistent with strangulation."

"Oh." The mayor looked nonplussed. "That's . . . wow." His phone buzzed on the desk, and when he reached for it, he bumped a five-by-seven frame with his elbow. The picture fell backward, revealing a family portrait of the mayor with his son and late wife.

Eric studied the image while the mayor responded to a message. The photo had to be at least five years old, before the family had been blindsided by Mrs. Jennings's aggressive cancer. She still looked healthy here, and Liam, who was now in medical school, appeared to be around eighteen.

Mayor Jennings pocketed his phone and righted the photo. "Sorry about that, Detective. Urgent message from my campaign manager."

"Not a problem." He slipped back into interview mode. "So you didn't see any marks on Allye's neck last night?"

"No, I didn't. But it was getting dark, and I could have overlooked them if they were there."

Eric zeroed in on the mayor's last words. "'If they were there?' Are you suggesting something might have happened after you

took her home? Because the bruises are certainly there now."
If Allye was protecting someone, it was possible the attack had
occurred later at her house.

"Of course—I'm not doubting what you saw. And I really don't
mean to suggest anything." Jennings frowned and lifted a hand
to his forehead. "I just don't know what to make of this situation. I found her literally within a minute or two of hearing her
scream, and there was no hint of anyone else nearby. You know
how quiet this part of town is at night."

Eric couldn't deny that. With the exception of the newspaper
office on deadline night, the businesses currently on the town
square tended to follow banking hours. Even the outliers were
usually closed by 6:00 p.m. By 6:30, the area was practically deserted on most evenings.

But that didn't preclude the possibility of a crime occurring.
Nor did the mayor's failure to hear anything else out of the or-
dinary. The attacker could have retreated quietly or even hidden
nearby until the coast was clear. Harder to believe he'd been able
to move a body so quickly and silently, but it still wasn't out of
the realm of possibility.

Or Allye might have actually fallen, and there was some other
explanation for the bruising on her neck.

But what about the conversation she'd overheard today? He
tapped his pen against the notebook. Should he bring that up
to Jennings?

Normally, he wouldn't divulge any more information than
necessary during an interview, but Jennings was his boss, indirectly at least. And he knew Allye. Rumor around town was that
the mayor was dating her mom and the relationship was getting
serious. Might as well get his take on the matter.

"I agree the whole thing sounds a little off. But here's another
piece to the puzzle." He flipped back a couple of pages. "Allye
says she was out taking pictures at the park today and saw her
attacker again—overheard a drug deal and a phone conversation.

She said he was talking about a mess-up needing to be fixed and the threat of police turning against someone."

The mayor's expression clouded. "Really? Does she know who he was talking about—or to?"

"No. But I don't like the sound of it."

"Neither do I. That's . . . concerning to say the least." Jennings frowned. "Was anyone with her that could corroborate her story? Or did she get any photo evidence?"

"No, unfortunately. She was alone and afraid to show herself."

"That is unfortunate. A photo would have been valuable proof." Jennings thought a moment, then let out a sigh. "Listen, Detective. I would never doubt Allye's word under normal circumstances . . ."

Normal circumstances? Eric left the question unspoken and waited for him to continue.

"But she seems to have been under a lot of stress or something lately. Her mother has been concerned about her. She says Allye's been forgetting things, not acting like herself. And with the knock on the head last night? Perhaps she—" He shook his head and waved a hand dismissively. "Forget I said all that. Surely she's not imagining things. And if you saw suspicious bruises . . ." He paused again. "I'm sorry. I really don't have an explanation for what's going on. All I know for sure is what I saw last night."

Eric glanced over the notes he had so far. He had a few new details, but everything matched what Moore had passed on from last night's call. Jennings glanced at his watch. He needed to get back on track and wrap things up.

"So Ms. Jessup refused to go to the ER, then you took her home and called the station?"

"Yes. She was obviously in no condition to drive. I made sure she got safely inside, then I called the nonemergency line and asked for someone to evaluate things, maybe take a look around."

"Even though you didn't think anything had happened?"

The mayor shrugged. "I promised Allye I'd report it—that was the only way I convinced her to go home and rest. And I'm a man of my word. I hated to use city resources on what was likely nothing, but with our low crime rate, I figured there would be someone who could spare a few minutes before the night was out. And what if I was wrong and something really had occurred?"

Eric held his gaze. "But you were convinced it hadn't?"

"As much as I hate to say it, yes. The timing just doesn't fit. And I can't unsee finding her crumpled at the foot of the stairs—just like you'd expect if she'd fallen down them."

"Fair enough." Eric clicked his pen twice, then pocketed it. He stood, the mayor mirroring his movement, and offered his hand. "Thank you for your statement."

Jennings gave him a firm handshake. "Thank you, Detective, for making sure Allye is taken care of. She's the closest thing to a daughter I have. I don't know what's going on, but I trust you'll figure things out."

No pressure.

Eric inclined his head. "I will do my best, sir."

8

AFTER FINDING NOTHING TO SUBSTANTIATE Allye's alleged experience at the park, Eric returned to town and headed for Dion's house. As he drove, he mulled through the details of Allye's case.

Much as he hated to admit it, the mayor's statement made sense. Allye's . . . didn't.

And yet he didn't feel comfortable dismissing the woman. Even without the concerning bruises on her neck, he'd known her for years. They weren't close friends by any means, but he was a pretty good judge of character and had spent enough time around her to know that she wasn't the type to blow things out of proportion. Yes, she came off a bit naïve at times, but she was smart and logical and very perceptive.

She was also an extrovert that could make friends with the grumpiest curmudgeon around. And her reputation was stellar. The worst thing he'd ever heard said about her was that she was too much of a Pollyanna.

And though he'd seen the fatigue Mayor Jennings mentioned, there'd been no sign of deceit or delusion when he spoke with Allye earlier today. But that didn't mean she wasn't mistaken. The mayor believed she'd had a traumatic fall, and trauma did weird things to people sometimes. And there was always the possibility that she experienced some sort of hallucination that left her with realistic-feeling, but totally bogus, memories from last night. Still didn't account for the bruising though.

And the conversations she'd claimed to have overheard at the park complicated things too. According to her, one of the speakers had reassured the other that whatever they were exchanging wasn't tainted. They hadn't outright said there had been tainted drugs floating around recently, but that would fit with the ODs the department had seen in recent weeks, Ashley Harrison's included. Regular meth users who didn't realize their drugs had been laced with fentanyl would be even more likely to overdose than someone who knew what they were taking.

Would Allye have any clue that kind of thing was going on? The police chief was waiting to get more results back before making a public statement about the possible fentanyl situation, so the average citizen shouldn't know about it yet. And if she'd just imagined a drug deal going down, that detail was conveniently on the nose. And then that cop comment . . .

This one was a puzzler, and he wasn't sure he'd be able to figure it out.

Darkness was falling as he pulled into Dion's driveway again. No lights shined from the house despite the early evening hour, but he'd try knocking on the door anyway. The crime scene tape had been removed earlier today, so Dion could theoretically have returned home and let himself inside.

But as he expected, his knock was met with silence. The teen was still missing.

Returning to his car, Eric settled into the driver's seat but didn't reach for the ignition. Instead, he checked his phone. No missed calls or messages. He tried Dion's number again, then the few remaining friends who hadn't responded to his earlier calls. All but one of them answered this time, but as with the earlier group, they claimed they hadn't seen or heard from Dion since school yesterday. Maybe they just didn't want to rat their friend out to a cop, but Eric didn't get the sense they were lying.

Heart heavy, he began entering a missing person report and getting Dion's info into the appropriate databases. The situation didn't meet the criteria for an AMBER alert, and there was still a chance the boy was completely fine, but Eric couldn't assume that was the case. He needed to find him ASAP.

Once everything was uploaded, including the most recent picture he had of the teen, Eric grabbed his notebook and pen. Again, he reviewed everything related to Dion and his mom. Added a few more notes to his most recent follow-up calls.

He stared at the paper. Clicked his pen. Once, twice, three times. There wasn't nearly enough information here. His brain flew through everything he knew about the situation, trying to fit the pieces together.

Dion's mom was dead of an overdose.

Click.

Lucky was safe. Dion in the wind.

Click.

Where had Ashley Harrison procured her drugs? Had her death hit the news? Did Dion know his mom was gone? Was the teen okay?

Click. Click. Click.

He dropped the pen and massaged his forehead. Before his meeting with Mayor Jennings, he'd checked in on Lucky. The social worker hadn't found an emergency placement for him yet at that point. If they were still at the social services office, maybe he could question the boy. Lucky might not know anything—or be willing to talk to him—but it might be his best shot at finding out something that would lead him to Dion.

A quick phone call confirmed Lucky and the social worker were still at the office. He started the car and backed out of the driveway, casting one last look at the darkened house before pulling away.

The social services headquarters was only a few miles away, and Eric arrived in less than ten minutes. He made his way to the third floor and rapped on an office door. Tracy Ann, a veteran social worker, answered.

"Detective Thornton, come on in." She stood aside to allow him entrance.

He quickly took in the office. One side of the room appeared to be a kitchenette and boasted a refrigerator and microwave. The other contained a desk centered under a window, a cot pushed against the wall in one corner, and a small play area nestled into another corner and framed in with a short couch.

Lucky sat in the play area, guiding a wooden train along a rug printed with a winding road.

"He hasn't said a word all day," Tracy Ann murmured. "Not even when we told him about his mama."

The words landed like a one-two punch to the kidneys. The boy had lost almost everything today. Depending on what happened with Dion, *almost* might be too optimistic.

Eric crossed into the play area and knelt in front of the boy. His knees crackled like a bowl of rice cereal, reminding him he hadn't eaten in a while. Next stop.

"Hey, there. Remember me?"

Lucky didn't look up from his train.

"I'm Detective Thornton. You doing okay?"

A barely discernible shrug.

"You have supper?"

A nod.

"Good. Listen, Lucky, I'm trying to find your brother. Nobody's heard from him, and I want to make sure he's okay. Do you know where he could be?" No response. "Lucky." Eric gently covered the boy's hand.

Lucky flinched away and scooted backward, leaving the train in Eric's grip.

Bad move. "Sorry." He moved the train back toward the boy,

but Lucky didn't reach for it. "Go ahead. It's okay." When the boy still didn't move, he decided to try one more time. "Lucky, I know it's been a really bad day, and we're trying to make sure you and your brother are taken care of. But I can't help Dion if I don't know where he is."

Lucky finally made eye contact. Held it. His expression gave nothing away, but at least it let Eric know he was listening.

"Do you know where he likes to hang out? Maybe the name of a friend he goes to see sometimes?"

He shook his head—a hesitant movement, as if he was afraid Eric would lash out at him for not giving the right answer.

Eric kept his face neutral. He was disappointed, but it had been a long shot. "Thank you for answering me. If you think of something, ask Ms. Tracy to call me." He nudged Lucky's hand with the train, and the boy took it this time, scooted backward another few inches, then began tracing the road again.

Eric studied him for a moment. The blank expression hid the fear and anxiety he had to be feeling. "You're gonna be okay, buddy." He prayed the words were true.

He rose and stepped out of the play area to where Tracy Ann was waiting.

"Thanks for letting me talk to him."

"Of course. I hope you find his brother soon."

"Yeah. Me too." He glanced at Lucky. "I know you guys are stretched, but if you can, would you keep me posted on him?"

"I'll do what I can. I haven't found a placement for him yet, so he may be staying with me tonight."

He thanked her again, then headed for the office exit.

"Will Dion take me home when you find him?"

Tracy Ann sucked in a breath, and Eric released the door-knob and turned to find Lucky watching him. He searched for a response that wouldn't crush the kid, but he wasn't going to outright lie to him. The truth was hard, but a lie would only give him false hope. And a short-lived hope at that. Lucky deserved better. "No. I'm sorry, Lucky. He's too young to be able to take care of you. You'll be going to a new home, but hopefully it'll be a better one and you two can be together."

The boy's shoulders slumped, and he turned away—but not before Eric saw the quiver in his lower lip.

He met Tracy Ann's eyes and saw the tears there. She still felt for these kids. The system hadn't hardened her like it had so many. At least while Lucky was in her care, he'd be well taken care of. For now, that had to be enough.

9

PRESSURE.

Allye tried to shift to a more comfortable position, but a weight seemed to rest on her. She couldn't lift her arms. Couldn't move her body.

"Boo."

She jerked fully awake at the whispered word. And froze.

A masked face hovered barely a few inches above hers. An unearthly green glow filled her bedroom, creating almost a halo around the intruder. He was on top of her, his weight pressing her hips into the mattress, hands pinning her upper arms.

"I got away with it." He rose slightly, though the pressure didn't ease.

With the increased distance between their faces, she found her voice. "Got away with what?" Her words came out with a breathy quality.

Instead of answering her, he lifted one hand and traced the bruised area of her neck. "We have unfinished business."

Him. It was him. Chill bumps rose over her entire body. A lump formed in her throat, nearly blocking her airway. She couldn't scream. Could barely think.

He'd come after her again. Here, at her house.

Her fight response finally kicked in. She screamed and simultaneously struck out with her left arm and kicked her legs. But her limbs tangled in the heavy quilt she hadn't realized still lay between her body and the intruder's, and what little noise escaped her bruised throat before his hand clapped over her mouth was pitiful.

He let her flail, seemingly unperturbed. After a long moment of desperate but futile fighting, she collapsed into an exhausted stillness. With her mouth covered, she could barely draw in enough air, and her chest heaved.

He lowered his face to hover just above hers again. "Are you finished?"

She didn't even try to respond, but a tear leaked from the corner of her eye.

"Good." He looked over his shoulder and nodded, then turned his attention back to her. "Now, I'm going to get up, and so are you. You try anything, and you *will* regret it. Get anyone's attention, and they will die. Understand?"

She managed a nod.

He lifted his hand, letting it hover over her mouth as if testing whether she would attempt another scream. When she remained silent, he stood and allowed her to do the same.

A wave of lightheadedness hit, but he gave her no time to linger. Wrenching her hands behind her, he shoved something hard against her back and marched her out of the bedroom. The night-light she kept plugged into the hallway outlet was out. Everything was dark other than the weird green glow that seemed to be following them now. What was that?

She stumbled as they entered the living room. The tight grip he had on her wrists kept her upright but wrenched her shoulders. A small cry escaped her lips, and the hard object dug into her spine.

"None of that, remember?" His hard whisper cut through the air.

"I'm . . . sorry," she gasped.

Without responding, he propelled her toward the front door. The pressure against her spine lifted, and she caught a glimpse of a gun as he reached around her for the knob. Cool night air greeted them as he opened the door and pushed her through. It snicked shut behind them, cutting off the green light.

She quickly cast her gaze around the area—unsure whether to hope for someone to try to rescue her or hope there wouldn't be anyone around to be put in danger. No lights shone from any of her neighbor's houses, and as far as she could see without her glasses, no one was out and about. Maybe that was for the best, but she couldn't help the despair that rose in her as her captor prodded her onward.

When they reached the edge of the porch, he abruptly turned her back toward the house. Without warning, he released her wrists and shoved her forward. She fell flat, unable to catch herself. Quickly, she rolled to her back, expecting a new attack.

But he wasn't there. Grabbing a nearby patio chair, she hauled herself upright and searched the semidarkness. Movement partway down the street caught her eye as a dark, blurred figure blended with the shadows. Then he was gone.

She sank into the chair. What just happened? Had he gotten spooked?

But there still didn't seem to be anyone about. A breeze ruffled her hair, and she shivered. The movement kicked her brain into gear. He'd let her go, but she was still outside and exposed. He could come back at any moment.

Springing to her feet, she launched toward the door and wrenched the knob. Locked.

Locked?

She tried again, twisting and pushing with all her might. Nothing budged. Something out in the yard snapped, and she spun to face it. The movement triggered a burst of dizziness, and she braced herself against the uncooperative door. She didn't see anything. No returning captor or any other threat.

But she couldn't stay out here. Nor could she get inside. And she didn't have her phone.

She had to get help. Surely the danger to other people was past if he'd chosen to leave, right? Before she could talk herself out of it, she scurried down the few porch steps.

The cold grass was damp beneath her bare feet as she crossed the yard to the other side of the duplex, where her best friend had lived before marrying Bryce. The new tenants had only recently moved in, but Allye had met them on a few occasions. They'd help her until the police arrived.

FIFTEEN MINUTES LATER, Allye was stationed on her neighbors' living room couch with a much-too-large, borrowed hoodie swallowing her. She'd spent a lot of time here during the two years Corina had lived next to her, but even if she hadn't, the place would feel familiar as it was basically a mirror image of her side of the building. She could use some familiarity at the moment.

Shannon Howard offered her a cup of hot cocoa. Allye accepted it gratefully, wrapping her hands around the mug and willing the warmth to seep into her. "Thank you. I'm so sorry I had to wake you up."

Her neighbor waved a hand at her. "Stop apologizing. I would be horrified if you were in trouble and didn't ask for help. It's bad enough something like that happened next door, and I didn't hear a thing. Besides, like I said earlier, I'd only just gone to bed. I wasn't asleep yet, and Cornell is on night shift this week. Is there anyone else you want to call while we wait on the police?"

Allye glanced at a clock. She couldn't make out the time without her glasses, but that didn't matter. Even though Shannon had still been awake, it had to be late. Bryce and Corina would be in bed. Her mom too. She shook her head. She'd get a lecture or two . . . or three, for not contacting them right away, but there was nothing they could do. Someone might as well get sleep tonight—and it didn't look like she would.

Police lights flashed outside the window. They were finally here. Allye started to rise.

"I'll let them in," Shannon said. "You stay right there."

She sank back into the cushions. She should greet the officer herself, but the ordeal had drained her more than she was willing to admit.

"She's in here, Officer." Shannon beckoned him in. Allye nearly groaned when Officer Moore cleared the doorway.

His gaze immediately landed on her, and he stepped closer. "Ms. Jessup, I hear you've had another incident?"

"Someone broke into my house." She'd already told the dispatcher that, but she had no idea what had been relayed to him.

"I'm sorry to hear that. Were you there?"

"Yes. I was in bed." She went through the details of what happened, hoping she wasn't forgetting anything important. As she talked, Moore's eyebrows drew together, but he didn't look up from the tablet he was taking notes with.

"Sounds like something spooked him," he said when she got to the end.

"I suppose? I didn't see anyone around, but that's the only thing that makes any sense."

Moore snapped the cover shut on his tablet. "Hopefully, he left evidence behind. I'll need to go over your house."

She grimaced. "It's locked."

"Locked?"

"After he left, I tried to get back in, but he must have locked the door behind us. My keys and everything are inside."

"Is there someone you can call who has a spare?"

"Oh! I guess I do." She gave herself a mental kick. "It's hidden in my backyard." A must, as often as she misplaced her keys or locked herself outside. She set the remainder of her hot cocoa on the coffee table and rose.

"Hold up," Shannon said. "It's too chilly for you to be walking around out there barefoot." She hurried down the hall and returned a moment later with a pair of flip-flops. "I'd lend you real shoes, but I'm pretty sure they'd be way too big."

"These are fine. Thank you. And thanks again for letting me wait here."

"Anytime."

Allye slipped on the sandals and led the way outside and around the back of the house. Moore followed her, flashlight in hand, and illuminated the area for her. She pulled the key from its hiding place.

"Do you want me to unlock the door, or do you want to?"

Moore extended his hand. "I'll take care of it. I need you to wait outside or back at your neighbor's while I examine things, then we'll do a walk-through together to see if you notice anything out of place."

"Okay." Allye viewed the dark backyard. She didn't want to bother Shannon any more tonight, but staying back here alone would give her the creeps. "Is it all right if I wait on the front porch?"

"That's fine." Moore headed for the door, leaving her to make her own way there.

She wasted no time circling back to the front of the house. At least there was the bit of light from the street. And the deterrent of the flashing lights from Moore's patrol car. She settled into the chair she'd sat in before and replayed the night's events in her mind. A shadow moved at the edge of the yard, and she nearly jumped out of her skin. But it was just a tree blowing in the breeze. No one was skulking in the shadows, waiting to grab her. Not that she'd be able to see them if they were there. She really needed to retrieve her glasses.

But her attacker was out there somewhere. He knew where she lived, and he'd made her a target. Despite the borrowed hoodie, she shivered.

10

AFTER WHAT SEEMED LIKE AN HOUR, Moore joined Allye on the porch. She stood and accepted her key from him but kept one hand on the back of the chair to help keep her balance.

"What did you find?"

"Not much. I dusted for prints, and we'll need you to provide yours so we can rule them out. It would be helpful if anyone who's regularly in your house could do the same."

"I can do that." And she'd have to ask her family to as well—or maybe not. She'd been too tired lately to have anyone over. Any prints they'd left might well have been eliminated weeks ago.

"Everything seemed to be locked up tight," Moore continued. "I didn't find an obvious point of entry."

"He locked the door behind us," she reminded him.

He made a noncommittal grunt. What did that mean? Instead of commenting on her attacker's odd action, he thumbed over his shoulder. "He had to have gotten in before that though. Did you have the doors locked when you went to bed?"

"Yes. At least, I think so." She normally kept the doors locked at night, but with her memory lately, she couldn't be absolutely sure.

Moore sighed. "If you're ready, we'll walk through together. Tell me if you notice anything out of place."

Before she could respond, another car pulled into her driveway. She and Moore both turned toward the newcomer, who climbed from his car and headed toward them. Allye squinted, but she couldn't tell who it was until he had almost reached them. Eric. The moment she recognized him, a bit of her fear and frustration ebbed away.

"I heard your address come over the scanner. What's going on?" There was concern in his normally curt voice, and he seemed to be assessing her for damage.

"Someone broke into my house."

"While you were at home?"

"Yes, but I'm okay. A couple bruises maybe, but he didn't actually hurt me." Scared about a decade off her life, but physically, he'd only been rough. He hadn't injured her, even though he could have easily done so.

"Good." He turned to Moore. "Status?"

Moore glanced from Eric to Allye and back and finally answered. "I just walked through the house. There's no obvious point of entry. Nothing seems broken. Ms. Jessup was about to go back in with me and check for anything out of place."

"Prints?"

The officer shrugged. "I took several samples, but the only place Ms. Jessup noticed him touch was the front doorknob—and there were no clear prints there."

"How would there not be prints on the knob?" Allye interrupted. "I saw him grab it, and he didn't wipe it clean after."

"Things aren't always as simple as TV makes it out to be." Moore's tone was bordering on patronizing. "And if he was wearing gloves—"

"He wasn't. I saw his hand in my bedroom and when he reached for the door." But then she remembered his touch. Against her face when he'd covered her mouth. Around her wrists. Her shoulders slumped.

"What?" Eric asked.

"It didn't feel like skin. More like a smooth, tight-fitting material. I didn't process that in the moment."

"But it looked like skin?"

"Yes, but the lighting was so weird—maybe they were just light-colored gloves? Or the clear rubber ones."

"Explain what you mean by weird lighting," Moore broke back in.

"There was this . . . green glow."

Eric and Officer Moore exchanged looks.

"A green glow," Eric repeated.

"Yes. It was . . . odd. And it cut off once we got outside. But I don't have anything in the house that would give off green light like that." She spread her hands. "I don't know where it came from."

Another look passed between the men, then Moore cleared his throat. "Are you on any medications?"

"Am I what?" As she said the words, she understood his meaning. "No. I mean, I do take something for migraines, but nothing that would alter my mental status." This couldn't be happening. They didn't believe her. Again. She crossed her arms. "I didn't imagine this."

Moore looked to Eric, and even without her glasses, Allye could see that the man was losing patience. Well, so was she.

"I. Didn't. Imagine. It." She started to sway, so she reclaimed her hold on the chair back.

"Ms. Jessup—"

"I can take things from here, Officer Moore," Eric said. "Copy me on your report."

"Glad to," Moore muttered as he stalked off the porch.

"Honestly." She'd never seen the man be so rude. Of course, she hadn't interacted with him personally very often.

"You're shaking. Are you sure you're okay?" Eric's quiet words helped calm her.

She took a deep breath and tightened her grip. "I'm good." Okay, maybe that was a stretch, but for the moment, she was fine. She should probably sit though.

Eric didn't look like he believed her, but he didn't call her on it. "I need to hear the details of what happened. Would you be more comfortable inside?"

"That won't contaminate evidence or anything?"

"Officer Moore's already done his inspection. After you give me the details, we'll do a walk-through together, but if you notice anything off when we enter the house, tell me right away and we'll note it before proceeding."

"All right." She pried her fingers from the chair back and quickly shoved both hands into the hoodie's front pocket where he wouldn't be able to see them shaking. Stepping around him, she led the way to the door. Moore had left it unlocked, and the knob turned easily.

A shudder passed through her as she stepped inside. The officer had also left the lights on, which she much appreciated at the moment. Even with Eric at her back, she didn't think she was ready to face her house in the dark.

"See anything?"

She jumped slightly at Eric's voice. "No. Sorry." She hadn't realized she'd stopped just inside the doorway with no explanation. She continued inside, then half turned back to him.

"I'm going to get my glasses first, if that's okay."

"Certainly."

"Make yourself at home." She headed for her room and tried not to think about what had nearly occurred there—and what *had* occurred there—only an hour or so earlier. Two steps into her bedroom, she stopped and cringed. It was a mess. Bed unmade with blankets spilling over the side. Clothing she hadn't had the energy to hang in her closet had transformed the corner chair into a mountain. And both her clean and dirty laundry baskets were nearly overflowing.

Even her nearsightedness couldn't hide how bad it looked. The thought of Officer Moore seeing all this was embarrassing. Worse, she'd be bringing Eric back here soon. Absolutely mortifying. She snatched her glasses from the nightstand, nearly knocking one of the half-empty water glasses off, and turned her back on the mess. Nothing she could do about it now.

On the way back, she caught sight of the dishes piled high in her sink. The weight in her stomach added a few pounds. If only she'd managed to keep up with things a little better . . . But she hadn't.

Yesterday was garbage day, so that at least was under control. And nothing smelled. That counted for something, right?

She dragged herself the rest of the way into the living room and collapsed in her favorite seat. Eric perched on the edge of a nearby sofa, his ever-present notebook in his hand and his eyes trained on her. His lips parted, then squeezed together again, as if he'd decided against saying something. The kindness in those normally piercing blue eyes threatened to break down the front she was putting up. *Don't cry. Not now.*

"Ready to tell me what happened?"

"I feel like we just did this."

He didn't smile at her attempted humor.

Suddenly nervous, she searched for something to occupy her hands. Her knitting bag lay next to her chair, along with the other bags she'd unceremoniously dumped when she arrived home earlier. More mess. But convenient this time. She grabbed her knitting and pulled out the glove she was working on. It was a pattern she'd done so many times, she could do it in her sleep—as long as her fingers didn't start spasming.

The feel of wool in her hands had an immediate calming effect. Needles softly tapping, she related the night's events, from waking up to her attacker and that ghastly green glow to when Eric arrived on her porch. When she finished, Eric scratched a few more words in his notebook, then stared at the page. When he met her gaze, she could plainly see the doubt there.

Something inside her shrank a little.

"You don't believe me either, do you?"

Eric let a few seconds pass, like he was searching for a kind way to call her a liar. Finally, he said, "I want to believe you, but think about what you say happened. You saw a green glow, someone broke into your house and acted like he intended to assault you, then started to kidnap you. But then he just ran off for no reason after locking you out of your house?"

Hearing it from his lips made her sound batty. "I admit it sounds crazy, but that's what happened."

"You've had a lot happen in the last couple days."

A lot that couldn't be explained. She understood the unspoken addendum.

A new wave of tiredness washed over her, and she let her knitting fall to her lap. "So that's it, then? You and Officer Moore will write your reports and note that I'm off my rocker. Case closed."

"Not quite. I'm going to do a walk-through with you like we already discussed, then we're going to make sure your house is locked up tight so you can get some rest tonight. Then we'll write our reports and run the fingerprints. Did Moore mention getting yours for comparison?"

"Yes. And if we don't find anything and there are no fingerprint leads?"

"Then we keep our eyes open and hope either something turns up later or you aren't bothered again."

She tried not to make a face.

"Sorry. We can only go so far without anything to go on."

Oops. A grimace must have slipped through. "I know."

"One other thing. Are you aware of making anyone mad lately? A customer. Angry ex?"

"No." As far as she knew, all her customers were satisfied. No need to tell him she hadn't dated in years. That sounded so . . . pitiful. Not that she hadn't had a few offers—okay, one plus a few matchmaking attempts by her mom—but after her last boyfriend had broken off their serious relationship and promptly announced an engagement to someone else . . . well, she'd needed a break. She just hadn't expected it to turn into three years and counting. But dating was out of the question right now. Even if she wanted to—which she didn't—she barely had the energy to keep up with normal life.

Eric stood. "Okay. I just had to ask. I know you're exhausted. Let's get the walk-through taken care of."

She set her knitting aside and scooted to the edge of her seat. Why was it so hard to muster enough energy to stand right now? *Just get up. Move!* Instead, she just sat there. Eric moved closer and offered his hand. She could—should—do it herself. But she was so tired. After only a short hesitation, she grasped his hand and let him help her to her feet.

Once she felt steady—which took a few seconds longer than it should have—she withdrew her hand. "Thanks."

"Of course."

Steeling herself against the embarrassment of her messy house, she led him through the rooms, retracing the path she'd walked with her attacker, then checking into the other areas as well. The search turned up nothing of note. And Eric either didn't notice or chose not to comment on her untidiness.

"Mind if I check your locks?" he asked when they were finished.

"Be my guest."

She propped herself against a wall while he examined the front door, then followed him into the kitchen. He unlocked the back door, opened it, bent to peer at the latch, then turned the lock and stepped outside. He pulled the door shut, locking himself out. But within seconds, he was letting himself back inside.

"How did you . . . ?"

He held up a credit card. "That lock is easy to disengage. A child could pop it with one of these."

"So that was how he got in?"

Eric shrugged. "Can't say for sure, but it would have been an easy point of entry."

"Lovely."

"You should install a dead bolt. Do you need help with that?"

"I'm sure Bryce will do it for me."

He gave her a quick nod. "Good. I recommend having it done sooner rather than later."

"Definitely." She'd ask him to come by as soon as she got permission from her landlord.

"I'll be going, then." But instead of moving toward the front door, he studied her. "Are you sure you're all right? If you want to call someone so you're not here alone, I can wait."

"No. I don't want to bother anyone else tonight. Thank you though. And—" She moistened her lips. "Thank you for not blowing me off—even though I know I sound crazy. But also for not placating me with empty promises."

"I wouldn't do that." He held her gaze, and for the briefest moment, she wished she could tell him about everything she had going on—not as a victim to a detective, but friend to friend. He would listen, maybe offer advice or comfort. She could use some comfort.

No. She put a hard stop on that line of thought. He didn't need her to dump all that on him. She'd be all right.

She lifted what felt like a shaky smile. "Well, goodnight, then."

"Get some rest, Allye."

11

ALLYE DRAGGED HERSELF out of her recliner at nine thirty Sunday morning after snoozing her alarm three times. Church started at ten, which meant she had twenty-five minutes to shower, dress, and eat if she wanted to be on time. Maybe she should skip the shower.

She headed for the kitchen and flipped the switch on the hot water kettle. The hint of a headache lurked behind her eyes—though it was nothing like the raging migraine that had knocked her flat and stolen nearly all memory of yesterday—and her hips and lower back protested a third night spent in the recliner instead of her bed. There was no way she could have even attempted to go back to sleep in her room Friday night, and she'd apparently fallen asleep in the chair again last night too.

She turned toward the table and let out a little groan. She just needed to stretch her muscles . . . and maybe pop an ibuprofen.

Once the pain reliever kicked in and she had her tea, maybe she'd feel more human and less like the grizzly Bryce and Corina teasingly called her morning persona. She sank into a chair and rested her forehead on her crossed arms while she waited for the water to boil. She didn't feel like a grizzly this morning. More like a half-drowned mouse. Her limbs felt numb and achy all at the same time. How was that even possible?

The water began to rumble in the kettle. She ought to choose her tea and portion it into the infuser basket, but she couldn't bring herself to move. The clock ticked behind her as if to prompt her to step things up.

One more minute.

It wasn't like running late was unusual for her.

Allye jerked her head up. The movement sent a shock of pain down her neck.

"Ow." She reached numb fingers to massage the area. She must have dozed off. With the realization, panic jolted through her. What time was it? She shot to her feet. Bad idea. Her equilibrium was off, and she grabbed the edge of the table to keep from falling. She blinked through the fuzz encroaching on her vision and turned to check the clock.

11:55.

She sagged back into the chair, disappointed. There'd be no church for her this morning. She'd missed last week too.

Classical music floated from the living room. Her phone. Allye stood—slowly this time—and let her vision clear. She smacked the on switch to her now-cold-again water kettle as she passed it. She wouldn't make it to the phone in time anyway. As she'd expected, the music stopped before she was halfway across the room. It began again almost immediately. She snatched it from the end table before it could throw the caller to voice mail again.

"Hello?" Her voice cracked on the word, and she grimaced. At least the pounding in her head wouldn't travel through the phone and give her away.

Corina's concerned voice came across the line. "Hey. You okay? We missed you this morning."

She blew out a disgusted breath. "Yeah. I overslept, then fell back to sleep." She left out the *at my kitchen table* part.

"Oh."

She pressed the heel of her hand against her eye. "Did you need something, or are you just checking up on me?"

"Both. Bryce wants to grill this afternoon. You interested in joining us?"

"Sure. What time? And what can I bring?"

"We'll eat about four, but you can come earlier if you'd like. And you don't have to bring anything."

"Okay." But she would. Corina should know better than to think she'd come empty-handed.

Corina hesitated. "You sure you're doing okay? You don't sound so good."

Should she tell her best friend about what had happened the other night? Maybe, but what if she didn't believe her either? And what if it had all been in her head? She didn't really believe that, but neither did she have an explanation for the weird events. And if Corina did believe her, she'd want to know why the police weren't taking her seriously. Which meant that Allye would have to admit to her health struggles.

Tell her.

She knew she should. But she just couldn't bring herself to do it yet.

"Allye?"

"I haven't had my tea yet, and I had a pretty bad migraine yesterday," she deflected, trying to lighten her tone. "Once I get some caffeine in my veins, I'll sound a whole lot better." Might feel a tiny bit better too.

"You should remedy that."

"That's my first priority when I hang up."

Corina chuckled. "Then I'd better let you at it. See you this afternoon."

"See ya." Allye disconnected the call and rubbed her forehead. Everything still felt foggy. Hopefully, the tea actually would help. And give her the energy to bake cookies or something.

She returned to the kitchen. Today called for an Assam tea—full-bodied, high caffeine, perfection. The water was just coming to a boil, so she selected and portioned out her tea leaves. The kettle's auto-off switch kicked in just as she was ready to pre-warm the teapot. She swished a little hot water in the pot, dumped it, then added the infuser basket. Her hand shook as she poured water over the tea leaves, but she managed to fill the pot without spilling much on the counter.

While the tea steeped, she sopped up her mess and began to search for something to eat. She didn't feel like cooking, so she settled for a leftover biscuit and a spoonful of peanut butter. Not ideal, but it would have to tide her over until dinner.

Once the tea was ready, she settled at the table with her meager brunch and tried to plan out her afternoon. She had nearly four hours to kill before heading over to Bryce and Corina's. Baking would take up some of that time, but she should attempt to do some photo edits.

And clean the kitchen. The mound of dishes glared at her from the sink like some sort of monster. Despite Friday's embarrassment, she hadn't had the energy to do anything but double-check her practically useless locks after Eric left. She'd slept with her phone in her hand, ready to dial 911 if her intruder returned. And doing anything yesterday had been impossible.

A bit of biscuit lodged in her throat. She quickly grabbed her teacup and gulped the hot liquid. It burned all the way down, but it took the food with it. Holding a napkin over her mouth, she coughed to confirm everything was clear.

Fear flickered through her. Difficulty swallowing could be another symptom . . . but everyone got choked occasionally. And the biscuit had been dry. Surely that's all it was. She shoved the fear aside but still took extra care as she slowly finished eating.

Next up: dessert for tonight. She took stock of her energy levels. A little better since she'd eaten and gotten a bit of caffeine in her system, but she still felt off. Better go with something simple. She did a quick online search and found a recipe that looked promising. She'd give it a try.

Before long, she had two pies in the oven. Timer set, she forced herself to load and start the dishwasher before heading to her spare-bedroom-turned-office with her refilled teacup. A few large or hand-wash-only dishes remained in the sink, but the monster was noticeably shrunken.

Now she would focus on edits for a bit. She hadn't missed any major deadlines yet, but she'd been edging awfully close on several projects. She couldn't afford to let her photography business tank. Not now when she desperately needed both the income and the flexibility it provided—not to mention the means to pay her health insurance premiums. Up the road, she might not have a choice, but she'd keep going as long as she could.

She tapped the mouse to wake her computer. She groaned. Update in progress. Just what she needed. It was nearing sixty percent, so maybe it wouldn't take much longer.

As she waited, she sipped her tea. The malty notes of the high-quality Assam soothed both her throat and her nerves. She let her gaze drift over the desktop. She'd managed to keep this workspace relatively uncluttered, but she desperately needed to dust. One more thing to add to the list. She probably had time to at least get the worst of it, but that would require the energy to get up and get a dusting cloth.

Instead, she grabbed her phone. Scrolling social media wasn't productive, but it didn't demand anything of her either. As she thumbed down her feed, a local alert caught her eye. *Missing Teen.*

She caught her breath. She recognized the boy in the photo. Dion Walker. Quickly, she tapped the link and pulled up the short article. No details other than his description and that he hadn't been seen since he left school Thursday afternoon.

Jesus, please protect him. You know where he is. Keep him safe until he's found.

She sent a quick text to her small group. Couldn't have too

many people praying. She pulled up a new tab and did a search for his name. No other articles or updates appeared, but she set herself a reminder to follow up and pray. Even if there weren't updates, it would help keep his situation from getting lost in her brain fog.

The computer screen in front of her went dark, then lit as the updates finally finished. Reluctantly, she set her phone and teacup aside. She had to get these edits started.

Password in. Program open. She was ready to go. Except she hadn't brought her camera case. Having the photos to upload would help.

She retrieved her camera case and returned to her seat. She removed her camera, then the memory card from it. Photos popped up immediately when she inserted the card, but they weren't from Jayden Alexander's senior session. These were the nature photographs she'd taken afterward. That's right—she'd swapped the cards before heading for the trail.

She dug in her camera bag but only found more new cards. What had she done with Jayden's? A hint of panic niggled at her brain. She forced herself to think through her actions from that day. She'd removed the card, placed it in the protective case the new one had come in, then . . . her purse! She'd slipped it into her purse.

Pushing past the lightheadedness that hit when she stood, she circled back to the living room and grabbed her purse. After a moment of fruitless digging, she dumped the contents onto an end table. She grabbed at her lip balm and a couple of coins as they rolled toward the edge. Two coins escaped her. They bounced loudly on the floor and skidded away to who knew where.

She scanned the odds and ends—and the few random leaves— that had been in her purse. No memory card. It had to be here somewhere. She shook her purse over the mess. Nothing but dust joined the pile on the table. Quickly, she began replacing items one by one. When all that remained were the leaves and a few gum wrappers, she stared at the nearly empty table, panic growing. She couldn't lose those photos.

Think, Allye! Maybe her purse had fallen over in the car?

She started toward the door, but the kitchen timer started beeping. *The pies.* Had to get them first. She rushed back to the kitchen and grabbed a pair of oven mitts. She checked the desserts and removed them from the oven.

Once they were safely cooling, she headed for her car. Twenty minutes later, she leaned her head against the seat back and tried not to cry. The memory card was nowhere to be found.

She knew it had been in her purse. She remembered the snap of the plastic case and the sensation of dropping it inside. So where had it gone?

All at once, it hit her. Her purse had dumped while she was hiding beside Spicebush Trail. She'd been in a hurry to grab everything and get out of there. She could easily have missed the memory card, especially if it had slid under a bush. Thank God it hadn't rained since then. Hopefully, the flimsy case was enough to protect it from any dew.

But her stomach clenched at the thought of returning to the trail. She couldn't go alone. That much was sure. She checked the time on her phone. Almost three. She didn't have time to go now anyway. While she hated to leave it there any longer than necessary, she'd wait until after dinner. Perhaps Bryce would go with her. She'd have to think of a reason to ask him that wouldn't require her to reveal everything that had been going on, but surely she could come up with something.

12

ERIC BENT OVER HIS DESK in the nearly deserted station. He'd been up most of the night, looking everywhere he could think of for Dion and rechecking some of the likelier places. After a few hours of sleep, he'd run by the teen's house again on his way to the Sunday morning early service. Still no sign of him. Then after church, he'd grabbed a fast-food sandwich and come back here to make sure his reports were in order and try to noodle through the mess of cases he had. But like it had all day yesterday, his mind kept bouncing between the missing teen and a certain redhead, no matter how hard he tried to focus.

He hadn't missed Allye Jessup's unceremonious entrance after retrieving her glasses Friday night. She had always been a little . . . well, *klutzy* was what some of the other guys had called her back in high school, but he'd never liked that term. Her propensity to graze corners and accidentally knock things off her desk was actually kind of cute, though he never would have admitted such a thing back then. She was Bryce's little sister after all. And with the three-year age gap between her and Eric, she'd been too young for him to consider dating. Even if they had been closer in age, she'd always been way out of his league—smart, witty, popular, and from a good family.

But she and her family had always been kind to him. Even when many of the "good kids" were told to avoid him because of his background, as if he'd had a choice about his parents and what they did. A burning started in his gut, as it usually did when he thought of them.

He forced his thoughts back to the present. Replayed Allye's return to the living room and nearly falling into a chair. Looking for all the world like her grip on the porch furniture was the only thing keeping her from toppling over during her conversation with him and Moore. The defeat in her posture each time he'd been unable to find anything to corroborate her story. But more than that, her normal enthusiasm for life and people was lacking. Something was going on with her. Perhaps the same something causing all these incidents?

Despite the lack of evidence, he'd been inclined to believe her accounts until Friday night. But as much as he wanted to deny she could be losing it, this latest story couldn't be anything but that—a story. None of it made sense. Yes, an attacker tracking down the victim that got away was, unfortunately, all too possible. But the rest of it was bizarre.

In a sense, he was relieved it couldn't be true. Because what could have and likely would have happened if that kind of man had actually broken into her home while she was there alone and helpless . . . He tried to shut down that line of thought. Between what he'd been exposed to as a kid and what he'd seen as a cop, he wasn't shocked by much. Disturbed and angered, yes, but those emotions were easily funneled into determination to bring justice to the victims.

But the thought of someone assaulting and murdering sweet, innocent Allye Jessup was more than disturbing. It made him want to vomit.

His phone vibrated on the desk, and he unlocked it to find a text from Bryce.

Early dinner at my place if you're interested.
Steak

Busy with a case

More like a dozen. Despite his hours sifting through notes and brainstorming theories today, he hadn't made any headway with Ashley Harrison's case. Or finding Dion. And between his search for the missing teen and following up on Allye's incidents, he'd gotten behind on the others over the last few days. Kincaid's size and budget had only allowed for one detective position, which meant he had to cover everything from vandalism to homicide. In the theoretical case of a homicide anyway. The only ones he could remember ever happening in Kincaid were in connection with the guy stalking Corina last fall.

You need a break

Bryce was probably right, much as he hated to admit it. Eric stared at the pile of scribbled notes in front of him. He wasn't getting anywhere. Maybe cutting out and actually taking a few hours off would give him fresh eyes for the morning. Technically, he was only supposed to be on call today anyway.

What time?

4:00

Will try. No promises.

See you then

AFTER TAKING A ROUNDABOUT ROUTE to drive by Dion's house again, Eric arrived at Bryce and Corina's house. The couple had married this past spring, then settled into Bryce's childhood home across the street from Corina's father. Those two had been through a lot in the past year—really the past decade or so. But they'd come out the better for it.

He parked on the street and turned off the engine. *3:58.* Right on time. The scent of grilling meat wafted toward him as he approached the porch.

He knocked on the door, then turned to scan the neighborhood. Everything seemed quiet. The house where Corina's stalker had set up headquarters last year remained empty, but the For Rent sign was gone. Hopefully, the new tenants would be upstanding citizens this time.

The breeze shifted, redoubling the scents of charcoal and beef. The door opened just as his stomach rumbled.

Corina grinned. "Hi, Eric. Glad you could make it. And that you brought an appetite." Houston, Corina's German shepherd, poked his snout around her legs and woofed.

"Thanks for the invite. Smells wonderful."

"Locally raised steaks with Bryce's secret dry rub. Come on through. He's out back with Wesley."

He followed her inside, pausing to give Houston's head a pat. As they entered the kitchen, he spotted Hailey Nieland, baby propped on one hip while she assembled a salad with her free hand.

"Eric, hey!" She dumped a jar of olives into the large bowl of greens. "It's been a while."

"Guess it has. How have you been?"

"Oh, pretty good." She added tomatoes to the mix.

He noticed Jenna was staring at him, so he attempted a comical expression. The baby giggled, exposing a toothy grin. A smile stretched across Hailey's face. She got her daughter's attention and signed something, pointed to Eric, then made the same sign again.

"What was that?"

"I told her you were funny. She doesn't know that one yet, so you're a great object lesson."

"Thanks." He flattened his tone, but he really didn't mind. He made the face again and copied Hailey's hand motion. Jenna rewarded him with another giggle.

"Not bad, Detective." Hailey reached for another ingredient.

"Want me to take her so you can finish up?"

"You can try, but she's being clingy today. I think she's got another tooth coming in."

Eric held out his hands, but the baby buried her face in her mom's shoulder. "I think that's a no," he said ruefully.

"Don't feel too bad. She wouldn't come to me either," Corina said from beside him.

Hailey dropped a kiss on Jenna's cheek. "It's okay. I've become the one-handed queen over the last year. Mommy powers." She winked at Corina. "Yours will be kicking in soon."

"Can't wait." A sparkle lit Corina's eyes, and her gaze lingered on her cousin's baby for a moment. Then she seemed to remember what they were all there for. She turned to Eric. "Why don't you head on out with the guys? We've got a few side dishes to finish up here."

"Anything I can help carry?" He scanned the room. His eyes narrowed as he caught sight of the dining room table. The end nearest the back door sported a few baby dishes plus a stack of six adult-size plates and a matching number of glasses and cutlery sets. Bryce and Corina. Wesley and Hailey. Eric and . . . ?

This had better not be some sort of couples thing with a surprise date for him.

He chose not to comment. Yet. No sense in spoiling the meal—but if that's what this turned out to be, he might have to set Bryce straight later.

Corina didn't seem to notice his reaction. She pointed at a collection of condiments on the counter. "If you want to carry those out to the picnic table with you, that would be great."

"Sure thing." He scooped them up and pushed the screen door open. Houston slipped past him. Oops. He glanced back.

Corina waved a hand. "He's fine. I'd have brought him when I came anyway."

Nodding, he stepped onto the back patio. Bryce looked up from the grill and lifted a spatula in greeting.

"Hey, man. Glad you made it."

"Hard to turn down your steaks." Eric deposited his load onto the cedar picnic table. "Gotta admit I'm relieved the ladies are handling the sides though."

Bryce laughed. "You and me both." His lack of skill with an indoor range was well-known.

Wesley looked up from a lawn chair and offered a quick greeting before returning his attention to his phone. His fingers flew across the screen. The guy had some serious speed-texting skills.

Houston nudged Eric's knee and dropped a worn tennis ball at his feet.

"Want to play?" He grabbed the ball and tossed it across the fenced-in yard. The dog was after it in a flash. Eric moved off the patio to keep the game away from the food. They played for several minutes, Houston making him fight for the ball each time he returned with it. After a particularly hard tussle where Houston pulled him off-balance, he threw the ball to the farthest corner of the yard. He was enjoying himself, but he needed a moment to catch his breath.

The back door opened, and Allye exited with a pie dish in each hand. The tension he hadn't realized he'd been carrying slipped from his shoulders. With Allye as the sixth adult member of their dinner party, he didn't have to worry about an unexpected blind date.

"Sorry I'm late."

"Wouldn't expect anything less," Bryce said with a grin.

Allye stuck her tongue out at him. "Not my fault this time. I got stuck behind a tractor. Hey, Wesley." She lifted a pie in greeting, then turned toward the table and caught sight of Eric. "Oh, hey. I didn't realize you were here." She shot him a quiz-zical look.

Right. He was still on the ground. He stood and brushed his hands on his jeans. "I was playing with Houston." The German shepherd returned with his tennis ball, but instead of offering it to Eric, he dropped it in the grass and jumped onto the patio to greet Allye.

She held the pie plates high. "Good afternoon to you too."

Eric clicked his tongue, and Houston dashed back to him. He ruffled the thick fur around the dog's neck, distracting him long enough for Allye to place her offering safely on the table and disappear back inside. With one final scratch behind Houston's ears, he straightened and rejoined Bryce and Wesley on the patio.

"That animal has some energy."

"No kidding. He doesn't show his age, that's for sure."

Wesley finally pocketed his phone, but as soon as he stuck it in his pocket, it rang. "Ugh. Sorry, guys." He shot them an apologetic look before stepping away to take the call.

Bryce stuck a thermometer into one of the steaks. "Almost done." He thumbed over his shoulder toward the house. "You know, Eric, you should ask her out."

"Who?"

Bryce gave him an are-you-being-serious look. "Well, I'm sure not talking about Corina or Hailey."

So much for this not being a blind-date setup. "You know I'm not much of a dater." He couldn't even remember the last time he'd asked anyone out, and it had been years since he'd had a serious girlfriend. That breakup had been completely unexpected, but in retrospect, Rachel's claim that he was too "emotionally unavailable" had probably been all too accurate. She'd found someone else and was now living her happily ever after. He was glad for her. She'd deserved better than he could offer her. So did Allye. "Allye could do a lot better than me."

Bryce grunted and wiped the meat thermometer on a not-so-clean towel.

Eric shoved his hands in his pockets. "Seriously. Your sister is way out of my league."

"Yes, she is. But I haven't met a guy yet who *is* in her league."

He supposed he could give him that. Allye was special, no doubt about it.

"And she likes you."

"What?"

"Allye had a crush on you back in high school, and she still does, if I'm not mistaken. But don't you dare tell her I told you."

Allye had a crush on him?

Bryce studied him, then shook his head. "Man, you really are oblivious. Just think about it. And if you decide you're interested, I'd be all for you two getting together."

"Hmm . . ." That was a curve ball he hadn't seen coming. The idea held more appeal than he would have expected. But considering Allye's current situation, he wasn't sure a relationship was a good idea for either of them. She was . . . vulnerable right now. And possibly unstable, though he hated to even think it.

His friend shook a spatula at him. "But whatever you do, you better not hurt her."

"That's the last thing I'd want to do."

Allye returned then, balancing an armful of glasses and plates. She stumbled, and Eric moved quickly to steady her.

"Let me," he said quietly. He took the plates from her and set them on the table, then returned to help her safely off-load the drinkware.

"Thanks." Her hands held a slight tremble, but she quickly buried them in her pockets and offered him a too-bright smile. "I should know better than to carry that many breakable things."

He eyed the polka-dotted scarf she'd arranged in some sort of decorative knot that obscured any lingering bruises on her neck, but before he could think of a response or ask how she was doing, the back door opened. Hailey and Jenna emerged with the salad, followed by Corina, who was balancing two serving bowls with a plate of rolls resting across their tops. Eric moved to close the door, glad for an excuse to get out of the way as the ladies descended on the table.

As he started to pull the door shut, he noticed the waiting pitcher of iced lemonade and a stack of napkins next to the baby dishes. He gathered up the lot of them and stepped back outside.

Wesley had rejoined the group and now held his daughter in his arms as he traded jokes with Bryce. Eric stationed himself beside them. No way was he pushing his way into the beehive of activity at the table where the three women were arranging sides and distributing plates and glasses.

Allye started back toward the kitchen. When she saw the items he held, she aimed herself his direction instead. "I'll take those."

He allowed her to claim the napkins and baby dishes, but when she reached for the large glass pitcher too, he shook his head. "I've got this."

She shrugged and turned back to the picnic table, but not before he caught the look of relief in her eyes. He'd made the right call. Even if it did mean having to wade into the synchronized table-setting dance that he didn't know the steps to. He quickly deposited the pitcher and retreated.

But the ladies were practically finished. A few seconds later, they all stood back, nodded simultaneously, and laughed.

Corina pressed her hands against her lower back and fixed her eyes on her husband. "Steaks about ready, Bryce? Everything else is."

"About to pull them off now." He made quick work of transferring the rib eyes to a serving platter and headed their way.

13

ALLYE FOUND HERSELF NEXT TO ERIC at the table. Bryce and Corina sat on the opposite side, with Hailey and Wesley across from each other on the end closest to Jenna's high chair.

Eric slipped a small chunk of meat from his plate and held it under the table. Houston inhaled it, his tail loudly thumping against Bryce's leg as he enjoyed the treat.

"You're spoiling my dog," Corina said.

"Is that a problem?"

She shifted sideways to look at the German shepherd. "I guess not." She turned her eyes to Bryce. "Not like my husband hasn't been spoiling him since we returned from our honeymoon."

Bryce didn't look up from his plate. "That is categorically false." He cut a corner off his own steak and offered it to Houston. "I've been doing it since we started dating again." He planted a quick kiss on Corina's cheek, and she leaned into him.

Allye grinned. "All right, you love birds. Remember there are other people present."

Bryce cocked his head. "You hear something, Corina?"

"Nope."

"Didn't think so." He kissed his wife again.

Allye kicked him under the table.

"Ow!"

She mimicked his head movement from a moment before. "Oh, that's funny. Eric, did you hear something?"

Eric just shook his head, but she saw the hint of a smile as he lifted a spoonful of mashed potatoes to his lips. Everyone else chuckled, and Bryce gave them a mock glare before throwing up his hands.

"Fine. No more PDA—for now."

Allye's phone rang.

"Rude," Bryce teased.

"It's Mom." She swiped to answer it. "Hey, what's up?"

"Hi. Where are you?"

"Eating at Bryce and Corina's."

"Oh. Did you forget about dinner?"

She groaned. "Oh, Mom. I'm so sorry."

Her mom's sigh came through the line. "It's okay."

"Could we do tomorrow? Or dinner Tuesday?"

"Tomorrow's out—I'm meeting with Thomas Marshall about a newspaper article he wants to run about local real estate, and I've got a house to show Tuesday evening."

"I could do early. Or late." She waited for her mom to think through her appointment schedule.

"Around eight?" she finally said. "We should be done by then, but I'll have to call you."

"That's fine." She paused. "I'm really sorry."

"Don't worry about it. I'll see you Tuesday."

"Okay. Love you."

"Love you too."

She blew out a breath and slipped the phone back into her pocket.

"What was that?" Bryce asked.

"Mom and I were supposed to go to Zhan's for dinner. I completely forgot."

"You've been doing that a lot lately."

"I've had a lot on my mind." She avoided looking at Hailey, but she could feel her cousin's gaze on her.

"Anything I can help with?" Corina asked.

Allye shook her head. "No. But I've had a lot of senior photo sessions lately, plus I've been working on my photos and knitted items for the Wool Fest next weekend. I'm trying some new ideas this year, and they've been more involved than I expected." All true, though neither of those were the real reason she was struggling. But now was not the time to go into all that.

"Let me know if you change your mind."

"Same here," Hailey said. Her tone held a slight undercurrent, but no one besides Allye seemed to catch it.

She bit back a sigh. Though she appreciated the offer, there was nothing either of them could do to fix her real problems—and delegating anything festival related would require more mental energy than she had to expend.

"Don't stress too much over it. Your displays are always stellar," Bryce said.

"Thanks." Despite the enormity of her other issues, she hoped he was right. She loved the annual weekend festival and hated that things weren't coming together like they usually did. Or maybe they were, but it really didn't feel like it.

She picked at her food as the conversation turned to other things, but she wasn't hungry anymore. Well, she hadn't really been hungry all day. Unfortunate, because this tasted great.

Allye glanced around the table. Everyone seemed to be fully focused on predictions for the upcoming football game, which she had no interest in. But she didn't mind—and she much preferred this topic to the previous one.

Hailey added a spoonful of mashed potatoes to Jenna's plate of soft foods. Without releasing the bit of roll in her hand, the baby stuck two fingers in the new option, tasted it, and flung the bread over her shoulder. Houston, who had strategically positioned himself near the high chair once the guys stopped feeding him, caught the scrap midair. Allye stifled a smile. The dog was smart. He knew where the most food was likely to fall.

Jenna raised goopy fingers in greeting when she caught her watching. Allye lifted her hands above the table and signed, *You like mashed potatoes?*

Grinning, the baby mimicked the sign for *potatoes*, then started babbling at her in an adorable baby version of ASL, with quite a few distinct signs in the mix.

Allye's gaze drifted to her cousin. Hailey was watching the exchange with pride. As she should. As soon as Jenna had been diagnosed with congenital hearing loss, Hailey had begun poring over ASL books and videos. Allye and the rest of the family had learned a few signs, some of them getting further than others, but Hailey had thrown herself into it and made sure to expose Jenna to the language as much as possible.

Hailey caught her eye and signed, *You okay?*

She nodded.

Her cousin made a sign she didn't recognize, but if her expression held any clue to the meaning, she'd probably signed a sarcastic *Really?* or something to that effect.

Now was not a good time for this conversation. Making sure no one else was paying attention, she finger spelled *L-A-T-E-R.*

Hailey responded with *Yes* and a sign that Allye suspected meant *later.*

She didn't want to talk about it later either, but later was better than now. She lifted her fork and took another bite of her steak. It was starting to get cold, which didn't help her lack of appetite. She swallowed, then pushed the plate back. Maybe she'd just plastic wrap it and take it home.

"If you're done, we going to get to try that pie?" Bryce pointed his fork at the dessert she'd brought.

She removed the foil cover from one of the pies and reached for the spatula she'd grabbed from Corina's kitchen earlier.

"Oooh, what is that?" Corina asked.

"Peach crumble pie."

"Sounds good," Eric said.

"I hope it is. Haven't tried this recipe before." She usually made a traditional crust for her pies, but that would have taken more energy than she had to spare today. This recipe used the crumble mixture for both the bottom crust and the topping. Simple, easy, fast. And hopefully, still tasty.

She served each of the others a large slice, but only cut a small one for herself.

Before Allye got a bite into her own mouth, Corina exclaimed, "This is wonderful!"

Eric swallowed and nodded enthusiastically. "I take back what I said. It's not good—it's amazing."

Wesley and Hailey echoed the sentiment. Bryce only winked at her and grunted, but at the rate he was clearing his plate, he shared their approval.

She smiled and lifted a spoonful. "Guess I'd better taste it, then."

"Not necessary. You probably won't like it." Bryce reached for her plate, and Corina swatted his hand.

"Behave."

Allye effected a somber tone. "I must make my own evaluation, dear brother." She popped the bite into her mouth. Sugar, spices, and peachy goodness pirouetted across her taste buds. "Not bad."

Her nonchalant verdict elicited laughter from the others.

"Seriously, Allye. I love this. What did you change in the recipe—and can you share it?" Corina asked as she dug her spoon back into her slice.

Allye almost chuckled at the fact Corina knew her well enough to assume she had tweaked the recipe, despite it being her first time making it. "Sure. It's just a simple one I found online, but I added a bit of coriander, ginger, and cardamom to the spices it called for." She took another bite and analyzed the flavor. "I like how it turned out, but next time I might sub brown sugar for some of the white though."

"I think it's perfect," Bryce declared.

"You want more?" She eyed his scraped-clean plate.

"I wouldn't turn it down."

She removed the cover from the second pie and dished him another generous slice. Good thing she'd decided to double the recipe. Corina hadn't mentioned how many they were expecting for dinner, but Wesley, Hailey, and Jenna—or just Hailey and Jenna when Wes was busy—were frequent additions to their impromptu gatherings. Making two pies was better than coming up short, and she'd figured she could leave any leftovers with Bryce and Corina.

After handing her brother's plate back to him, she turned to the others. "Anyone else?"

Hailey held up her hand. "It was delicious, but I'm totally stuffed."

Wesley started to answer, but his ringing phone cut him off. He stepped away from the table and answered it.

"How about you?" Allye turned to Corina.

Her friend pretended to be considering. She looked down at her still nearly flat belly and nodded as if coming to a decision. "Baby says we should have a little more."

"And my little niece or nephew gets whatever they want."

Bryce released a groan. "You're going to be *that* kind of aunt, aren't you?"

"Mm-hmm." She leaned across the table to slide a second piece onto Corina's plate. She grabbed the pitcher of lemonade. Might as well refill their glasses while she was up.

Corina turned to Bryce. "So you don't think I should have more pie?"

Bryce waved his hands. "That is absolutely not what I meant."

She winked at Allye. "Sure sounded like it. A girl could get offended."

"Better watch it, Bryce," Eric said dryly.

He sent him a withering look. "You too?"

Eric shrugged and focused on scraping the last of his pie from his plate. Hailey snickered.

Bryce dropped his shoulders and sighed in mock defeat. "Can't win with all of you against me."

Corina leaned into him. "I love you. You know that?" She kissed him. And stole a spoonful of pie from his plate while she had him distracted.

"I saw that," Bryce murmured when the kiss ended.

Corina shoved the spoon into her mouth and dissolved into giggles. Hailey and Allye joined her laughter, and Jenna raised her hands and squealed, obviously enjoying the adults' antics.

Wesley rejoined them, frustration creasing his forehead. "We're going to have to go. There's been an incident with one of my clients' accounts."

Disappointment settled over Hailey's face, but she quickly cleared her expression. "Let me get Jenna cleaned up."

Once the three of them had taken their leave, Allye tapped the edge of Eric's empty plate. "Sorry. I got distracted. Did you want another slice?"

"I really shouldn't." He glanced from his plate to the pie dish. "But I think I will anyway. Just a small one, please."

Satisfaction filled her. He really did like it. She quickly cut a slice that wasn't quite as large as Bryce's. It was definitely pushing the limits of what could be considered small though.

Allye settled back into her seat, grinning as the conversation and banter rose again. Eric was mostly quiet, but he was clearly amused and occasionally joined in too. She loved this. Family. Friends. Time spent enjoying each other's company.

During a lull when Bryce had excused himself for a moment and Corina had stepped away with a phone call, Allye sneaked a look at Eric. He was petting Houston, but his expression indicated he was somewhere else—and judging by his frown, it wasn't a good place.

"Everything okay?"

His hand stilled atop Houston's head, and it took a second for his eyes to focus on her. "Sorry. Just thinking about a case."

"You look bothered. Need to talk about it? I mean, I know you probably can't share details—not with me anyway—but maybe talking would help? Or not." She felt her cheeks flame as she backtracked. She didn't know a lot about police work, but that was probably overstepping.

He didn't quite smile, but his frown disappeared. "It's okay." Houston nudged him, and he resumed stroking the dog. After a moment, he said, "I'm worried about a missing teen. His mom OD'd a few days ago, and no one seems to have seen him anywhere."

"Dion?" She covered her mouth. The alert hadn't said anything about his mom. Poor kid.

Eric's intense gaze shot to hers. "Yes. Do you know him?"

She shook her head. "Not really, but I saw an alert for him this morning, and I remember his face. He used to attend youth group, didn't he?"

"He did. His brother, Lucky, still rides the church bus on Sunday mornings. Or did." He sighed. "Not sure if he'll be able to come now that he's in foster care."

"I didn't realize those two were related." She sometimes volunteered with kids ministry, but Lucky was in the class below the one she usually helped in.

Bryce rejoined them, and they let the subject drop. Before long, it was time to clean up. The four of them worked together to get everything into the kitchen, dishes washed, and leftovers put away. Once they were finished, Allye leaned against a wall. Exhaustion pulled at her, but she refused to acknowledge it. She still had to go to the park and search for her memory card.

She summoned what she hoped would pass for a cheery expression before launching into her request. "We've still got an hour or so of daylight left. Anyone want to go for a walk at Kincaid Lake?" She pretended not to notice the look Eric shot her. Instead, she fixed her gaze on her brother.

But he was already shaking his head. "Sorry, Allye. Corina and I have something we have to take care of. Wish we could."

"Oh, that's okay." She smiled, though she didn't feel it. She really didn't want to go alone.

"You and Eric could still go," Corina said.

This time, her gaze shot to Eric's. Was Corina trying to . . . ? She glanced back at her friend. Yep. There was a mischievous twinkle in her eye. A lump settled in Allye's stomach.

She forced the smile to remain on her face as she pushed away from the wall and began gathering her bags. "I still nee—want—to go, but I'm sure Eric has other things to do."

Corina turned to him. "Do you?"

Eric's expression gave nothing away. "I do. But a walk first might be nice, especially after that meal."

"You really don't have to go," Allye insisted. She was not going to let Corina put them on the spot.

He studied her for all of two seconds, then picked up her pie dishes. "Let me get this for you at least." He nodded to their hosts. "Thank you for dinner. It was delicious."

"Yes, thanks," Allye echoed.

"Any time," Corina said. She pulled Allye in for a hug and whispered, "Don't be stubborn."

Stubborn? About what?

But when her best friend released her and rolled her eyes pointedly in Eric's direction, Allye knew exactly what she meant. She just shook her head. Matchmaking couldn't happen. Not now. But she also couldn't reveal why.

"I gotta go. Love you guys."

"Back at you," Bryce said.

Eric followed her outside, pie plates in hand. Once they were safely out of earshot of her family, he said, "Are you sure you don't want company?"

No. She absolutely wanted company. But she didn't want to invite more than friendship. She couldn't. But she was too tired to figure out how to politely decline without lying to him. She kept walking toward her car.

"Allye."

The way he said her name made her step hitch. She took a deep breath. "It's okay, Eric. Really. You don't need to feel pressured to go because of what Corina said." She popped the trunk of her Jetta and tossed everything but her purse inside. She turned and grabbed the pie dishes he held. He didn't let go.

"That isn't what I asked."

She stifled a sigh. "Fine. I would love to not go alone, but seriously, I'm a big girl. I'm used to going places by myself."

He frowned. "Is that wise considering everything you have going on?"

"Are you saying you believe me now?"

"I believe something is going on, and you probably shouldn't be out in the park alone just in case."

Just in case her attacker showed? Or just in case she had another "episode"? She didn't have the heart to ask for clarification. *He's right though.* She knew he was. Whether she was in physical danger or going crazy, she didn't need to be out on the trails alone. And she didn't want to be.

"Are you okay, Allye?" he said quietly when she didn't respond. "No offense, but you look exhausted. Maybe you should just head home."

She tugged the empty dishes from his fingers and tossed them in beside her bags. Her shoulders slumped as she faced him again. "It's not that I just want to take a walk. I lost a memory card with an important photo shoot on it Friday. I have to try to find it. If you have time"—she felt her shoulders drop a bit further—"I'd appreciate not being alone."

His gaze softened at her admission. "I have time."

14

ERIC FOLLOWED ALLYE TO KINCAID LAKE. She had refused his offer of a ride. Though she didn't say it, he suspected it had less to do with wanting to drive and more to do with not wanting to leave her car at her brother's and incite a round of teasing. He'd played dumb to Corina's not-so-subtle matchmaking attempt, but he hadn't missed it.

Allye signaled before turning at the park's entrance. While she'd pushed the speed limit a bit on the way over, nothing about her driving was erratic. No sign she was drowsy or in any way impaired.

That was a relief. He hadn't been sure allowing her to drive was a good decision, but it hadn't been his choice. Still, something was obviously going on with her. But what?

He backed into a parking space next to her and exited his vehicle first. When her door opened, he offered his hand.

"I can stand."

"I know." He didn't withdraw his offer. And she took it, resignation on her face. The vehicles on either side left little space between them as he pulled her to her feet for the second time in two days. A hint of jasmine and mango tantalized his senses. He'd noticed the scent on her before, and he liked it. It fit her well. Or at least, it fit her usual fun-loving and caring personality well. But her current pallor and hesitancy worried him. "It's okay to accept help, you know."

"But it isn't easy." Her words were barely a whisper.

The tremor that went through her worried him. He gave her hand a light squeeze, then shifted it so she could lean on his arm instead. "Let's find your card so you can get home and rest. Do you have any idea where you lost it?" He led her from between the cars and scanned the area. Despite the beautiful weather, only a handful of people were around.

She sucked in a breath. "Probably when my purse dumped . . . while I was hiding by the trail."

"We'll check there first, then."

They made their way to Spicebush Trail. The temperature dropped a few degrees as they entered the shaded path.

A little way in, Eric helped her over a fallen branch, then broke the silence between them. "I've been wanting to ask you. How did you get my number the other night?"

Her face flushed. "I, uh, just knew it."

"How did you 'just know it'?"

"I might have memorized it in high school."

High school? "That was over a decade ago. How did you know it hadn't changed?" The red in her cheeks deepened. She was adorable when she was embarrassed. He straightened at that thought. Where had that come from?

She attempted a nonchalant shrug. "I happened to see it pop up on Bryce's phone a while back."

"I didn't realize you were so good with numbers."

She shrugged again but didn't offer a response, and they lapsed back into silence. A few minutes later, she pointed. "I think it was over there."

They approached the bush she indicated, and he let her pull away from him but stayed close behind her as she departed from the trail and knelt down to search. The area behind the bush did show signs of her presence the day before. Nothing too obvious—especially from the trail, which would explain why he hadn't seen it Friday—but subtle depressions in the flora and a still-shiny safety pin caught his eye. He crouched beside her and picked up the pin to dispose of later. If it was Allye's, he doubted she would want it back after it had lain in the dirt for two days.

"Anything?"

"No." Her worry was clear. "If it's not here, I don't know where to look."

He sifted through some of the nearby leaves, then moved a few steps away. "This yours?" He held up a tube of Chap Stick.

She took it and examined it. "Yes."

"So your card could have rolled farther than the area you're looking in."

"True." She felt under the base of the bush, then moved to his left. They searched together for a couple more minutes before she released a triumphant cry. "Found it!"

"Is it okay?"

She popped the case open and felt the memory card. "Looks okay and feels dry."

"Great." He stood and held out his hand. She took it without hesitation this time and allowed him to pull her up. They returned to the trail, and he looked back the way they came. "I think we're about halfway through. Do you want to complete the circuit or turn around?"

"Forward is fine. I wish I had my camera though. I didn't continue on Friday because . . ."

Because her attacker had gone that way. Or at least, that's what she'd thought happened. No need to get into all that right now. Instead, he nodded understanding and guided her down the trail.

"It's so pretty out here," Allye breathed as they walked.

It was a beautiful area, he couldn't deny that. He didn't often take time to enjoy nature. Most of his free time was spent either fixing up his house or helping with the teens at church.

Perhaps he should consider an occasional walk out here to clear his mind.

They rounded a bend in the trail, and Allye pulled him to a stop.

"What is it?"

"That would make an excellent print."

He followed the direction of her gaze, but although it was as pretty as the rest of the trail, he didn't see what was so exceptional about it.

"Come on." She tugged at his arm.

"You don't have your camera."

"I can use my phone. It might not be print quality, but it's not bad. I'd still like to get a few shots."

"As long as you feel up to it."

She mumbled something, but he didn't quite catch it as she led him off the trail. She released his arm, pulled her phone from her pocket, and began taking photos.

He stood back, watching but trying to stay out of her way. She was smiling, but he doubted she realized it—she seemed totally immersed in the world of photography. No doubt she loved what she did.

After what had to have been fifty photos, she slowed and leaned against a tree.

"Doing all right?"

"Sorry. Just need a breather."

He closed the distance between them. "Take however long you need."

The smile she gave him was tired but genuine. "I could spend all day out here with my camera. At least when I'm feeling—" Her mouth snapped shut.

"When you're feeling what?"

She shook her head. "Never mind." She scanned the wooded area, avoiding his gaze.

What had she been about to say? He bit down on the question.

They might be friends, but they weren't close friends. And this wasn't a case. He didn't have a right to the facts or her thoughts. But he did wish he could make sure she was okay.

"What's that?" Allye pointed off to the right.

He snapped his head in the direction she indicated. A dark lump protruded from behind a tree about five yards away. He should have noticed it before now, but he'd been so focused on Allye, he hadn't been paying much attention to their surroundings.

"Stay here." He moved cautiously toward the foreign object. As he drew near, he could see it was a bedroll—a dark gray sleeping bag rolled tightly around a black pillow. He didn't touch anything, but he noted the location to report to the park service. Kincaid Lake provided camping spots, but this wasn't one of them. The items didn't appear to be brand-new, but neither did they look like they'd been out in the weather very long. Someone had either hiked off trail and dropped them, or they were camping here illegally. Based on the compressed vegetation, he'd guess the latter.

He snapped a photo and made his way back to Allye. "Sleeping bag," he said in answer to her silent question. "Looks like someone's camping out here."

She shivered. "Isn't it a little late in the year for that?"

"You'd think." Nighttime temps this time of year often dropped to the low fifties or into the forties. Avid campers in the area still enjoyed the overall moderate weather, but they usually had access to a campfire. There'd been no makeshift fire pit or other sign of illicit burning near the bedroll. Whoever was staying out here was apparently smart enough not to risk detection or a forest fire in an attempt to stay warm, but Eric imagined the nights were less than comfortable. Of course, if the person stayed high or drunk, they might be oblivious to the cold—putting them in more danger.

Nothing he could do though. Allye was his primary responsibility at the moment, and Kincaid Lake wasn't within his jurisdiction. He'd pass off their findings to the park service and see that

Allye got home safely. He'd prefer to do both before their illegal camper returned.

He extended his hand toward the trail. "Ready?"

"I suppose." She cast one last look at the campsite before leading the way back. Eric stayed close, ready to catch her if she stumbled, but they made it to the trail without incident and continued on their way.

As they neared the final bend before the trailhead, crunching leaves signaled a newcomer's approach. They drifted to the right to make room, and a lanky teen with a backpack and ball cap soon rounded the bend. He kept his head down as he passed them, but Eric caught a look at his face.

"Dion?"

The teen immediately broke into a run.

15

ERIC TOOK OFF AFTER THE FLEEING TEEN. "Wait here!" he called
to Allye.

The kid was fast, but Eric wasn't about to lose him so quickly. A
few yards down the trail, Dion shucked his backpack. Eric hurdled
it and kept going. His feet pounded the earth. He was gaining on
him.

As Dion rounded a bend, Eric put on a burst of speed. He
cleared the curve in time to spot the teen attempting to disappear off-trail. He charged that direction.

"Dion. Hold up."

The teen ignored him. Eric was only a few feet behind him
now. Without warning, Dion changed directions. Eric pivoted,
a bit too fast. He tripped. Flung his hand out and managed to
grasp the boy's ankle.

They both went down to the forest floor, Dion flailing.

"Get off me!"

Eric held tight as he pulled himself up from his prone position.
"That's enough." He infused the words with as much author-
ity as he could muster. The teen kicked and managed to break
Eric's hold, but as he attempted to rise and take off again, his foot
caught on a root, and he went back down.

Eric was on him instantly. Doing his best not to hurt the boy, he pinned him to the ground.

"Dion, chill. It's me."

After one final thrash, the teen finally stopped struggling and closed his eyes.

"I've been looking all over for you. You okay?"

Dion didn't answer, and Eric gave his shoulders a light shake. "Hey. Help me out here. You hurt? In trouble?"

His eyes popped open. "No. I'm fine. Why you chasin' me down?"

"Why did you run?" Eric fired back.

"I dunno. You scared me." Right. Because it was normal to take off running when someone said your name.

"You done running now?"

"Yeah." The word was mostly a groan.

Eric released him and sat back. He left just enough distance between them to appear unthreatening, but not enough to allow Dion an easy escape should he decide to take off again.

But the fight seemed to have gone out of the teen. He sat up and draped his arms over his knees.

"Where have you been?"

"Around."

"That's not an answer."

Dion shrugged, avoiding eye contact.

"We found a bedroll off the trail a little ways. That yours?"

Another shrug.

"How long you been staying out here?"

"Few days."

"Hey." At the seriousness in his tone, Dion finally met his gaze. "Do you know about your mom?"

The teen's face blanched, then hardened. "Yeah."

"I'm sorry."

"She deserved it." Dion swiped at his nose. He was trying awful hard to look like he didn't care. And failing miserably.

Eric clenched his teeth. He couldn't comment on whether Ashley Harrison had deserved her fate, but her boys sure hadn't.

Light footsteps sounded on the trail, and they both turned to see Allye approaching with Dion's discarded backpack.

"Everything okay?" she asked hesitantly.

Eric glanced at Dion. "Yeah. We're about to come out."

"I'm not going anywhere," Dion mumbled.

"You can't stay out here alone."

"I've been just fine."

"You're fourteen. Leaving you out on your own isn't an option."

"I'm not going to a foster home. Been there, done that."

"I didn't say anything about a foster home."

"And where else would you send me? I don't have a dad, and Mom's dead." His defiant tone almost covered the hurt he had to be feeling.

Eric pulled in a deep breath. "Look, it's getting late. How about you stay with me tonight, and we'll figure out next steps tomorrow."

Dion stared at him.

"I promise, no social workers tonight." He wasn't leaving him here alone regardless, but Dion's cooperation would make things much easier. He'd contact Tracy Ann, but he knew how hard it was to line up care on short notice. He was confident she'd let him handle things tonight. Morning would be soon enough to get the ball rolling on a more long-term solution.

After another moment, Dion jerked a nod. "Okay."

Allye's relieved exhale carried across the space between them, and Eric silently released his own. He stood and grabbed the ball cap Dion had lost in their struggle. He offered it to him. "All right, then. We'll get your stuff and head back to town. Grab a bite to eat on the way." Like with his brother, the mention of food sparked something in the teen's eyes. But he didn't comment. Just took his hat and began trudging in the direction of his makeshift campsite.

Eric returned to the trail, pausing long enough to heft Dion's backpack onto his shoulder. He offered his other arm to Allye but kept his eye on the teen. "You up for a bit more walking, or would you rather wait here?"

She tucked her arm into his. "I'd rather not be alone."

"Fair enough." They followed Dion back down the trail. The teen made no attempt to run off again, but neither did he seem inclined to conversation. Eric let him be for now. He'd try to get some answers after the kid had something in his stomach.

Allye remained quiet as well. Her slightly labored breathing concerned him. So did the increasing pressure on his arm as she began to lean more heavily on him. But she didn't complain.

When they eventually reached the parking lot, Eric eyed her car. "You sure you're okay driving home?"

"Yes. Thank you for coming with me." She gave him a tired smile, then reached for Dion's hand and squeezed it—obviously surprising the teen. "I'm so glad you're okay, Dion. I'm praying for you and your brother."

A nod was his only response. She pressed his hand again, then allowed Eric to help her into her car. Once she had the engine started, she rolled down the window and waved to them. "Bye, guys."

"Night. Drive safe."

"I'll do that, Detective." Her smile edged a bit into impish territory with the last word, but it only made her more adorable.

Hold up. He shook his head and backstepped from between the vehicles. While she pulled out, he unlocked his trunk and placed Dion's backpack inside. "You can toss your bedroll in there too."

Dion looked like he didn't want to be separated from his things, but he complied without complaint.

Eric clapped him on the shoulder. "Climb in."

"What's wrong with her?" Dion held the question until they were both inside and the vehicle was in motion.

"Not sure." Eric swung onto the main road. "Maybe nothing.

But we'll make sure she gets home okay, then we'll get food." Dion snorted, and Eric gave him a sidelong glance. "What?"

"Sounds like an invasion of privacy."

Eric's fingers tightened on the wheel, but he kept his tone light. "Nope. Just being a friend." If Dion thought following Allye home was an invasion of privacy, he wasn't going to like when Eric questioned him about his whereabouts the last few days and what he might know about his mom.

Dion let the issue drop, and they soon caught up to Allye's red Jetta. They followed her to her house and watched from the road as she slowly exited the car, gave them a wave, unloaded her trunk, and disappeared inside.

"What are you in the mood for?" Eric asked as he pointed his car toward the center of town.

"Doesn't matter."

"Hamburger? Pizza? Chinese? Totally up to you."

After a pause, Dion mumbled, "Pizza's fine."

"You got it." They'd get takeout from Zhan's. Filling. Satisfying. And there might even be leftovers for later.

16

ALLYE BARELY MADE IT INSIDE HER HOUSE. As soon as the front door closed behind her, she let her bags slide to the floor and considered joining them. She was absolutely exhausted, and her mind was reeling. Dion had been camping out on Spicebush Trail. And while she was so very grateful they'd found him safe, she'd had an awful realization. He'd been the one on the trail with her attacker Friday afternoon. The voice was the same, and so were his shoes.

What was he mixed up in?

She probably should have told Eric—correction, she knew she should have. But she was so tired of not being believed. And Dion had never been comfortably out of earshot on their return to the parking lot. Besides that, she'd had to focus on actually getting back. She'd been pushing herself well before they started the second loop around the trail. It was embarrassing how difficult that hike had been for her.

And things were just going to get worse.

"You don't know that," she muttered to herself, but the melancholy of the thought latched on, adding another weight to her weary body as she leaned against the door. The symptoms she'd noted over the last several weeks—no, months now—paraded in bold print through her mind. Recent unverifiable incidents aside, the conglomeration added up to a diagnosis she was quite familiar with.

She'd been eight when her aunt was diagnosed with multiple sclerosis, but she remembered her mom's reaction when she heard the news. Remembered independent, fun-loving Aunt Jo slowly losing her ability to play with them or even care for herself. Remembered when she was hospitalized repeatedly over the years for the pneumonia that eventually took her life.

Tears threatened, and she pressed her fists against her eyes. MS might not be fatal in itself, and from what she'd researched, it was more treatable today than in the past. Still, anyone who tried to say it wasn't scary needed a reality check.

Maybe she was wrong. Maybe she was just losing it and none of the physical symptoms were real. She snorted. Like that was any better.

But it could be something else. Something more manageable, even curable. Or something worse.

She groaned and pushed off the door. She hated the negative thoughts. They weren't productive, weren't helping her or anyone else. But they were there just the same.

More slowly than she would have thought possible at the beginning of the year, she trudged to her room and collapsed onto her unmade bed. Despite her fatigue, her thoughts continued to spiral with the frightening possibilities of what her life might look like in the coming months and years. Fears for herself tumbled over one another and collided with worries of how best to alert Eric to Dion's possible involvement with her attacker. The sun set, then twilight faded, leaving her in total darkness.

Her phone, still in her pocket, buzzed. With an effort, she tugged it out and read the text from Hailey.

Praying for you.

That started the tears flowing for real. This time she let them. They'd probably result in a massive headache, if not a migraine, but she'd deal with that later.

Between sobs, she gasped out a prayer of her own. "God, I really, really need your help. I know you're in control of whatever is going on in my life and my body, and I trust you. I do." She sucked in a breath. "But this is also really, really hard."

The tears continued, but her words were spent. Even as she soaked her pillow, she took comfort in knowing God understood her situation and what she would say if she could. He knew.

Eventually the flow subsided, leaving a raging headache in its wake as she'd feared. But she didn't regret the tears. They'd helped. A little.

But the longer she lay in bed, the worse her head hurt, and the drier her throat became. Her face felt stiff and itchy from her cry. She reached toward her nightstand, feeling for a water bottle or glass with anything in it, but she'd cleared them all off when she did dishes earlier.

She procrastinated moving for another couple of minutes before working herself into a sitting position. The immediate nausea and dizziness almost pushed her right back down. She lowered her head into her hands and prayed for it to pass.

When the worst of it dulled, she gathered her courage and stood. She swayed and bumped the nightstand. Something clattered to the floor and rolled, but no way was she about to bend down for anything.

With a hand on the wall for support, she made her way to the bathroom for some pain relievers. She swallowed them with water from the sink, wishing she had a glass to fill for her room but not wanting to brave the walk to the kitchen. She needed to start keeping a case of water bottles in her room. One more thing to add to the "later" list.

She splashed her face with cool water and drank a couple more handfuls, all the while avoiding her reflection. No doubt her face was as red as her hair and puffy to boot. She could pass on that image.

Once back in bed, she started making a mental checklist for tomorrow. She didn't think she had any appointments, but she'd confirm that in the morning. Unless she'd forgotten something, editing Jayden's photos would be priority—assuming the memory card hadn't suffered damage during its time in the woods. She should have checked that as soon as she arrived home. Too late now. She wasn't getting back up.

After editing, she'd move on to her festival products. Wool Fest was this weekend, and she had a booth reserved for all three days. She'd been collecting photos and knitting whimsical gifts and accessories all year, but her stockpile still seemed much smaller than usual. Maybe some of the photos she'd taken on her phone today would be high enough quality for postcard prints. Those tended to sell well, since they were an inexpensive option, and people loved looking through them.

Somewhere in there, she'd need to contact Eric about Dion. And she couldn't forget dinner with Mom again. Or was that supposed to be Tuesday? Gah. She'd have to text her and confirm. Should have put it in her phone as soon as they discussed it.

Tuesday would be a whopper of a day regardless. MRI day. She both dreaded and looked forward to it. The not knowing was killing her. But once she knew, there would be no going back. If the MRI showed what she feared, she'd have to prepare to accept the diagnosis—even if more tests were required before it was official. She'd have to tell her family. Her mom.

She wasn't ready for that.

17

ZHAN'S WAS PACKED WHEN THEY ARRIVED, and by the time Eric and Dion made it home with their to-go order, it was getting late.

Eric dropped the pizza boxes on the table and retrieved plates from the cabinet. The cashier at Zhan's had given them disposable ones, but he preferred real dishes. Even if it did require washing them afterward. He handed one to Dion. "Help yourself." While the teen filled his plate, Eric moved to the refrigerator and grabbed cans of Coke for both of them. "Sorry I can't offer you a variety. It's this or water."

"Coke's fine." Dion looked like he was barely restraining himself from digging into the food on his plate.

"Go ahead and eat."

That was all the permission the teen needed. By the time Eric served himself, Dion's first slice of pizza had vanished, and he was quickly working his way through a second. Eric pretended not to notice. He'd ordered more than enough for the both of them.

Once Dion's pace began to slow, Eric folded his arms on the table. "We need to talk man to man."

Wariness immediately rose in the boy's eyes. "What about?"

"Your mom. I need to know where she got her drugs. You have any idea who her dealer was?"

He looked away. "What's it matter now? She's dead."

"It does matter. Someone is responsible for her death. And if we can stop the dealers, we can prevent more people from dying."

Dion shrugged and slowly ripped a piece off a napkin. "Soon's you stop one, another pops up. Druggies always find a way to get their fix. Mom always did."

"Doesn't mean we ignore justice or stop doing our best to stop it." He waited but got no response. "You didn't answer my question though. Do you know who her dealer was?"

"No clue."

"Do you do drugs?"

Dion's gaze shot back to his. "No!"

That struck a nerve. Eric tried to appear nonthreatening. "No offense meant. I'm not accusing you or trying to trap you. Just asking."

"Answer's still no. I saw what they did to Mom. I'm not that stupid."

"Good. I'm glad to hear it. Lot of people follow their parents' examples whether they're making smart decisions or not."

Dion relaxed ever so slightly at the affirmation, but he continued tearing the napkin, filling his plate with wispy shreds.

"So if you don't know her dealer, do you know the names of any friends she might have gotten drugs from? Or who might have an idea where she got them?"

"I stayed as far away from her friends as I could."

"She ever mention their names?"

"First names is all I know. Sarah. Amber. Might have been a David."

"Okay, that helps. Any others?"

"Dunno. Like I said, we just tried to stay outta their way."

"You and Lucky?"

"Yeah." He glanced up from the destroyed napkin, true concern in his eyes. "He doing okay?"

"Yes. I saw him Friday night. He's being taken care of. I think he misses you though."

"I'm all he's got."

Eric already knew that, but hearing it from Dion felt like a gut punch. He let a few seconds pass before redirecting the conversation. "Another question for you. How'd you know about your mom? Her name hasn't been released to the news yet."

Dion stilled. Eric waited him out. He hated what the boy was going through. But he had to do his job, and right now, he had precious little to go on.

"Dion?"

"I saw her," the teen finally mumbled.

"When? When did you see her?"

"Couple hours before I called."

"*You* called?" They'd been waiting on a warrant to track down the anonymous caller just in case it had been someone involved in Ashley's death. Looked like that wouldn't be necessary.

He nodded but didn't look up. "Didn't know what else to do."

"You pretended to be a neighbor?"

Another nod.

"Why didn't you just say who you were?" And why wait?

"I didn't know what to do," he said again. "Knew she was long gone already, so it wouldn't have done any good to call for an ambulance. And I didn't want CPS coming after me and Lucky. But he wasn't in the house then, and you found him before I did."

"What would you have done if you'd found him?"

He shrugged.

"You two are too young to be on your own, Dion. Lucky needs a roof over his head and regular meals. Stability. You deserve those things too."

The teen had started to bristle, but at Eric's last statement, he softened. But then he shook his head.

"You know foster homes aren't like that. We get a roof, sure.

And food most of the time. But they ain't stable. You get yanked from place to place. And some of the parents are downright mean."

Eric wished he could refute Dion's words, but they weren't totally untrue. Although the system was meant for good, there were often a lot of broken pieces. "I'm sorry you've had bad experiences. But I can promise you there are good homes out there, and we'll make sure you're taken care of."

"Nice try, but you don't control the system."

"No, but that doesn't mean I'm powerless. I will take action if I find out there's neglect or abuse going on in a foster home. And I know the local director. She won't put up with it either if she finds out her kids are being mistreated."

"So you say." He spoke the words under his breath, but Eric caught them.

"I mean it. You still have my number?"

"Yeah."

"Memorized?"

He hesitated, then nodded.

"I want to hear from you. And not just if things are bad—although I certainly want you to call me if you need help. But you can call if you just want to talk too. I'll pick up if I can, and if for some reason I can't, then leave me a message, and I will call back. Promise."

He didn't look convinced, but he didn't argue.

And it really was late now. Eric should probably ask him for more details about how he'd found his mom, if he'd touched her body or moved anything, but at this point, it wouldn't hurt to wait until tomorrow. The kid could use a good night's sleep. He'd been through a lot the past couple of days—and Eric wasn't naïve enough to think he'd had it good before that.

He slapped his thighs and stood. "I think it's time we get some sleep. I don't have a spare bed, but you can have mine for tonight. I'll take the couch."

Dion's head shot up, his eyes round. "I don't want to take your bed. It's your house."

Eric waved him off. "You're my guest for tonight. The couch won't kill me. Sometimes I fall asleep there anyway."

"But—"

"No *buts*. And listen, while you're here, I want you to make yourself at home. You get hungry or thirsty, help yourself to whatever's in the kitchen, even if it's the middle of the night. Got it?"

Dion nodded.

"All right. Let's get you settled in."

18

ERIC DRAINED HIS SECOND CUP OF COFFEE. He was normally an early riser, but wakefulness had hit even sooner than normal this morning. Probably had something to do with sleeping on the couch. He hadn't been lying when he'd told Dion he sometimes fell asleep there. But he also hadn't bothered to mention that he normally woke back up and moved to his much more comfortable bed to finish out the night.

He glanced at the clock. Better get Dion up. Much as he hated sending him into the system, he didn't have a choice. But he could see to it that the teen got a good breakfast before Tracy Ann arrived for him.

He pulled eggs and a package of bacon from the refrigerator and weighed them in his hands. Wake Dion now or let the scent of sizzling bacon do the motivational work? He thought about his own early days of living with his grandpa. He'd been a little younger than Dion the first time around, but he remembered the feeling of waking up to the smells of a hot breakfast for the first time in his life. It wasn't just the relief of not wondering if he'd go hungry—though that was part of it. It was the hope that maybe, just maybe, someone actually cared about him.

Yeah. For today at least, he'd try to give Dion that.

Ten minutes later, he placed a lid on the skillet and pushed it to the back of the stove to stay warm. Then he headed down the hall and knocked on his bedroom door.

"Dion? Time to get moving." He waited a moment, but no sound came from beyond the door. He cracked it open. "Dion?" Still no answer. Kid must sleep like a rock. He pushed the door the rest of the way open. An empty room stared back at him. He took in the sloppily made bed and not-quite-closed window. He groaned. This was not good.

He crossed to the window to peer outside. As expected, there was no sign of Dion in the backyard or sauntering away through the adjoining properties. Turning from the window, he scanned the bedroom again. Nothing of Dion's remained, not even a candy wrapper.

He'd go outside to see if there was any indication of which direction the teen might have gone, but he didn't have high hopes of discovering anything useful. With Eric's house situated on a connecting road in a quiet neighborhood at the edge of town, Dion would have had plenty of options to choose from—and that was assuming he was on his own and hadn't called anyone to pick him up. Even if he was on foot, he could be quite a ways away from here if he'd left as long ago as Eric suspected based on the chill permeating the room. And it was still early. The neighbors likely hadn't seen anything that would help point Eric in the right direction.

On his way to the door, he grabbed his phone and keys. He'd have to call this in to the department as well as inform Tracy Ann that her scheduled pickup was now on hold. Hopefully, she hadn't said anything to Lucky.

He jumped into his car and debated which direction to go first. Would Dion head back to Kincaid Lake? Or toward town? He doubted the kid would return to the place Eric had found him, but there were countless places both in and around the park where he could attempt to disappear. But then again, he might try to hitch a ride in town or find a friend to stay with. That would be safer. Depending on the friend.

Town was closer. Might as well head that way first. He dialed Tracy Ann and pulled onto the road while waiting for the call to connect through his Bluetooth speakers.

"Hello."

"Hey, Tracy Ann. It's Eric."

"Eric. Great. I'm just about to head your way. Everything go all right last night?"

His fingers tightened on the wheel. "Last night was fine. Or so I thought. Just went in to wake Dion up, and he's gone."

"Oh no."

"Yeah. Window's open, and his stuff's missing too. I'm heading out to look for him now."

"Please keep me updated. I'll be praying."

"Good." He should be doing that too. "I'm so sorry."

She sighed. "Happens more often than you'd think. Don't beat yourself up. He'll turn up eventually."

"Yeah." That's what they'd have to cling to and work toward. But they both knew many runaways didn't.

He ended the call with Tracy Ann and turned his full attention to his surroundings. Not much traffic going through the neighborhood this time of day, and while he passed an occasional morning jogger or dog-walker, he saw no sign of a teen boy shouldering a backpack and bedroll.

As he left the residential area and turned toward town, he put in the call to dispatch. Details given, he prepared to thumb the end call button on his steering wheel.

"Oh, hold up."

"Yeah?" he asked.

"Kev said he was about to radio you. Call just came in . . . Oh man."

"What you got?"

"Head out to Kincaid Lake. Hikers found a body in the woods."

THE BODY WASN'T ON STATE PARK LAND. Although the hikers had started out in the park, they'd strayed from the path and ended up on private property. Which put jurisdiction squarely with Kincaid police.

"ME been here yet?" Eric asked the officer standing guard.

"Not yet. On his way."

He scanned the area. A middle-aged couple he didn't recognize huddled together under a sycamore. Must be the ones who'd discovered the body. He couldn't touch the victim until the medical examiner had done his thing, but he'd take a cursory look at the scene and snap a few photos before interviewing the couple. Hopefully, the tree cover here had provided enough protection from Friday morning's rain to preserve any evidence left behind—assuming this guy hadn't been dumped more recently than that.

Eric signed the crime scene log, slipped on a pair of booties, and ducked under the tape cordoned around the area. The wind shifted, and the smell of death blasted him full on. Ugh.

Closing off any emotion, he squatted beside the body and gathered what details were obvious on the surface. Caucasian male. Tall. Probably in his early twenties. Had to have died at least a few days ago. The evenings had been cool, but the days warm, and the body was beginning to show early signs of decay and a bit of scavenging.

Looked like he'd been unceremoniously dug from a shallow grave. Probably by coyotes, if Eric had to guess. The local population had exploded over the past several years. Thankfully, they didn't seem to have done too much damage, at least not from what he could see. One leg of the filthy jeans was shredded. The navy T-shirt sporting a music band he didn't recognize seemed to be intact. Both were obviously bloodstained beneath the dried mud and dust still clinging to them.

He used his work phone to snap photos of the victim's body and the immediate area before turning his attention to the couple. Puffy eyes and runny mascara indicated the woman had been crying. Both of them looked a bit gray.

The man straightened as he approached.

"Hello, folks. I'm Detective Thornton. You discovered the victim?"

"Yes." The man took the lead.

"Can I get your names?"

"Mark Loesing, and this is my wife, Barb."

Eric spent the next fifteen minutes interviewing them, but it was obvious they knew little more than he did. They were camping at the park, had gone off-trail during their early-morning hike, and stumbled across the body. They'd had to move around a bit to find cell phone signal before calling it in, then they'd returned to the scene to wait for the police to arrive. They claimed they hadn't touched anything, for which Eric was grateful.

After getting their contact information and requesting they remain in town, he cleared them to go. Another more formal interview might be necessary later, but there was no reason to keep them at the scene.

As the couple trekked back toward the park, Eric reentered the cordoned-off area to join the ME, who'd arrived while he conducted his interview.

"Starnes."

"Thornton," the ME responded without looking up. "Two early morning callouts in less than a week is pushing it."

"My apologies."

Starnes harrumphed like Eric had killed the guy himself just to force the ME out of his office before he'd had a chance to finish his first pot of coffee.

Eric angled to see over the man's shoulder, trying not to cast a shadow on the body in the already filtered light of the woods. "Anything of note?"

"Besides the fact that he was murdered and it didn't happen here?"

19

DION HITCHED HIS BACKPACK higher on his shoulders. Part of him wished he could have stayed at Eric's place. He quickly squelched it. Detective Thornton had always been good to him, but he was still a cop. Even if he wanted to keep Dion more than one night before turning him over to the system, he'd change his mind in a hurry once he discovered what Dion had been up to over the last year. What he was responsible for.

His hands balled into fists. He hadn't known.

He shouldn't have tried to argue with the big guy. He wasn't usually an idiot.

No, he was just a bottom-of-the-chain drug dealer who hated drugs almost as much as Detective Thornton. He grunted. Maybe he was an idiot. But his job had kept food on the table for him and Lucky when Mom blew her entire paycheck on meth. He'd never sold to her, and she never questioned where her boys' food and clothes came from. Things were working out just fine until she'd found his stash last week. Of course she'd stolen it. All of it. Then kicked him out when he confronted her. He'd had to wipe out his meager savings to cover the loss so the three of them didn't end up on a hit list.

And then she'd promptly OD'd because the drugs were tainted

—though he hadn't realized that until Bernie told him a few days ago.

He hadn't told Eric the whole story about finding his mom. Couldn't share all those details. But they replayed in his mind now. He'd sneaked back in during the night to check on Lucky and try to recover some of his merchandise. At first, he thought his mom was just passed out on the couch, but when he couldn't find Lucky, he'd tried to wake her up. She was cold and stiff. He'd forgotten about looking for any remaining drugs and just hightailed it out of the house. It took him the rest of the night to figure out what to do, but he'd finally gone back in and used her phone to call in the wellness check so they wouldn't be able to trace it back to him.

He'd hung around to watch the cops arrive, keeping his distance to avoid being spotted. That had backfired. By the time he saw Lucky slipping out of the neighbor's tree house and making a beeline for his bedroom window, it was too late to stop him without calling attention to himself.

He should have tried anyway. They might have been able to make a break for it before anyone realized there were kids in the household.

Now Lucky was in a foster home, Dion was on the run from one of the only decent adults he'd ever known, and he had to report to the big guy. Or at least, bigger than Marco had been. He wasn't sure who the real big guy was, and he didn't want to know. Safer for him and Lucky if he didn't. But he was stuck in this thing, and now he was totally on his own. At least his mom had somehow kept the house while she was alive.

This wasn't how things were supposed to happen.

How many of his so-called friends would have died if she hadn't stolen his stash before he had the chance to off-load it? Would they have taken less than Mom and been okay? Or would he be responsible for multiple deaths?

The new package hidden in a wad of clothes at the bottom

of his backpack made it feel like he was hauling a bowling ball around. If only he could just bury it out in the woods somewhere. But that wasn't an option.

Maybe if he could make up what he'd lost—save enough—he could find Lucky and escape this town. Go somewhere Bernie wouldn't think to look for them. He just couldn't owe them anything when he disappeared. As long as they didn't consider him a threat and he could figure out a way to leave payment without taking new inventory, maybe they wouldn't bother seriously trying to find him. He and Lucky could be free. Go legit.

The improbability of being able to get that far ahead made his shoulders sag, but he shook off the fear of failure. He would do it. He had to. If not for himself, then for Lucky. His brother deserved better.

20

ALLYE AWOKE WITH A START, chased into consciousness by frightening images of her attacker squeezing the breath from her as green smoke billowed behind him.

But he wasn't here. She was in her bed, blessedly alone.

And everything ached. Her head was the worst offender by far—until she stretched and triggered a charley horse in her left calf. She yelped and instinctively curled into a ball, massaging the area until it relaxed.

Well, she was fully awake now. And by the light streaming through her window, she guessed it was nearing noon. So much for an early start to her day.

Ignoring the temptation to give up and remain where she was, she slipped on her glasses, then sat up and swung her legs over the side of the bed. Dizziness joined the pounding fury in her skull. She was so tired of this.

"Get used to it," she muttered as she stumbled to the bathroom. She caught a glimpse of herself in the mirror and for once was glad she lived alone. Talk about looking like death warmed over.

Desperate to dull the migraine, she retrieved her prescription and popped one of the pills, ignoring the instruction to take with food. She'd eat in a few minutes.

She pushed through the absolutely necessary parts of her

morning routine, minus the shower she probably needed after the hike yesterday. Despite the energy it took, having a clean face and brushed teeth did help her feel slightly human again.

That done, she moved to the kitchen. She wasn't hungry, but she knew better than to let the meds wreak havoc in her stomach. And she really needed some caffeine. That was nonnegotiable.

By the time she settled in at her desk with the curtains drawn to shut out excess light, it was after one o'clock. She practically melted into the amply padded chair. She was already bushed, and the migraine meds had hardly made a dent in the pain. Staring at a screen would be torture. But she had to make headway on these projects. Wool Fest was a hard deadline. Technically, she had more wiggle room with Jayden's photos, but the sooner she got them done, the sooner she would get paid. So there was that.

She swapped her everyday glasses for a pair with rose-tinted migraine lenses. Hopefully, they would provide enough protection to allow her to get some work done. She jiggled the mouse to wake the computer and braced herself. The brightness still made her wince.

This was a bad idea.

"But what else am I supposed to do?"

She didn't bother answering herself. If she waited to work when she felt good, she might never get anything done. She'd push through as long as she could. Pay the price later if she must.

Praying it would work, she inserted the recovered memory card and waited for the computer to read it. As the photo previewer popped up, she released the breath she'd been holding. There they were. Uncorrupted. Perfect. Well, as perfect as raw photos could be.

Now for the fun part.

For the next hour or so, she lost herself in the world of photo editing. The distraction did as much as the meds and caffeine to bring the migraine to a manageable level—or at least a level she could pretend to ignore.

As she edged up the vignette effect on a shot of Jayden with the lake in the background, the doorbell rang. Her hand jerked, sending the effect to max. Ugh. She quickly undid the action and pushed from her seat. Too fast. Dizzy. Ugh. Ugh.

The bell rang again.

"Coming," she mumbled. She finally reached the door and threw it open. "I heard you the first time."

Eric paused, his finger on the doorbell. "Sorry." He didn't return her smile.

"What's wrong?" A hundred scenarios went through her head. Was Bryce okay? Corina? Mom?

"May I come in?"

She stepped aside and let him pass. "What's going on? Is my family okay?"

"Yes," he was quick to reassure her. "They're all fine. It's just . . ." He sighed and motioned her to sit, but she wasn't ready to do so until she knew what this was about. His gaze landed on her glasses, and his brows drew together.

"They're for migraines," she said in answer to his unspoken question.

"They help?"

"A little." *Get to the point.*

He nodded and took a deep breath. "The reason I'm here is that we found a body this morning. The autopsy hasn't been done yet, but the initial assessment is consistent with your description of what you saw behind your studio the other night."

She sank into her recliner. "A body? As in, dead?"

"Yes. Would you recognize the victim you saw?"

"No." She didn't even have to think about it. "It was starting to get dark, and I wasn't at a good angle to see him. I only got a good look at the attacker." She'd seen him all too well.

"That's what I was afraid of. Any idea what the victim was wearing?"

She thought a moment. "Jeans and a dark T-shirt, I think. Couldn't tell you what color."

"Did you notice anything on the shirt? Logo, text?"

"I don't remember. But he was half curled up, like he'd been trying to protect himself from the blows." Her voice shook, and she wasn't sure he heard the last few words. She twisted her hands. "But his head didn't look right, and he wasn't moving."

"I'm going to need you to walk me through everything again."

"Okay." *God, please help me remember any pertinent details.* She shot the silent prayer upward as she reached for her knitting bag. But it wasn't by her chair. She looked around and spotted it in the pile of bags she'd left just inside the door last night.

Eric pulled out his pen and notebook. *Notebook!*

"Hold on!" She launched from her chair, remembering too late to take it slow. Unwilling to let on about the wave of dizziness, she kept going and made it into the kitchen and out of Eric's sight before having to grab on to a chair back to steady herself. While she waited for the spell to pass, her gaze roamed the table. There. As soon as the dizziness was manageable, she grabbed the spiral-bound notebook peeking from under yesterday's breakfast plate that she'd missed when she loaded the dishwasher.

Notebook in hand, she returned to the living room and thrust it into Eric's hands. "Friday, before I went to bed, I wrote everything down that I could remember. I was afraid with my—" She cut the words off before she admitted too much. "I was afraid I might forget something important."

"That was a good idea." He looked pleased, and she felt her cheeks warm. He flipped the cover back and began reading.

She felt herself sway slightly. Better not just stand here. She retrieved her knitting, then sat next to him on the couch where she could see the pages as well. She hated that her writing was shaky, but it was still legible. That was the important thing.

Eric reached the last page, which only contained a few lines. He paused there for a moment, then flipped backward as if searching for a detail. He clicked his pen a few times. "There was a third man present at the initial attack. And your attacker had someone with him at the park as well. Same guy?"

Not something she'd considered. She worked a few more stitches of the nearly finished glove she hoped to sell at her festival booth. As her fingers flew automatically through the familiar motions, she pictured the man who'd been leaning against the back wall of the building. He'd been in the shadows, and her focus had been on the attacker and victim. When the attacker turned toward her, she'd run.

Her needles slowed, and she sighed as she lifted her eyes to Eric. "I want to say no. My impression of the guy behind the building was that he was older—not old, but an adult. I'm not positive of that though because I didn't get a good look at him and I didn't hear his voice. The guy at the park sounded like a teenager." She hesitated. "And there's something else."

"What?"

"The one in the park? His voice sounded a lot like Dion's, and he was wearing the same shoes as Dion was yesterday."

Eric's spine straightened, and he stared at her. "Why didn't you tell me that before?"

"I didn't recognize his voice that first day. It's changed since the last time I saw him. When we found him yesterday, it dawned on me, but I didn't know how to bring it up then. Not when he was right there and nobody believed me about last week anyway."

He didn't quite wince at that last sentence, but his cheek twitched. "I would have preferred to know."

"I'm sorry."

"And for the record, I do believe you."

"Now that you have a reason to?"

He didn't answer that immediately.

She sighed and resumed knitting. "I shouldn't have said that. With how crazy everything sounded, I don't blame you for being skeptical. Especially after the break-in."

His gaze shifted to her notebook, and he flipped to the last page with writing and checked the next as well. "You didn't document that."

"It happened after I wrote down the first two encounters. I never got around to adding it." She'd been too preoccupied with everything else, not to mention her discouragement over the police's reaction to her statement.

"Tell me again what happened that night."

Her hands began to tremble, and she dropped a stitch. She tried to reclaim it, but her hands weren't steady enough, so she set the project aside before she could do more damage.

"Are you all right? You're pale."

She wasn't sure how to answer that. She didn't want to dig into those memories right now. Not after the nightmare she'd woken up from. But she knew she needed to. Maybe she could approach it clinically. If it meant they might be able to catch this guy, she'd do whatever it took.

Eric placed his hand over one of hers, surprising her. But his touch calmed her too and gave her the courage to launch into her memories of that night. She recited everything she could remember—from waking up to that ghastly green glow to finding the door locked after she'd been abandoned on the porch.

When she finished, she stole a look at him. She couldn't read his expression. He'd said he believed her about the first two encounters with her attacker. Did his confidence extend to this one too? She knew how bizarre it sounded. If she hadn't experienced it, she wasn't sure she'd believe it either.

He released her hand and began writing in his own notebook. The absence of his touch left her feeling chilled. That was just weird.

She rubbed her hands together to warm them—and maybe to distract herself from the awkwardness that Eric seemed oblivious to. Maybe she should offer him tea. That would give her something to do while he puzzled through the information.

Before she could voice her offer, his pen clicked twice, and he spoke. "So he was wearing a mask? Why? You'd already seen his face."

She stilled. That hadn't occurred to her. But Eric had a point. Why bother to wear a mask? Her attacker likely knew she lived alone. He also knew she knew what he looked like, and he clearly wanted her to know it was him.

"I don't know," she said finally. "He wasn't trying to hide his identity." No, he'd taunted her with it. "But then again, nothing he did made sense. I thought he was going to kill me or . . ." She couldn't finish the thought, but judging by the way the notebook bent under the pressure of Eric's grip, he knew exactly what she hadn't said.

"And you're sure it was him?"

"Yes."

"You recognized his voice, then?"

"Yes. At least, I think so," she corrected.

"You think so?"

"He was whispering," she admitted. "So I guess I didn't hear his true voice. But his actions and words made his identity obvious." She could almost feel his hand on her skin, and her stomach turned.

Click. "Okay. What else was odd about his behavior?"

"Besides the way he locked me outside and then disappeared?"

"Yes. Is there anything else he did—even something small—that was off?"

She searched her slightly fuzzy memories. Between how frightened and caught off guard she'd been, she wasn't sure she would have noticed anything else off. She hadn't even processed the fact he'd been wearing gloves until afterward. The gloves made sense. He wouldn't have wanted to leave fingerprints behind. But the mask? Maybe he hadn't wanted to risk being seen as he entered or exited?

He didn't seem the type to be overly afraid of that. After all, he'd murdered a man behind her studio, before nightfall, and he hadn't bothered to wear a mask then. So why had he worn one in her house?

Focus. Was there anything else odd? She replayed the moments in her mind, allowing herself to feel his hand over her mouth, his breath on her cheek. The sick knot in her stomach grew.

Eric's hand closed over hers again, snapping her back to the present. "It's okay. You don't have to go there again right now."

She sucked in air. "Sorry. I don't know why thinking about that night is so much harder than remembering the first time. I mean, he tried to kill me when he caught me by my studio. At least, I think he did." She rubbed her neck but quickly lowered her hand when she realized she'd drawn Eric's attention to the lingering bruises. The flash in his eyes betrayed his anger on her behalf. "But he didn't hurt me Saturday night, even though he could have." Pushing her down hardly counted, despite the few hidden bruises she sported from the fall as well as from the way he'd ground the barrel of his gun into her spine.

"Both were traumatic," he said quietly. "But the second attack was more personal. He came after you in your own home. Invaded your private space and threatened to harm you."

"But then he just ran off. He didn't warn me not to talk, and he didn't follow through with the things he implied." She heard the frustration in her own voice. "I'm so, so thankful he didn't, but I don't understand why. Why go to all that trouble and then leave me behind? He didn't get anything out of it besides the satisfaction of seeing me scared. So what was the point of putting me through all of it?"

21

ALLYE'S QUESTIONS CONTINUED TO RING in Eric's mind as he combed the streets of Kincaid, searching again for Dion. What had been the purpose of Friday night's break-in? Assuming it had all happened in the first place. With a body in the morgue testifying to the veracity of her initial report, he hesitated to dismiss her other accounts out of hand. But he still couldn't deny how preposterous some of the details sounded. Most of it they could explain away. Even the guy's abandonment of her could be chalked up to him getting spooked by something Allye hadn't seen or heard. If only it weren't for that green glow. But that element coupled with the other would overshadow everything else she claimed had happened that night, and they'd cast serious doubt on the other encounters.

If they caught this guy—which he fully intended to do—Allye would be the star witness in the murder trial. And he could only imagine how viciously a defense attorney would rip her and her testimony apart if he caught wind of this story. And he would. There was a police report on file.

Eric scrubbed at his hair. He didn't even know whether he believed the break-in had happened. He believed she believed it. But after the trauma of seeing a murder in progress and being attacked herself? Hearing her attacker's voice again on the trail could have triggered a night terror of some sort. That would make a lot of sense actually. He could work with that assumption. After all, he'd seen the marks on her neck the day after the initial encounter. Something had obviously happened.

But a defense attorney wouldn't leave it at that. He'd pounce on the green glow and use it as proof that Allye's testimony couldn't be trusted. Her credibility, perhaps even her sanity, would be questioned.

And there was nothing Eric could do about that. His job was to figure out who committed a crime and to collect enough evidence for the courts. Allye's testimony was part of that, but especially now that they had a body, he would have more to work with.

There was strong evidence their John Doe's murder hadn't occurred out in the woods, at least not where he'd been dumped. There was no sign there'd been a struggle in the immediate area, and Starnes had pointed out a notable discrepancy in the amount of blood on the victim's skin and clothes compared to the almost negligible amount found elsewhere in the grave. Plus, he'd discovered bits of gravel stuck to the man's back, inside his waistline and pockets, and in his hair—gravel that matched what was outside Allye's studio.

"Lord, I could use some extra help with this one. I need to find this guy and find the evidence to convict him—with or without Allye's testimony." He executed a left turn. "And, Lord? Help Allye too. Something is going on with her, and the stress of all this can't be making it better." He raked his gaze over the sidewalks and down side streets as he passed them. "While I'm at it, protect Dion too. If Allye's right, he's playing with fire. Keep him safe and help us find him before he gets into worse trouble."

Dion's likely involvement with drugs weighed on him. He wasn't surprised, really. Family cycles were hard to break. But he'd hoped for better for the teen. Tried to make a difference in his life and the lives of other teen and preteen boys in the community, like Officer Mike had done for him. Lot of good he'd done. Some of the boys did all right, but so many of the ones without strong family support dropped out of the church program soon after the pressures of high school hit—or as soon as they were old enough that their parents no longer needed free babysitting.

He'd seen something in Dion though. The kid had courage, determination. A fierce desire to make something of himself. And to protect his little brother. Eric believed his denial of doing drugs himself. Probably foolish of him. He knew better than most how convincing an addict's lies could be. But his gut said Dion was telling the truth, and he'd seen no signs of drug use in the hours they'd spent together last night. His eyes had been clear, pupils normal. No telltale sores or track marks. No trembling as if he needed a fix.

But Eric hadn't gone through his belongings for "product." He'd trusted him. That had been an oversight on his part. No, he hadn't had a warrant, but he wouldn't have been looking for prosecutable evidence either—just assurance that no drugs were being brought into his home last night.

He sighed. If Dion was dealing, good chance he'd been lying about not knowing who'd supplied his mom with the drugs that ended her life. He might have sold them to her himself. Eric prayed that wasn't the case. Legal ramifications aside, it would be a heavy burden the teen would carry for the rest of his life.

As he reached the outskirts of town, he finally acknowledged that he wouldn't find Dion today. He'd known when he left Al-lye's that spotting him on the streets would be a long shot at this point. The teen had likely found shelter or at least a new hiding place by now. And he was smart enough to know he was being looked for.

Eric executed a three-point turn and headed for the police

station. He had a lot to do. Allye had promised to drop by around four to look through mug shots. If they were lucky, her attacker's face would be among them. That would make this whole thing much easier. If not, his next order of business would be to contact one of the larger departments in the area and see if they might be willing to lend their forensic artist to work with Allye on a sketch of her attacker.

One way or another, they needed to identify this guy and find him fast. Regardless of whether Allye's Friday night break-in had actually happened, he had no doubt she would be in real danger once news got out that they were actively investigating the murder she witnessed.

AT FIVE MINUTES TO FOUR, Allye loaded her bags into her car and climbed in beside them. She took a few seconds to catch her breath before inserting the key into the ignition. *Click.*

Really? She tried turning the key again, but the engine refused to wake. She eyed her dashboard. Checked the headlights. And groaned. She must have left them on yesterday. She did vaguely remember the car dinging a warning as she got out, but she'd reached back in to grab her keys from the ignition and assumed that was the sole problem. Apparently not.

She turned the lights off—not that it mattered at the moment—and tried to think. Bryce and Corina would both be at work. Mom had indicated she had a busy day today. She looked to her neighbors' driveway. Cornell's car was here, but if he'd been working nights, she didn't want to disturb him. And Shannon's car was gone.

There were other people she could try, but finding someone available could take a while. Defeated, she leaned her head back and dialed Eric's number.

"Hello, Allye."

"Hi. Um, I have a little problem."

His concerned answer came quickly. "Did something else happen?"

"Not a problem like that," she assured him. "But my car won't start. I think the battery's dead. I'm going to have to find someone to help me jump it before I can come to the station. I'm so sorry."

"No worries. Why don't I come to you instead? I have a few things to finish up here, but I could head your way in about an hour. I'll bring the mug shots for you to look at, and I'll jump your battery while I'm there."

"You don't have to do that."

"I don't mind."

"I would really appreciate it, then. And you could stay for dinner. It won't be anything fancy, but it's the least I can do if you're making another special trip out here." She paused for a half second as her good sense caught up to her words. "I'm sorry. You're probably busy or have other plans. I blurted it out without thinking. Just ignore that—"

"Allye. Hold up." She could hear the smile in his voice. "I do have a lot to do with these cases piling up, but I still have to eat."

"Would you like to stay, then?" She could kick herself for how hopeful she sounded. After all, she was just offering him dinner as a thank-you.

"I'd be honored."

"It's a—" She bit her tongue before the word *date* came out of her mouth. "A plan, then."

"Be there at five." He ended the call, and Allye dropped the phone from her ear.

Had she really just invited Eric Thornton to dinner? And he'd accepted? Eight or ten years ago, she'd have been ecstatic. She'd been a hopeless romantic back in high school, but even now, the thought excited her more than it should. Of course, she reminded herself, it *wasn't* a date, and she was in no position to start a relationship anyway. This was a thank-you dinner following official police business. Nothing romantic about it.

She snorted at the ridiculous image of the two of them sitting catty-corner at her kitchen table, candles burning as she and Eric bent their heads over an album of mug shots. Yeah, she'd leave the candles in the drawer.

But she did need to get dinner started and straighten the kitchen before he arrived. It was still a mess, and she didn't have the slightest idea what to make. She stifled another groan and reached for the door handle. An hour. She had an hour. She'd whipped up a meal in less.

Back inside, she eyed the disarray of her kitchen. No time to put everything in order, but she could prioritize. And cheat if necessary. She cleared out the dishwasher first, then placed anything dirty inside—including the hand-wash-only pots and pans that she would have to pull back out before running it. No time to fully clear the table, but she relocated the piles of mail and receipts to her desk and moved everything else to one end. It would have to do.

Ignoring the urge to sit for a few moments, she instead made a quick decision about tonight's menu. She pulled out a gallon bag of frozen broth and transferred it to a large pot. She added extra water and a few spices, then placed the pot on the stove. The broth would thaw in a matter of minutes, and with a few carrots, some leftover rotisserie chicken, and her grandma's measured-with-the-heart dumpling recipe, she'd have a comfort meal ready in no time. She leaned against the counter and glanced at the time. Might even be able to get a pan of brownies in the oven before Eric arrived. If not, there was always ice cream.

Promptly at five, her doorbell rang. She slid the brownie batter into the oven and set a timer. She knew better than to answer the door first and hope she'd remember when she returned to the kitchen. That done, she hurried to let Eric in.

She greeted him with a smile, noting the tablet tucked under his arm in lieu of the photo album she'd been expecting. Of course mug shots would be electronic now—even more of a blow to her silly romantic dinner imaginings from earlier. She returned her gaze to his face, and she found him grinning.

"What?" She tucked an escaped curl behind her ear.

He bit his cheek like he was trying not to laugh. "You've been baking."

"Yes?" She sniffed the air. The brownies hadn't been in the oven long enough to spread their aroma throughout the house, but the chicken and dumplings smelled delicious.

He grazed her hairline, then held up his finger. Brownie batter.

Her hand flew to her hair. Just as she made contact, she realized she still had batter on her fingers and had probably just added another glob to her curls. *Floor, swallow me up now.*

It didn't. Unfortunately. Heat rose in her cheeks as she rushed to wipe the remaining batter on her apron. Which was covered in flour. That was probably what Eric had originally been referring to. *Oops.* She raised her eyes to meet his, an apology on her lips.

But his lips were twitching, and there was a glint of merriment in his eyes she'd rarely seen from him. He was obviously trying to hide his amusement, not willing to embarrass her further. The gesture put her at ease.

"I, uh, hope you like brownies. Baked and sans hair?" She couldn't help it. She burst into laughter, and Eric joined her. "Come on in."

She ushered him into the kitchen and pointed to the cleared side of the table. "Have a seat. I'm going to make myself presentable."

"You look fine."

"I'm floured. And chocolate-covered, apparently."

"A chocolate-covered hostess isn't the worst thing I could have arrived to," he said.

She laughed. "Maybe not, but I still don't want it in my hair.

I'll only be a moment." She fled to the bathroom and almost cracked up again at her reflection. Besides the batter smeared in her hair and flour covering her apron, she had cocoa powder and more flour streaked on her cheeks and forehead. How had she managed that? Better question, how had Eric managed to keep an almost-straight face?

22

"THAT WAS ABSOLUTELY DELICIOUS. THANK YOU." Eric polished off the last of his ice-cream-topped, double-fudge brownie. He was so stuffed.

"You're very welcome." Allye looked pleased at his compliment, but she was obviously tired. More like exhausted.

He needed to redirect them to the purpose of his visit so they could get it over with and he could leave her to relax. "We should probably get started. Do you want to look through the mug shots here, or would you be more comfortable somewhere else?"

She eyed the tablet sitting to his right. "How many are there?"

"More than a few."

She sighed. "Let's move to the living room, then." She topped off his coffee and refilled her iced tea before leading him into the other room. She plopped onto the couch, where they'd sat together this morning.

He joined her and powered on the tablet. As he navigated to the program, he explained how it worked. Allye nodded understanding.

"Okay." He placed the device in her hands. "Have at it."

They spent the next hour browsing through photos. He noticed Allye frequently rubbing her eyes, and her hands shook—at points, badly enough that he had trouble focusing on the tablet screen.

Something was wrong.

Finally, he couldn't take it any longer. "Allye, what's wrong?"

"What do you mean?" She picked up her glass and stood, swaying slightly. "Can I get you a refill?"

"No, thanks."

"Well, I need one. Be right back." She was gone before he had a chance to object.

The weight in his stomach grew. Allye wasn't generally an evasive person. Not unless she was protecting someone.

He waited until she was again settled next to him. "You didn't answer my question."

"Which was?" She took a sip of her tea.

"I asked you what's wrong."

"I've told you everything I know."

"Not about the case. What's going on with you?"

"It's nothing." The glass wobbled slightly in her hand as she returned it to the table. "You sure you don't want anything else? There's plenty of dessert left. Coffee too."

He shook his head.

"Let me get that out of your way, then." She rose halfway and reached for his mug.

"Stop."

She paused, fingers gripping but not lifting the dish.

He softened his tone. "Please. Talk to me."

She closed her eyes and took a few shallow breaths. After a couple of seconds, she released her hold on the mug and sank back into the cushions.

Silence stretched between them. He waited.

Finally, she moistened her lips. "I'm being tested for multiple sclerosis. I have an MRI scheduled for tomorrow morning."

The softly spoken words slammed into him.

He had to search for a response. "Allye, I'm sorry." Man, that sounded lame.

"It might not be that, but I've been showing symptoms." She shrugged. "And my aunt passed away from MS complications, so there's family history."

"Bryce didn't mention anything."

"I haven't told him. Please don't say anything. He and Corina have enough on their minds right now."

"What about your mom?"

She shook her head. "She's already lost one child—not that MS is a death sentence, but it's life-altering for sure. And it was her sister who had MS. She'd freak. I don't want to put that on her until I have an official diagnosis. Especially when there's a chance it's something . . . less serious."

So she was doing this alone. He'd seen how Allye tried to shoulder her family's burdens, but this was extreme.

"Don't worry about it."

Don't worry about it? "Allye—"

"Really, Eric. I didn't tell you so you'd feel sorry for me. I'll be fine."

"Even if you have MS?" He reached for her hand. She didn't pull away, but he felt the tremor.

She swallowed. "Even then."

They sat in silence for a minute. Two. Finally, he asked, "What kind of symptoms are you dealing with? If you don't mind telling me, that is."

"Extreme fatigue. Numbness and tingling, muscle spasms, more frequent migraines." She sucked in a breath. "I get dizzy and light-headed easily—especially when I stand up or am standing for an extended period of time." She lifted her free hand. "And the shaking, of course. Lack of coordination is another common symptom of MS, but I've always had that." She attempted a laugh.

He didn't return it. "How long has this been going on?"

"Several months. Maybe longer, but that's when I started

paying attention and realized the symptoms were multiplying, not going away. I've been blessed with doctors that take me seriously, and they've fast-tracked what they could because of my family history, but it's still a long road to a diagnosis."

She'd been dealing with this for months? All on her own? He'd known she would do anything for those she cared about—even risk her own life like she had last fall when Corina was trying to escape a killer. But this? He gave her hand a light squeeze. "You don't always have to be the strong one."

"Someone has to."

He couldn't stop himself. He cupped her chin in his palm and looked deep into her eyes. "But it doesn't always have to be you."

She gave him a sorry excuse for a smile. "You're one to talk. Mr. Big Bad Policeman who doesn't need anyone."

"Yeah." He dropped his hand and leaned back to put a little space between them. He let the silence linger a moment. "You'll have to tell them though. If it does turn out to be MS." *God, please don't let it be MS.*

He barely heard her whispered "I know" before she picked up the tablet and began scrolling through mug shots again. Message received—she was done talking about her personal problems.

ALLYE'S HANDS CONTINUED TO SHAKE as she dried and put away the supper dishes. She didn't really have the energy to spare, but she needed to burn off a bit of her anxiety before trying to retire for the evening.

But the work wasn't distracting her from her problems. Her conversation with Eric replayed in her mind as if through a loudspeaker. While she'd admitted some of her situation to Hailey the other day, she hadn't given voice to her worst fear—that she might be facing MS. She hadn't wanted to share that with anyone until she knew for sure, one way or another.

What must Eric be thinking? They were friends, but not close friends. And she'd admit, if only to herself, that she'd long wished to be more. That was unlikely now. She didn't think he was the kind of guy to run from a relationship requiring immediate consideration of the "in sickness and in health" part of marriage vows, but she wasn't so sure she was willing to ask it of anyone.

But at least she didn't feel quite so alone anymore. Telling him had been an unexpected relief, even more so than her brief conversation with her cousin. She didn't like keeping secrets—not from her friends and especially not from her family. But she hated the thought of burdening them even more.

The last dish safely in the cabinet, Allye leaned against the edge of the counter and closed her eyes. She was so tired, she was almost afraid to move. How bad would it be to sleep on the kitchen floor tonight? She could just slide down the counter and—

Her phone began to ring from the other room. She released a groan and considered letting it go to voice mail. But it could be important.

She pushed off from the counter and retrieved her phone. "Hailey, what's up?" She tried to infuse a bit of energy into her voice.

"Hey. Just wanted to see how you're doing."

"I'm doing okay."

"Okay, okay? Or are you just being polite?" She continued on before Allye could answer. "Because if you're just being polite, you can stuff it. I want the truth."

Allye sighed. "The truth? I still feel lousy."

"And you don't know what's causing it?"

Yes. No. Maybe. How was she supposed to answer that?

"Come on, Allye."

Was she ready to share? Not really, but confiding in Eric had broken the ice. She'd said the words once—admitting what she feared didn't seem quite as scary now. So she did. She blurted it all, unable to stop once she'd begun.

After she finished, there was a long pause on the line.

"I'm so, so sorry."

"No, I'm sorry." Allye sniffed. "You've got your hands full with Jenna. I didn't mean to burden you with my junk."

"Listen here, Allye Jessup. We're family—more than that, we're friends. Did you consider me a burden when I called you, scared about Jenna's diagnosis?"

"Of course not. But that isn't—"

"It is exactly the same. And if you remember, I asked for the truth." Her voice softened. "I'm here for you—whether that means providing a listening ear, or helping you get to appointments, or coming along for moral support when you decide to talk to your mom."

"Thank you," she whispered.

After she ended the call, she dragged herself to her bedroom. Again she had no energy to change. She fell into bed as she was.

Silence enveloped her. She stared up at the ceiling. She kept telling people she was fine—or would be. She told Eric she'd be fine even if it turned out she had MS. Was she telling the truth?

"God, I'm scared." Terrified, if she were being totally honest. Not of death really—whether at the hand of a criminal or potential complications of a disease. She knew where she was going no matter how short or long her life was. In that, she really would be fine. But fear still hovered over her.

Of what? Of what she might have to go through? Of not being able to fulfill her life's purpose—whatever that was? Of being a burden on her family? Or of the very real possibility that she'd never have a family of her own, never find someone who would dare to love her despite her illness?

Yeah. Maybe a bit of all of that.

She rolled to her side and curled into a ball. Pain shot through her neck and down into her right arm.

Things weren't supposed to be this way. There was so much she wanted to do, to accomplish. So much she felt responsible for. So many people she cared about.

She wasn't ready to give up on any of those things. Dread pressed in on her—almost tangible, as if her attacker was squeezing the life out of her right now. Her lungs refused to fill. She grabbed a fistful of blanket and tried to ground herself.

The words from one of her favorite psalms popped into her mind. *"When I am afraid, I put my trust in you."* She turned the words over in her mind, then forced them through her lips. Focused on a tiny blotch on the ceiling. Repeated the words. The pressure around her chest loosened slightly. She repeated the words once more, willing herself to mean them.

It helped. She drew in a deep, ragged breath. And another.

For a few moments, she lay still. Then a spasm started in her leg. She twisted in an attempt to ease it. That pain wasn't going to go away by calming her anxiety. "I still trust you," she mumbled.

Sleep. She seriously needed to rest her mind as well as her body. Last thing she needed was to be a vibrating bundle of nerves for the MRI in the morning.

23

DESPITE ZHAN'S PIZZA being located barely three miles from her house, Allye still managed to show up late nearly every time she and her mom met for a dinner date. She'd arrived ten minutes early today. And she'd only had to plan for an extra thirty minutes to do it. She'd needed to get out of the house and distract herself from worrying over the yet-to-be-revealed MRI results.

Her mom wasn't here yet, so she snagged their favorite table and ordered tea for both of them, sweet for herself, unsweet for her mom. Allye had cut back on her sugar intake lately, but Zhan's sweet tea was a treat she wasn't quite ready to give up.

Despite the late hour, the restaurant still had a reasonable number of dine-in customers present. The tables close to theirs were empty, relegating the various conversations to an unintelligible hum punctuated by frequent laughter. It had been several days with no sightings, weird or otherwise, and Allye could almost convince herself things were normal.

She smiled. This place felt like home. She'd done a photo shoot here earlier in the year. Zhan's had wanted new promo photos, and she'd wanted to use them as a setting for a "Spirit of Kincaid" series she had planned. The result had been a lovely collection of portraits and candids showing customers and restaurant staff laughing, chatting, and enjoying each other's company over the best carbs in town.

The waiter arrived with the teas, and she went ahead and put in their food order as well. As he disappeared back into the kitchen, she checked the time on her phone. One minute before her mom was supposed to arrive.

And there she was. Allye waved, and her mom's face broke into a smile when she saw her. Nothing about Julie Jessup looked old-fashioned, yet she still managed to resemble a cross between a classic movie star and a New York attorney, complete with red lipstick and a graceful power stride.

"Hey, Mom."

"Hi, honey." She wrapped Allye in a hug. After a few seconds, she pulled back slightly but didn't release her. "Are you feeling all right? You look exhausted."

Allye forced a smile and hoped it looked genuine. "I didn't sleep well last night, and today was a busy day." Not a lie.

"We could have rescheduled."

"Nonsense. I can handle dinner." For now. "Besides, we missed Sunday already, and you know I love our monthly dates." That brought the smile back to her mom's face.

"I do too." She gave Allye's arms a light squeeze before letting go and taking the seat across the table.

Allye breathed a silent sigh of relief and changed the subject while she had the chance. "I ordered our usual."

"Wonderful." Mom pulled a packet of sweetener from her purse, poured exactly half of it into her glass, then swirled the tea with her straw to dissolve it.

"How was the showing?"

She lifted one shoulder in a delicate shrug. "I don't think the buyers were impressed, but we'll see. They said they'd discuss it and call me tomorrow." She took a sip of her tea. "If they turn it down, you might want to take a look at it. It's small enough to be cozy and simply overflows with personality."

Allye suppressed a sigh. As a real estate agent, her mom seemed nearly offended by Allye's choice to rent rather than own. She knew buying was the better investment, but committing to a mortgage on her own was a big deal—not to mention a decent down payment would have practically wiped out her bank account. Instead, she'd thrown about half her savings into starting her photography business and found a reasonable place to rent. The fact Corina lived nearby and eventually moved into the other side of the duplex didn't hurt any. Being next door to her best friend once again had been nice while it lasted.

She tuned back in as her mom finished describing the cottage-style home. "It sounds wonderful, but it's not a good time for me. I've got a lot on my plate. I don't think I could handle the upkeep by myself."

Her mom's crimson-tinted lips drew together. "I could help if you have questions, and I'm sure Bryce would be willing to help with the maintenance—especially if you choose something close by."

"I'm not his burden, Mom. He has his own house and family now."

"You know he would never consider you a burden."

No, he wouldn't. Didn't mean she wouldn't be one though. Especially if her health continued to decline. She gave herself a mental shake. She wasn't going to dwell on that tonight.

Their pizza arrived, and Allye welcomed the interruption. She helped herself to a large slice of the Olive Special—complete with Castelvetrano, Mission, Gaeta, and Kalamata olives, and of course, Zhan's signature heavy dousing of Parmesan.

Her mom shook out a napkin and placed it on her lap before selecting a slightly smaller slice for herself. "So any hot dates lately?"

Allye hid her grimace behind her pizza. Maybe her lack of a house title was a better topic. "Again, no time." No time. No energy. No guy. Her thoughts shot to Eric. Okay, so there might be a possibility there. Didn't eliminate the other two issues.

"Don't get so busy you miss out on life, Allye." Her tone turned serious. "I know you're passionate about your business, and you should be—you have real talent. I talk about your photography every chance I get. But I worry about you too." Allye opened her mouth to respond, but her mom kept going. "Don't take me wrong, I would never say you need a relationship or a house to be happy. But I also know how much you've always wanted to have a family."

Allye swallowed the lump in her throat and chose her words carefully. "And I still do. But there's plenty of time. This has been an intense season for me, and dating doesn't fit into my life right now."

"And that's okay. But"—her mom's expression softened—"it's more than that. You're forgetting things, missing church, and you've been so tired and preoccupied lately—not just tonight. I don't want to see you get burned out or destroy your health for your career."

My health is the problem, not my career. The words were on the tip of her tongue, but she bit them back. They would require her to disclose her secret, and she wasn't ready to do that. Instead, she mustered a smile, hoping to placate her mom and bring the conversation back to safer ground. "This is a big week, especially with Wool Fest coming up. Next week, I should be able to slow down a little bit."

"Please do. I'm not trying to be pushy, but I love you, and I know how easy it is to overextend yourself."

"I love you too, Mom. And I'm trying to take care of myself—I really am." It wasn't working, but she *was* trying. She finished off her slice of pizza and reached for another. "Speaking of Wool Fest, are you coming? I think you'll like my booth's setup this year."

"I wouldn't miss it. I always love what you have to offer."

"How'd your interview go yesterday?" Allye ventured. She was truly interested, but she also wanted to keep the topic of conversation off herself.

"All right, I suppose." She shot her a rueful smile. "I don't know if I gave Thomas anything worth printing unless he just has a really slow week of news. But I didn't have anything exciting to share. Things are somewhat slower than I like, with people a little more hesitant to buy than they were a few years ago, but that's part of the business."

The waiter stopped by to refill their glasses, and her mom excused herself to the restroom.

Allye lifted her glass with trembling fingers. She'd successfully changed the direction of their conversation, but she needed a moment to regroup. Keeping such a big secret from her mom was not something she enjoyed. They usually shared everything going on in their lives. It was so hard not to ask her advice about doctors and medications or, like tonight, to pretend things were okay when they weren't and come up with excuses for the things she couldn't do.

Soon, she told herself. She'd know something soon, and then there would be no more secrets.

Once Mom knew what was really going on, she would understand Allye's reticence to date or purchase a home. She'd also be a lot more worried than she was right now.

That was the part Allye dreaded.

"Allye!" A deep, jovial voice pulled her from her thoughts, and Allye looked up to find the mayor striding toward her.

"Mayor Jennings, how are you?"

"Great, as always. I've been meaning to check on you." He looked around and lowered his voice as he reached her table. "No more episodes, I hope?"

She blinked. "Episodes?"

"Like what happened with you falling Thursday night," he clarified.

"Oh yes—I mean no." She slowed when his brows knotted in confusion. "I mean, yes, I know what you're referring to, and I have had a few run-ins with that guy, but I'm okay," she hurried to assure him. "But no, no 'episodes.' I didn't fall Thursday either. The police found evidence to prove it."

The confused look didn't leave his face. "But I found you. You'd obviously fallen."

"I'm still not sure how I ended up at the bottom of the steps," she admitted. "Maybe the guy got scared off when he heard you. But I know what I saw, and there's been a body found matching a description of the man I saw being beaten." Just saying those words left an acidic taste in her mouth. She grabbed her glass and took a drink to wash it away.

The mayor slipped into a seat beside the one her mom had vacated. "Are you sure about all this?"

She nodded. "The police had me go through mug shots to try to identify my attacker, but he wasn't in there. Next step is to work with a forensic artist to try to get a sketch of him."

"Are you absolutely sure about what you saw? I know you're under a lot of stress with your health right now. That could affect your perception of things."

She gaped at him. He knew about her health issues? How?

Mayor Jennings gave her a concerned fatherly smile. "Don't get upset with him, but Wesley mentioned your health struggles the other day." Apparently he'd read the question in her face. She'd never been good at hiding what she was thinking. He patted her hand and continued. "I know that has to be such a weight on your mind, and medical problems and stress can work together to create . . . scenarios that feel real but aren't quite what they seem."

Was he calling her delusional? Officer Moore had practically done so the other night, but this was Mayor Jennings. Surely he knew her better than that. And Moore's insinuation was before they'd found the body. It took her a moment to find her voice. "That's true, but there is evidence to confirm that a crime occurred."

"I'm not saying one didn't. If there's a body, something had to have happened to him. But that doesn't mean you witnessed it.

And if word gets out that you might have seen the murderer, it could put you in serious danger unnecessarily."

"I think I already am in danger. I've been attacked again."

"Again? What else happened?"

"He broke into my house Friday night. Scared me half to death, but I'm okay. He didn't hurt me."

"Broke into your house? The same man?"

"Yes, but like I said, he didn't actually hurt me. I'm not sure why he was there."

The mayor ran a hand through his thinning hair. "This is serious, Allye. I don't like it. You're too vulnerable living there alone, and your health only makes things worse."

"I know," she admitted reluctantly. "But I can't do nothing. A man is dead, and this guy has come after me twice. He knows where I live."

The mayor thought for a moment. "If the situation were different, I'd recommend you do all you can to ensure justice is served. But so many details of what you've experienced don't add up. The way I found you, the green glow. I think you need to seriously consider whether you really witnessed what you think you did before you make yourself a target." His gaze shifted, and a smile lit his face. "Julie! I didn't realize you were Allye's companion." He rose and embraced her mom.

Allye watched them, feeling like her insides had frozen. She hadn't mentioned the green glow. How did he know about it? As they started to turn back to her, she snatched another slice of pizza and took a large bite. She wasn't at all hungry now, but she needed something to help hide the shock she knew would be all over her face.

"I'd invite you to join us, but it's our monthly mother-daughter date," her mom was saying.

"Of course. I'm not staying, just happened to see Allye here and thought I'd say hello while waiting on my take-out order." He flashed her a grin as if they'd been talking about the weather rather than murder. "I hope you ladies have a wonderful time." He winked at her mom. "And I'll see *you* in a few days."

"I can't wait. Goodnight, Raymond." She was all smiles as she retook her seat. "He's such a wonderful man."

"He could have joined us if you wanted him to." Not that she wanted to talk to him right now, but perhaps once her shock wore off, she could have asked him where he'd heard about the green glow.

Mom waved her hand. "We have plans for Saturday evening."

"What kind of plans?" Allye was impressed that she managed to keep her voice even. She didn't want to tip her mom off that something was amiss. Or might be.

"He said it was a surprise but to dress up. I'm looking forward to it. Now, how about dessert?"

Allye didn't feel like dessert, but it was their tradition, and her mom would surely suspect something if she turned it down. They decided on the tiramisu to share. The dessert wasn't covered in Parmesan like most of Zhan's menu items, but the restaurant took their reputation too seriously to leave their signature ingredient out completely. Somehow they'd managed to make the flavor combination work, and it had become a local favorite.

For the next several minutes, her mom chatted about work and mutual friends, but Allye found it difficult to follow the conversation. How had Mayor Jennings known about the green glow? She mentally rehearsed their conversation to make sure, but no, she definitely had not mentioned it. Could he have heard about it from Officer Moore or Eric? She hadn't told anyone else that detail—not even her neighbor right after it happened. But if the mayor had heard about it from the police, why had he acted as if he didn't know she'd experienced a break-in?

Before she found an answer to her questions, the waiter approached them with two pitchers. "More tea, ladies?"

"Please." Mom turned that megawatt smile on him, and he actually blushed. What was he? Seventeen?

A drop of condensation slid down the side of one pitcher and landed on the small pile of extra napkins.

The waiter straightened. "Can I box the pizza for you, or are you still working on it?"

Allye glanced at her mom, who nodded. "That would be great, and we'd like an order of tiramisu, please."

He left with their pizza, and Allye attempted to focus on the story her mom was relating. She was hopelessly lost.

Her mind drifted again. It wasn't just the offhanded way Mayor Jennings had mentioned the green glow that bothered her. Why did it seem like he just wanted the whole situation to go away? She couldn't make sense of why he not only was unconcerned about a murder—and an attack on her—happening barely a block from his office but also felt so strongly against her involvement.

He was running for a state seat, and much of his campaign focused on how safe he kept his town. Perhaps he saw the situation as bad publicity? She'd never seen him as one to gloss over the town's problems though. He had a reputation for meeting challenges head on—fixing things. If he was hoping to cover up the fact that major crimes were going on in the area, he wasn't the man she and the majority of Kincaid thought he was.

She really hated to think that might be the case. Maybe his relationship with her mom was clouding his judgment? Allye's personal connection to him wasn't quite what she'd call a father-daughter bond, but he did seem to care about what happened to her.

When an opportunity arose, she rerouted the conversation. Perhaps her mom knew something that could help her make sense of the situation, but she'd have to be careful about how she worded things to avoid spilling her own secrets.

"You've been dating Mayor Jennings for a while now. How have things been since he started his campaign?" She hoped the question sounded casual.

"With how busy election season has kept him, we haven't seen each other as often as we'd like, but it's been going well, all things considered."

That hadn't exactly been what Allye was getting at, but she lifted her tea to take a sip while she tried to think of a better way to ask about *him*.

Her mom glanced at Allye through her eyelashes and ran a finger around the rim of her own glass. "Just between us, I wouldn't be shocked to receive a proposal soon."

24

ALLYE DROPPED HER GLASS. Sweet tea and ice cubes sloshed across the table, spilling into her mom's lap. Her mom sprang to her feet, whisking most of it away with her napkin before it could soak into her expensive cobalt suit.

"Oh no." Allye grabbed the pile of napkins—already half soaked—and tried to head off the stream still dripping to the floor. The napkins helped, but they weren't nearly enough. "Sorry. Sorry." Why did she have to be so clumsy?

"It's okay. No harm done." Her mom blotted the remaining drops on her skirt, then added her napkin to Allye's efforts. "I needed to have this suit cleaned anyway."

The waiter appeared beside them, towel in hand. "Here, let me."

They stepped back and allowed him to mop up the puddle on the table.

"I'm so sorry."

"No problem. Would you like to move to the next table while we get this area cleaned up?" He gestured to an area behind him where their boxed pizza sat.

Allye's cheeks burned as she took a seat at the new table. If they hadn't already ordered dessert, she'd be tempted to toss a couple of twenties on the table and make a beeline for the door.

Her mom laughed, not seeming to share her embarrassment. "That wasn't the reaction I expected you to have."

Oh. That.

She wanted to deny the admission had anything to do with her clumsiness, but it had. Twenty minutes ago, it wouldn't have bothered her. She'd have been happy for them. Now . . . now she was so confused. She tried to pull her thoughts together. Her mom was still waiting for a response. "I guess I didn't realize you two were getting so serious. You really think he might propose?"

"I have no way of knowing for certain, but like I said, it wouldn't shock me."

"If he does, what will you say?"

Her mom either didn't notice or pretended not to notice the slight edge to her voice. Her shoulders lifted in a graceful shrug. "I think I'd accept."

Allye's stomach bottomed out.

Her mom studied her, likely taking in the alarm that had to be splayed across her face. "I'm lonely, Allye. When your dad first died, I had you and your brothers. The last few years since you moved out, I've busied myself in church work and the housing market. Now that things are slowing down, I'm beginning to notice how quiet the house is."

"I could visit more." Allye knew as soon as the words left her mouth how oblivious she sounded. Game nights with the daughter weren't a replacement for a husband.

Her mom reached across the table and patted her hand. "I'd love that, but I'm ready to move forward when he is."

She swallowed. "Are you sure about him?"

"He's a good friend. I've always thought highly of him. Your dad did too."

So had Allye before all this started. Maybe she still should.

"Do you have a problem with Raymond?"

Yes. Maybe. She wasn't sure. And she certainly couldn't go into the details of her concerns without owning up to what she'd been facing lately. She wasn't about to open that can of sardines right now, especially not in public.

The waiter deposited their tiramisu and a fresh glass of tea. Allye picked up a spoon, grateful to have something to occupy her hands. She stole a glance at her mom, who was still waiting for an answer to her question.

Allye sighed. "I don't know. I've always looked up to him, thought he was good for this town. But . . ." How did she say what she was thinking without giving too much away? "Do you think he's changed lately?"

"What do you mean?"

"I don't know. He just seems different."

Mom took a bite and thought for a moment. "Well, he has seemed a bit distracted. But like I mentioned earlier, the campaign has kept him busy. Running for state senator is much more involved than running for mayor in a small town. I think he thrives on the excitement and challenge, but it's taken a toll on him too. I think it would on anyone."

True enough. Allye dug her spoon into the tiramisu. "For the record, I'm not opposed to you getting married again if you choose to. I just don't want you to get hurt."

Her mom gave her a sad smile. "I appreciate that. And 'for the record,' I'm not planning on getting hurt, but hurt is a part of life. Our family has seen more of that than most." She blinked against a sheen of tears. "But I refuse to live in fear."

Allye nodded, swallowing back her own tears. They finished off their tiramisu in companionable silence, but Allye hardly tasted the creamy dessert. She had a lot to process, and her headache had progressed from teasing to a boxing match.

The waiter returned with the check and exchanged it for the empty plate. "I'll leave this for whenever you're ready, but take your time."

Allye reached for it, but her mom got to it first.

"I've got this one." She placed several bills in the black book and handed it back to the waiter. "Keep the change."

Allye took one last sip of her tea, and they rose to leave together. Once in the parking lot, Mom pulled her into a tight hug.

She returned it full force. As they pulled away, she couldn't help whispering, "Do you love him?"

Mom met her gaze, a smile tugging at her lips. "Yes, I believe I do."

As Allye climbed into her car, her thoughts whirled, and she wasn't sure which to snatch for further examination. Her mom was in love with Mayor Jennings. Was that a good thing or a tragedy waiting to happen? Was he who everyone seemed to think he was? Was he involved in something nefarious?

Her head continued to pound. Maybe she'd misunderstood her conversation with him. She needed an objective person to talk to. She glanced at the clock. It was nearing ten. Too late to call Eric?

She didn't want to chance waking him if he was asleep. But maybe she'd text when she got home.

IT HAD BEEN A LONG, frustrating day. Eric hadn't slept well last night after scouring the internet for information on MS. He'd tried to keep his mind from constantly straying to Allye and her test, but it had been a struggle. He'd almost texted her to ask how it had gone, but he doubted she had the results yet.

Instead, he'd thrown himself into his investigations, even returning to the station after dinner. With nearly everyone else gone for the day, he'd finally hit a rhythm, his concentration only broken when he received Allye's text asking if he had time to talk. But he still had no new leads on any of his big cases. The labs were backed up as usual, so there'd been no confirmation on the identification of the presumed drugs he'd collected from Ashley Harrison's house. Dion was still missing. Their John Doe had yet to be ID'd. The forensic artist he'd hoped to contract to work with Allye was out of town until next Monday.

He resisted the urge to pound on his steering wheel. Investigations took time. He knew that. Usually, he was okay with it. But these cases were different. Some of them were connected—and people he cared about were in danger. He needed these cases wrapped up yesterday.

Allye's street loomed ahead, and he flipped on his right turn signal. Whatever had her unsettled probably could have been handled over the phone, but he sensed she needed a face-to-face, and he'd be lying if he said he didn't want to see her, especially after what he'd discovered about MS last night.

He'd known the disease was bad. He hadn't realized how debilitating it could be as it progressed.

Allye had said it could be something else, but he'd heard the resignation in her voice. She knew.

He wanted to be there for her as she faced this, but something inside him shrank back. Was he really that shallow? No. Allye needed a friend to support her. He could do that—would willingly do it. But he'd have to keep his feelings in check. No matter what Bryce had said, he couldn't allow their friendship to progress to more. She deserved better than him and all his baggage.

With that depressing thought foremost in his mind, he parked on the street across from Allye's house. She'd turned her porch light on to welcome him, and before he reached the door, Allye had it open. "I'm so sorry to keep bothering you."

"You're anything but a bother." He eyed the shiny dead bolt on her door. "How's the new lock?"

"Good, I guess. Only took Bryce a few minutes to install it this afternoon." She made a face. "Had to dance around why I suddenly wanted one though." She motioned him toward what was becoming his regular seat.

"Maybe you should just tell him."

She sighed. "I almost did. Then he started talking about Corina and the baby. They're finally settling into a normal life, and I don't want to pull them into this."

"I can guarantee you Bryce wouldn't want you to risk your safety for his comfort."

"Nothing's happened in the last few days, and I have good locks now." She frowned. "Don't look at me like that. I'll think about it, okay?"

Not quite okay, but he decided to let it drop for now. "Okay. So what's going on?"

She started toward the seat beside him, then seemed to re-think her choice and dropped into the recliner instead. He almost wished she had joined him on the couch. The recliner was close, but the space it left between them felt like a barrier.

"Let me start off by saying, this may be nothing. But my head is muddled, and I need your perspective."

He inclined his head, waiting for her to continue.

"I talked to Mayor Jennings tonight, and it was . . . odd." She paused as if searching for words, then blurted, "Something isn't right. He tried to discourage me from pursuing answers about the attacks, said I could be putting myself in danger unneces-sarily if I'm mistaken about what I saw. But I did see it. There's evidence of that now."

Eric blinked. Why would the mayor try to discourage a wit-ness? That didn't make any sense. "Could he have gotten the im-pression that you were personally digging for answers? Because I would strongly discourage that too."

"No. At least, I don't think so. I was only telling him that there is evidence now and that I'm working with you to try to identify my attacker."

"Perhaps he misunderstood."

"I don't see how. He seemed to be warning me against claiming I knew anything—like he was afraid I'd make myself a target and could get hurt because the murderer might think I could identify him when I really couldn't."

Her words came out in rush, and Eric had to take a moment to untangle them. He thought he knew what she was saying. "Okay," he said slowly. "Well, first off, I believe you witnessed the murder. Full stop. So your testimony isn't an 'unnecessary' risk. But he isn't wrong about the danger. Drug dealers—which is what your attacker seems to be, based on the conversation you heard in the park—can be ruthless. And if we're correct, this guy has already murdered at least one man—with his bare hands. That's aside from the overdose deaths that this drug ring may or may not be responsible for."

Allye visibly swallowed. "I know. But isn't that all the more reason to make sure he gets caught before anyone else dies?"

"Of course. I wasn't saying you should cower from the danger, only that you should be aware of it."

"And I am."

"Good. You need to watch your back until this guy is caught and we have everything figured out." He paused and leaned toward her. "Do me a favor. Promise me you won't go anywhere alone for a while—try not to be alone if you can help it."

She tilted her head, a half smile curling her lips. "You do realize I live alone, right?"

"I'm being serious."

Her smile drooped. In fact, her whole body seemed to droop from the weight of their discussion. "So am I. I know it's not ideal, but I don't have much choice. All my friends and extended family members have jobs or other commitments. And between all the normal things that keep me running, I'm slipping in doctor appointments and tests right and left."

He really didn't like it, but she had a point. "At least do what you can. Keep your doors locked, even when you're at home. Try not to go out alone, but if you have to, tell someone where you're going and be extra aware of your surroundings."

"All right. I can do that."

She sounded calm, but he noticed the trembling in her hand

when she tucked her hair behind her ear. Was that from nerves, or was it due to her illness?

"But back to Mayor Jennings. Should I be concerned about him, or am I overthinking things?"

He leaned back. "I wouldn't think too much of the mayor trying to encourage you to be cautious. From his point of view, it very much looked like you suffered an accidental head injury. I can see why he'd have doubts."

"There's more though." Allye's tone put him on alert. "When he was listing the reasons why I needed to rethink whether my memory could be trusted, he mentioned the green glow."

His brow crinkled. "From your break-in?"

She nodded. "How did he know about that? I certainly didn't tell him."

"Are you sure you didn't mention it to him? Or to your mom?"

"Positive. I had just told him about the break-in, and he acted like that's the first he'd heard about it—but I didn't say anything about the green glow. And Mom doesn't know about any of this. The only people who should know that detail are me, you, Officer Moore, and my attacker." She paused. "If you didn't tell and Officer Moore didn't . . ." She left the rest unsaid.

Eric clicked his pen a few times. Her insistence on still keeping all this a secret from her family was not good, but that wasn't his call. "Okay," he said finally. "I'll check with Moore if I can get ahold of him. Sometimes he's a bit of a gossip around the station, but your break-in happened on the last shift before he left for vacation. If I know him, he was in a hurry to get everything logged and get home as soon as he clocked out. I doubt he told anyone."

"And if he didn't?" Allye's words were soft.

He blew out a breath. "If he didn't, then we may have a major problem."

25

ERIC STRODE INTO THE MORGUE early the next morning. Starting his day with witnessing a set of autopsies wasn't at the top of his list of favorite things. But maybe it would shake something loose regarding John Doe's and Ashley Harrison's cases.

Maybe. Maybe not. If they were correct about their John Doe being one and the same with the victim behind Allye's studio, then the examination might not reveal much new information. But the confirmation would be helpful, even if it only established that the estimated time of death matched.

He expected the same would be the case with Ashley's—providing confirmation of his current theory rather than new information to run with. Unfortunately, the most helpful information on Ms. Harrison's cause of death would likely be found in the toxicology report, which could take weeks to get through the state labs and back to him. It would probably be in a race for last place with the other results he was waiting for. Sometimes he hated how the system worked.

Several hours later, he was on his way back to the police station. As he'd thought, the autopsies had revealed little new information. He'd get the official report, minus the toxicology results, within a few days. But the ME had verbally confirmed that the physical examinations did indicate that John Doe had been beaten to death and Ashley Harrison had overdosed.

Now he just needed to find the responsible parties. And Dion. He still hadn't been able to find a trace of him. Yesterday he'd made another round of calls to the boy's friends. As before, they claimed not to have any idea where he might be.

He was tempted to go back to Kincaid Lake and comb the park for him. He'd do it in a heartbeat if there was any indication that's where the teen had gone, but there was none. Still, he had put the park service on alert. They now had Dion's photo and would detain him if he was spotted. For the moment, he'd have to rely on them doing their jobs while he did his.

As he neared the station, his thoughts turned to his last conversation with Allye. He didn't like the thought of the mayor being wrapped up in something shady, but he had a responsibility to investigate. He'd left a message for Moore after leaving her house last night. He was half hoping the man would admit to having run his mouth to someone. That might be enough to explain things and put their minds at ease, but he had no idea if Moore would ignore his calls while on his California vacation. They might have to wait for that answer until he returned next week.

Eric could just outright ask the mayor how he knew. If he had somehow come across the information innocently, he could set their minds at ease with a simple explanation. But if he was guilty of something, he'd just lie. And Mayor Jennings was cool under pressure. That quality had served him well during his political career, but it could make it a lot more difficult for Eric to detect deceit.

Plus, if he was somehow involved with whatever this was, a confrontation would tip him off that they suspected him.

An incoming call disrupted his thoughts as he pulled into a parking space. The display showed Moore's number. He quickly punched the button to answer. "Thornton."

"It's Moore. Sorry I'm just getting back to you. Forgot my phone in the hotel last night, and it was dead when I got back. Didn't turn it back on until this morning."

"No need to apologize. I'm the one interrupting your vacation, and I'm sorry about that. I'll try to keep this quick. Did you tell anyone about the incident at Allye Jessup's home the other night?"

Moore snorted. "Is that what we're calling it? No, I didn't. I put it in my report—which I sent to you like you asked—but that's it."

"No one at the station? Even Darla?" he clarified.

"Nope. I had to pack and get to the airport. Didn't have time to talk."

"Okay. That's what I needed to know. Thanks for returning my call."

"Sure thing. What's this about?"

No way he was going into that with Moore. If the mayor was innocent, then he didn't want to malign him to another officer—especially one who liked to gab. If he wasn't, then he certainly didn't want to take a chance on something being said that might tip him off.

"It may tie in with something I'm investigating," he hedged.

"You think something actually happened there?" Moore sounded incredulous.

"I do. But I'm not sure what." Time to end this conversation. "Thanks again for calling me back. I'll let you get back to your vacation."

"Glad to help."

Eric ended the call and stared at the brick building he worked out of.

So Moore wasn't responsible for spilling the beans. That left Eric and Allye, and neither of them had told anyone. Yes, Eric and Moore had included Allye's statement about the green glow when they filed their reports, but he doubted anyone had read them yet. Sure, the chief *could* have, but—

The chief. He was the mayor's uncle—although with the large

age gap between Chief McHenry and the mayor's mother, the two men were pretty close in age. They had grown up more like cousins than uncle and nephew.

That could explain things. Or severely complicate them.

Mayor Jennings could have asked the chief for the details about Allye's situation. As mayor, he technically was Chief McHenry's boss, and he had a right to be apprised of what was going on in their investigations. Chief could have pulled all the reports, not just the one from the first night, and then mentioned that detail to him. No harm, no foul.

But if Jennings didn't believe a crime had been committed as he claimed, why would he have asked for the information?

Perhaps he'd only been curious if Eric had uncovered anything new since his interview. Or, considering his relationship with Allye's mom, he could have followed up out of concern. Either possibility was reasonable. But like Allye said, knowledge of the green glow couldn't easily be divorced from knowledge of the break-in.

So why had Jennings acted as if the break-in was news to him?

Eric could only think of one plausible answer. The man knew more than he was telling. Which meant that he was probably up to his eyebrows in whatever was going on.

A heaviness settled on Eric's chest. He'd wanted to believe Mayor Jennings was innocent. Everyone who knew the man respected him, even his political enemies. The man was practically a shoo-in for state senate, and he could do a lot of good there. But if he had criminal ties . . .

And what about Chief McHenry? Eric sure didn't want to believe his boss was anything but the epitome of integrity, but he wouldn't be doing his job if he didn't consider the possibility. The chief and the mayor had been close growing up and were still good friends on top of their familial ties. Even if he didn't know what Jennings was possibly involved in, would he allow Eric free rein to investigate?

He would need to tread even more carefully now.

Until he was sure that the chief hadn't been compromised, he'd have to be extremely cautious about what he told him and what he included in his reports.

ALLYE SHIFTED in the semi-comfortable seat at her follow-up appointment to discuss the MRI results. She'd spent the morning and early afternoon organizing her items for her festival booth—making sure everything that was finished had been safely boxed for transport and that she had the necessary pricing labels printed and sorted into the correct boxes for easy setup. She'd hoped focusing her energy on that needed task would alleviate her nerves as she anticipated this appointment. It had helped. A little.

But now that she was here, they'd returned full force. Her hands trembled, and she considered sitting on them as the pause between pleasantries and getting down to business stretched a little too long. *God, I meant it when I said I trust you no matter what.*

Finally, the doctor turned from her computer screen and back to Allye. "Well, there's no sign of demyelination," she announced.

The term sounded vaguely familiar from her aunt's experience or maybe from her previous visit, but she couldn't place its significance. "I'm sorry. I can't remember what that means," she admitted.

"Essentially it's damage to the myelin layer protecting your nerve fibers. A definitive MS diagnosis generally requires evidence of that damage."

"So the results mean . . . ?"

"While there's still the slightest chance you could have MS, it's very unlikely."

Allye blinked. She'd wanted to believe it wasn't MS, but she hadn't allowed herself to hope too much. She studied the doctor's face. She wasn't smiling. "What's wrong? This is a good thing, right?"

"Of course. But you still have unexplained symptoms—serious symptoms. With the MRI, we also checked for tumors."

Allye caught her breath.

"We didn't find any," the doctor hurried to assure her. "But sometimes, they aren't easy to spot."

Allye took a moment to digest that. The possibility of a tumor hadn't occurred to her. Was that any worse than MS? Maybe. At least she might have some chance against a tumor.

"So what's next?"

The doctor slipped off her glasses. "Although these results indicate it is very unlikely you have MS, I think it would still be wise to do a spinal tap to further rule it out. But in the meantime, we'll run other tests as well."

Great. "Looking for what exactly?"

"I won't lie to you. There are many things that could be causing your symptoms. With your family history, we focused on that when normally we would have eliminated some of the other possibilities first. Now we'll be backtracking." She tapped on her keyboard. "I've put in the referral order for the spinal tap. When you leave, we'll give you the phone number to schedule that. I also want to go ahead and do more blood work."

"If the spinal tap doesn't show anything, what other kinds of things will we be testing for? I'd like to know what I could be up against."

The doctor sighed. "We'll be checking for Lyme disease regardless because it can also cause the spinal tap to come back with a positive result. If the test is negative, we'll still do further tests for Lyme, but with this other blood work, we'll also look into the possibility of certain vitamin and mineral deficiencies, as well as test for a handful of autoimmune and other inflammatory conditions."

Allye struggled to focus. She'd never dreamed there were so many other things that could be causing her symptoms. Of course, she'd simply assumed the diagnosis would be MS.

When the doctor asked if she had any other questions, she shook her head. Later, she would likely have a whole list of them, but she needed to let everything sink in first. For now, she had enough info to go on—hopefully, she'd remember the important things or be able to find them in her doctor's notes online.

Once she was back in her car, she rested her head on the steering wheel. She needed a few minutes to think and pray before beginning the long drive home. Without lifting her head, she murmured, "Well, God, it looks like this isn't finished yet. I still don't know what the future holds or what's going on, but I'm grateful it probably isn't MS. Thank you for that."

She knew—more from the doctor's tone than her words—that there could still be something just as bad or worse going on, but she couldn't deny her relief. A bit of her burden had lifted.

This deserved a celebration. And she knew exactly what she'd like to do. She started her car and backed out of her parking space. First order of business would be getting back to Kincaid before rush-hour traffic hit.

26

ERIC FOLLOWED SEVERAL UNIFORMED OFFICERS from Chief McHenry's office and forced himself not to let the door slam behind him. An hour absolutely wasted. Because of one officer's carelessness during a routine callout, they'd all had to sit through an hour-long lecture about procedure. He suspected the chief had included him as a reference rather than a target of the training, but he'd still lost an hour of valuable time.

He'd barely reached his desk when his phone vibrated. He quickly answered, not bothering to check the caller ID.

"Thornton."

Allye's voice came over the line. "Hey, Eric. Are you busy?"

"Yes." Was he ever not?

"Oh." Her disappointment was clear.

He didn't need to take out his frustration on her. Trying to soften his tone, he asked, "What do you need?"

"I was hoping you might have time to join me for a photo shoot at Kincaid Lake. I promised I'd try not to go off alone, but no one else is available, and I'm anticipating a fantastic sunset that could be a great last-minute addition to my booth." She paused the rush of words before adding, "But if you're busy . . ."

"You're going out there either way, aren't you?" He felt the beginning of a tension headache coming on.

"Maaaybe."

He rubbed his forehead, his eyes trailing over the notes that still needed to be entered into the system. But after his realization this morning, he wasn't sure doing so was a good idea. If the mayor was getting info from his uncle, Eric didn't want to make it available any sooner than he had to. And Allye did not need to be out in the park alone.

He sighed. "You at home now?"

"Yes."

"Stay put. I'll pick you up in ten."

"I'll try to be ready."

Less than thirty minutes later, Eric was pulling her equipment from the back of his car. On the way, they'd eaten sandwiches Allye had prepared beforehand. Good thing too. With her call coming right after the chief's end-of-day lecture, he hadn't had time to even think about dinner.

The sun hung low, but they still had plenty of time before color would begin to streak the sky. Allye held out her hands for the camera bag and tripod, but he shook his head.

"Nothing doing." He slammed the trunk and gestured toward the lake. "Show me where to go."

After a second's hesitation, Allye took the lead. He followed, scanning their surroundings as they went. There were a few people around—a man walking a dog, kids on the playground with their mom nearby. No one that appeared suspicious. No one that matched Allye's description of her attacker. His shoulders relaxed slightly.

As they neared the lake's edge, she paused and angled her head, shook it, then moved a few more yards. She repeated the evaluation until finally a smile broke across her face. "This is it."

Eric glanced at the lake from this position. Looked about the same as the other places she'd tried, but he said nothing, just swung the tripod from his shoulder and offered it to her. More quickly than he'd have thought possible, she had it out of its carrying case and assembled.

"Impressive."

"I know." She grinned and reached for her camera bag. Chuckling, he released it to her. She set the bag on the ground and removed her camera. She inspected it—lens, battery, memory card—before attaching it to the tripod.

"Now what?" he asked when she finished her adjustments.

"Now we wait." She lowered herself to the grass and sat cross-legged facing the water.

"Fair enough." He turned his back to the lake and took a leisurely look around. Still no sign of trouble. Or of Dion. But that would be too much to expect. "So you really wanted to come out here just to catch the sunset?"

"Well, not just that. I'm sort of celebrating too."

He swiveled back to her, his hopes rising. "Celebrating what?"

She pushed her hair out of her face but kept her gaze on the lake. "The doctor is pretty confident I don't have MS."

"Allye, that's wonderful!"

"Yes, it is." She finally looked up at him. A sheen of tears glimmered in her eyes, but she was smiling. "We still don't know what I have, but I'm glad to take that win for now."

He wanted to ask what was next, if the doctors had any idea what else might be going on, but he held his tongue. He sensed she didn't want to face the unknowns right now. She was celebrating, but her victory was tenuous. Instead of voicing his questions, he glanced around them once more before joining her on the ground.

"I love this place," Allye murmured. "Even though we lived so close, sometimes we'd camp here on long weekends or just come for a day trip. Dad loved taking us kayaking on the lake."

He absorbed her recollections, the wistfulness in her voice. He hadn't known Allye's dad—the man had been killed in action before Eric came to Kincaid to live with his grandpa full-time—but he could hear her love for him. His own father had never been interested in family outings. Drugs, booze, anything to escape reality—those were the things his dad cared about. Mom had been the same. Try as he might, Eric couldn't dredge up a single instance they'd spent time together that hadn't involved one or the other of them making a detour to meet their dealer, being at least half stoned already, or raging mad because they weren't.

"You okay?"

Allye's concerned voice pulled him from the black hole he'd begun to sink into. "Yes." He loosened his clenched jaw and forced himself to relax. There was a reason he didn't allow his thoughts to linger too long in that period of his past.

"You ever go camping as a kid?"

"Nah. My parents weren't into that, and Gramps was past his prime by the time I moved in with him." He hoped she'd leave it at that, but of course she didn't.

"You never talk about them—your parents, I mean."

He tried not to bristle. He really didn't want to get off on that topic. "Not worth talking about."

"Do they live around here?"

"No."

From the corner of his eye, he could see her studying him, but she apparently got the hint. Instead of pushing further, she redirected the focus of conversation. "What keeps you here? Bryce commented the other day how he always expected you to return to the city after high school."

"I can see where he got that idea. Fact is, I fully intended to move to a place with a bigger department—maybe one in Cincinnati—and work my way into the narcotics division."

"Why didn't you?"

"Gramps had a massive heart attack right before I graduated from the academy. Needed someone in the area to keep an eye on him."

"And when he passed?" She had known Gramps from church. Most of the congregation, including Allye, had attended his funeral several years ago. Eric had been touched by the show of support.

He shrugged. "By then, I'd hit my stride. Found I liked working in Kincaid." He'd found home here. A bit of community, though he'd be the first to admit he still felt a bit like an outsider sometimes. But now that he thought about it, maybe he'd been the one holding back.

Oblivious to the turn his thoughts had taken, Allye focused on his last words. "And now you're a detective. Do you like the change?"

Did he? He shifted to a more comfortable position as he considered her question. "It's not what I thought," he said finally. "But I wouldn't give it up to return to patrol. I just wish it were possible to close these cases more quickly."

"You mean it's not like on TV—case closed in fifty minutes, tops?"

He chuckled. "Definitely not."

Her expression sobered. "Has Dion been found?"

That was a whole other concern. He blew out a breath. "No. We reissued the alert, but he seems to have disappeared."

Her hand settled on his knee, the touch featherlight. "I'm sorry. I'll keep praying."

He hadn't stopped. The kid had him worried. Nearly as much as Allye's situation did. At least, to their knowledge, Dion wasn't a target. With his associates, that could change at any moment though. He was playing with fire. Sooner or later, he would get burned.

"Tell me something, Eric."

"What?"

"I don't know. Just something about you." She still hadn't removed her hand from his knee.

"Okay." What kind of request was that? He thought for a moment. "I memorized one hundred digits of pi when I was a freshman in high school."

"Seriously?" She sounded mildly interested. Or like she could fall asleep at any moment.

"Mm-hmm."

"Remember any of it?"

"Three point one four."

"Even I remember that much."

He could practically hear the eye roll. His lips twitched.

"Eric!" She lightly swatted at him, but he caught her hand and recited the next five digits while tapping each of hers. She stilled.

Without letting go, he transferred his attention to her face. "I could go on, but you might miss the sunset."

Her eyes shot to the sky, which was just beginning its brilliant transformation. She scrambled from the ground, then paused and blinked. She swayed slightly.

Eric was instantly on his feet. He gripped her arms to steady her. "Take it easy."

She blinked a few more times and took a deep breath. "I'm okay. Just stood up too fast." She extracted herself from his grasp and moved behind her camera. Though her face was half hidden, he didn't miss the flush creeping up her neck.

He stood close, not so close she'd feel like he was hovering, but close enough to catch her if she started to fall. But she didn't.

Instead, Allye's tiredness seemed to melt away as she snapped picture after picture of the scene, sometimes pausing to readjust her tripod or swivel the camera to capture a different slice of the beauty before them. Confident she'd gained her footing, Eric stepped back, thumbs hooked in his belt.

The sunset *was* breathtaking tonight, but she was more so. He found himself watching her more than the sky. She didn't seem to notice, or didn't mind if she did. And as she worked, she got chatty—asking him questions, throwing out fun facts about the park, reminiscing about other photo shoots. He responded when appropriate, but mostly he just watched and listened, enjoying her obvious delight. For a few moments, at least, she was her old self. Sparkling and bubbly. And, oh, so beautiful—not that she'd ever ceased being that. But her unbounded joy combined with the kiss of the setting sun on her fiery hair made him more aware of it than he'd ever been before.

He slipped his phone from his pocket and aimed it at her, clicking a few photos as she turned toward him, a radiant smile on her face.

"What are you doing?"

"Nothing." He grinned and slid the phone back into his pocket.

"Uh-huh." Her lips twitched as she returned her attention to her camera.

When the last remnants of the sunset's brilliance had faded to the somber blue of twilight, Allye turned to him, wistfulness in her expression. "I guess that's that."

"You took a lot of pictures."

"Yeah, I always take more than I think I'll need. Especially with the changing colors of a sunset, you never know which will be 'the one.'" She shrugged and gave him a sly grin. "Of course, I'm not limited to just one."

"How can you even choose?"

"It's not easy sometimes," she admitted. She turned her gaze back to the darkening sky. "Looks like it'll be a clear night. Wonder if we'll have a full moon. That would make for some excellent photos too—a bright shining moon reflecting off the water."

"You aren't scared of werewolves?" He tilted his head.

A mischievous smile lit her face. "Not with a big strong detective by my side."

"You trust me to protect you? Against werewolves?"

"Of course." She tapped her camera. "And I'd take lots of pictures. Think of what the newspapers would pay for those kind of photos." She stepped toward him and mimed tracing a headline. "Man Defeats Werewolf in One-on-One Fight."

"Oh, so you're not even going to try to help me?"

Her eyes widened, and she blinked in mock surprise. "You'd need help?"

He threw his head back and laughed. Her giggle turned into a snort and made him laugh harder.

When his eyes fixed on hers again, only a hint of merriment remained there. She was staring at him with an intense longing and . . . sadness?

He closed the remaining space between them. Tucked a wayward curl behind her ear. She placed a hand over the spot he'd touched, her eyes never leaving his.

"For you, I'd fight off an army of werewolves." The words were ridiculous. But he meant them. And she didn't laugh. Her eyes fluttered shut, her lips parting as she swayed toward him.

And then he was kissing her. She was kissing him.

It was sweet and beautiful and terrifying—all wrapped together.

When their lips parted, her wide-eyed gaze met his. Neither of them had been expecting that.

"I, uh—" He took a step back, hoping the distance would help him clear his head. "I should get you home. It'll be dark soon."

Something flickered in those big green eyes, but she only nodded. She readjusted her glasses with trembling hands, then turned to collect her equipment.

A gunshot split the silence.

Eric dove for Allye as her camera exploded mere inches from her fingertips.

27

ALLYE SCREAMED.

Before she had time for any other reaction, Eric plowed into her. She hit the ground hard. The breath whooshed from her lungs.

Eric covered her body with his. "Stay still," he whispered.

Stay still? She couldn't move—couldn't breathe. Her head buzzed from adrenaline and the pain of getting the wind knocked out of her. After what felt like an eternity, she managed to suck in a breath. Good grief, she sounded like she was dying.

Eric shifted above her. "Were you hit? Are you hurt?"

"I don't think so," she managed to gasp out. "What happened?"

"Someone put a bullet in your camera," he said tersely. He cocked his head. Listening for threats? Allye tried to hear above the pounding of her pulse. She hoped his ears were working because hers were practically useless. He shifted again, just slightly. This time, she caught sight of his gun. When had he drawn that? Didn't matter. She was just glad he had it.

As her breathing and heart rate returned to normal, so did her hearing. No more shots disturbed the serenity of the area. Insect chirrups and the soft slap of waves against the shore were the only sounds she registered.

Finally, Eric turned his head back to her and whispered, "Stay down. I'm going to make sure it's safe." He stood cautiously. Allye held her breath. Nothing happened. No bullets ripped through the night. No . . . anything.

She started to rise, but Eric motioned her to wait. She followed the direction of his gaze. Someone was heading their direction. She squinted, but between the low light and her now-smudged glasses, she couldn't make out much besides the fact he had a flashlight and appeared to be in uniform.

He stopped several yards away from them. "Park service. What's going on out here?"

Eric identified himself and Allye. "Someone shot at us."

"Either of you hurt? Need an ambulance?"

"No. Her camera took a direct hit, but he missed us."

"Where's the shooter?"

"No idea. We never saw him. There was a single shot, we dove to the ground, then nothing."

"Okay. We need to clear the area to make sure he's not still around. The two of you can wait in the back of my SUV until we're certain the threat is gone."

Eric extended his hand to her. She wasn't sure her shaky legs would hold her, but she let him help her up. As he did, he whispered, "Lean on me if you need support." He offered her his arm.

Relief flooded through her. "Thanks. I just might." This was no time to insist on independence. Not if she didn't want to risk falling flat on her face. She wrapped her arm around his and latched onto his wrist, hoping her grip didn't look as white-knuckled as it felt as they followed the ranger to his vehicle. They climbed into the back with instructions to remain there.

Once they were settled, she removed her glasses to clean them. But when she looked at them, she grimaced. That wasn't a smudge. A flying bit of camera must have scraped a deep gash across one of the lenses. She'd have to have it replaced—there wouldn't be any repairing it. Another thought hit her, and she shuddered. If she hadn't been wearing glasses, she might be missing an eye right now.

"You really okay?" Eric asked. He leaned close to study her in the near darkness. "You have blood on your cheek."

She instinctively reached for it and flinched at the sting. She touched the area more gingerly. "Just a scratch, I think. It doesn't feel deep."

"Good. I'm sorry about your camera—and the photos."

"It's okay. I'm just glad it wasn't one of us." She did hate losing her primary camera, but it was insured. And there would be other sunsets. But people weren't replaceable. If the shooter had aimed just a few feet to the side, she could be dead. A few feet more, and Eric might be.

She shuddered again, and he pulled her into a hug. She allowed her head to rest on his chest. He was tense, but his heart beat strong and steady beneath her ear. She matched her breaths to his and felt her anxiety ease a bit, though she was still shaking.

Thank you, Jesus, that we're okay. But if you don't mind, could you keep this from happening again?

This wasn't the first time she'd experienced a shooting incident, but she sure hoped it would be her last. Especially since this bullet, unlike the ones that had wrecked Corina's storefront last year, had likely been aimed at her.

"Not on my bucket list," she muttered.

"What?"

"Getting shot at—it wasn't on my bucket list."

Eric snorted. "I would hope not." His words sounded brusque, but his rigid posture relaxed slightly. After a brief pause, he asked, "What is something on your bucket list?"

She suspected he was trying to distract her from the situation, but why not play along? "Something on my unofficial, unwritten bucket list?" She thought for a moment. "I'd love to photograph an active volcano."

"An active volcano." He sounded thoughtful as he repeated her words. "Any particular one?"

"Haven't thought that far ahead. What about you? Something on your list."

Silence stretched between them. Long enough, she didn't think he was going to answer. "I want to be a dad one day," he said finally. "A good one."

She wanted to look at his face. Study his expression. But she loathed surrendering the comfort of his arms. Instead, she just said, "I think you will be."

Before the conversation could go any further, Eric straightened. Allye sat up, keeping her hand on his arm, and followed his gaze. The ranger was back and approaching the SUV—Allye's bags and equipment all bundled in one hand. He opened the door on Eric's side.

"Coast is clear, folks. Looks like whoever took a potshot at you didn't stick around to have another go. Couldn't find any sign of him except for the obvious damage to your equipment."

Eric's face was stoic as he took in the news, but Allye could feel the tension radiating through him. This wasn't good.

But there wasn't much they could do about it tonight. They gave their statements and contact info, then the ranger released them to head home.

It was a quiet ride back to her house. They were both still processing what had happened. While she could process things verbally just as well or better, she sensed Eric was in the mood for silent analysis. She could give him that. He'd likely saved her life tonight.

How had such a perfect evening morphed into disaster? And why? She kept coming back to why. Had someone tried to kill her tonight and missed? Why hadn't he fired again? Yeah, it was getting dark, but she and Eric had been out in the open with nothing to hide behind. It was like the break-in—except this time, she had a witness. There would be no debate about whether something had actually happened here tonight. That was some consolation.

But she still didn't know who was targeting her this way, or why they were doing it. It didn't make sense. If they wanted her dead, they'd had plenty of opportunity to make that happen—the night they'd broken in, this evening, and any number of times in between. Either they kept chickening out during their murder attempts—which she figured was highly unlikely—or whatever was going on was more complicated than it appeared on the surface. And as much as she'd prefer to think otherwise, she doubted it was over.

When they finally arrived back at her house, Eric insisted on walking her inside and clearing the house before leaving her alone. After assuring himself that no danger lurked behind her piles of laundry and stacks of empty delivery boxes, he reluctantly left with strong instructions to make sure her new dead bolt was locked behind him.

She did as he asked, then stood at the door, listening until the sound of his engine faded away.

Now what? Despite her tiredness and the late hour, she was pretty sure she was too wound up to even attempt sleep. The last thing she wanted to do was spend more hours lying in bed with her racing thoughts and relentless symptoms vying for attention.

Normally, she would be working. She'd spent countless nights editing photos, creating salable products, or designing creative advertisements for her business. But she knew she didn't have that kind of energy tonight, and her head was killing her.

A cup of tea, meds, and a movie might be her best option. If she was lucky, she'd fall asleep in her recliner.

Decision made, she headed to the kitchen. Medication was first priority. She retrieved the bottle from her purse and shook it. Empty. How had she missed that? Or had she just forgotten she'd taken the last one? She wasn't sure. She made a mental note to call for a refill tomorrow. At the rate her migraines had been hitting lately, she couldn't afford to be without her medication. Sighing, she retrieved an over-the-counter pain reliever and downed that instead.

That done, she placed the prescription bottle where she'd be likely to see it first thing in the morning and shifted her focus to making tea. While she waited for the water to boil, she selected a handful of noncaffeinated ingredients to create tonight's comfort blend. A spoonful of rooibos, some dried berries, hibiscus, a bit of ginger . . .

She added a few more ingredients and eyed the infuser basket. Something was missing. She opened her spice cabinet and scanned the contents until her gaze landed on a jar of cinnamon sticks. That was it. She broke a few chips off one of the sticks and added them to her little compilation.

Once the tea finished steeping, she retreated to the living room and turned on a favorite movie.

For the first half of the film, she knitted in between sips of tea and tried to lose her brain in the romantic cozy mystery she'd seen a half dozen times already. But when the main characters shared their first kiss, her hand went to her lips. She'd kissed Eric tonight. She really, really shouldn't have done that.

She hadn't meant to. She'd just lost her balance when she closed her eyes. At least, that's what she was going to keep telling herself.

Regardless, he'd kissed her. And that hadn't been an accident.

They weren't even dating. And she wasn't the type of girl to kiss on a first date. Not to mention a non-date.

And then there was the way she'd allowed him to hold her in the SUV. Her cheeks burned. There hadn't been anything inappropriate about his touch, she reminded herself. He'd held her like a brother would—in fact, Bryce would have done exactly the same if he'd been there.

But it hadn't been Bryce. It had been Eric. And she definitely didn't view Eric as a brother—especially after that kiss.

She groaned. She needed to pull herself together and stop acting like a lovestruck flibbertigibbet. So they'd kissed. Lots of people kissed and thought nothing of it.

But she wasn't lots of people. It did mean something to her. And while Eric might have only held her in a big-brother sort of way, his touch had been gentle. And he'd been considerate enough to offer her discreet assistance when she'd needed it.

Her phone dinged with a text message, pulling her from her embarrassment. Who would be sending her a message this late in the evening? She entered her passcode and pulled up the texting app. There was a new message from an unknown number, and it didn't show any preview text. Frowning, she tapped it.

Two photos appeared—one of her mom leaving her realty office, another of Bryce and Corina sitting on their back patio. None of them seemed to have any idea their picture was being taken.

As she stared at the photos, a second text appeared.

Retract your statements, or next time, it won't be a camera.

28

ALLYE CONTINUED TO STARE at the text messages.

No, no, no, no.

She had to tell her family—warn them.

The time caught her eye. It was late. They'd all be in bed by now. Should she wake them?

She reread the message. Forced herself to think logically. The photos might be recent, but it had been hours at minimum since they'd been taken. And she doubted whoever sent the threat expected her to be able to do anything about her statement tonight.

Her family wasn't in immediate danger.

But that did little to calm her nerves. They *were* in danger. And it was all because of her.

What should she do? She couldn't lie to the police—couldn't let a murderer and drug dealer keep ruining some lives and outright ending others. But she couldn't let her family be harmed either.

Her brain finally kicked in. She needed to call Eric. Show him these texts and ask what he recommended she do. Before she could second-guess herself, she paused the movie and dialed his number.

He answered quickly. "You okay?"

Relief swept through her at the sound of his voice. "Yes, I'm fine—I think."

"You think? Did something happen?"

"I just received a text message threatening my family."

"What did it say? Better yet, forward it to me." He gave her the number of his work cell.

"One second." She sent the messages through. "The photos came through first, then the threat."

He grunted. "I'm assuming you don't recognize the number?"

"No."

"Probably a burner phone, but I can try to track it down if you give me the number."

She pulled the phone from her ear again and read him the number. In the quiet that followed, she could hear his pen clicking.

"This changes things, Allye. I know you've been trying to shield your family from this, but they need to know so they can watch their backs."

"I know," she whispered. "I'll tell them in the morning."

"Do you need me to come with you?"

She hesitated. Did she want him to go with her? Yes. Full stop. Did she need him there? No. She could do this alone. No need to pull him from his work. "I can handle this."

"I know you *can*. That wasn't what I meant. Would you feel better having someone along that knows what's been going on and won't react emotionally?"

"I mean, yes, but—"

"Then I'll be there. Tell me when and where."

"I'll have to let you know. I don't even know if I'll be able to get everyone together or if I'll have to go to them separately." She massaged her forehead. "Why threaten them? Why not just kill me and be done with it?"

"For some reason, they seem to want you alive." He sounded puzzled. She had to admit it didn't make any sense to her either. Her attacker, like most drug dealers, seemed to have no problem with murder.

"But still, why not at least threaten *me*? Why go straight to my family?"

"What would you do if the threat had been aimed at you? Would you even consider asking us to drop the investigation, as far as it concerns the events you experienced?"

She barely had to think about it. "No."

"And somebody knows that. Someone involved knows you and knows you well enough to predict that a threat to your family would be much more effective than one to yourself."

"Mayor Jennings?" She could hardly picture it, but he was the only one she could think of. Even with his apparent slipup last night at Zhan's, it was still hard to wrap her mind around the possibility that he could be involved in something like this.

"We need more evidence before we throw accusations around." He paused. "But he seems the most likely suspect so far. Whoever it is already went to a lot of trouble to try to gaslight you. Now they know that isn't going to work, and more drastic measures are necessary."

"What should I do?"

His pen clicked again. "You can't give them what they want. But we can play this smart."

"How? I don't think I have the capacity for smart right now." Her head hurt, and it wasn't just from tonight's earlier events.

"We'll start with warning your family, like we already planned. Bryce knows how to watch his back."

Corina too, after all she'd been through last year. Allye wasn't so sure about her mom. Her head pounded harder as another realization hit.

"My mom and Mayor Jennings are dating." The words tasted like acid. If her teapot weren't already empty, she'd be pouring another cup to rinse her mouth out.

"I've heard that." *Click, click.* "Is their relationship serious?"

"Mom seems to think so."

He blew out a breath. "That's another complication we didn't need."

"Could that possibly play into things? He doesn't want me dead because of how it would affect her?"

"But now she's being threatened."

"Maybe it's an empty threat."

"Maybe. But we can't bank on that."

"I know." She sighed. "And Mom's a straight shooter. If I tell her we suspect the mayor, she's going to want to confront him directly."

"That would be a really bad idea. We don't want to tip him off."

Allye couldn't agree more. "But if I don't tell her we suspect him, she'll probably end up confiding in him about whatever I do tell her. But I can't *not* tell her. She needs to know she's in danger—especially if the mayor's involved. She trusts him, Eric."

He thought for a moment. "Okay. We're agreed nothing is to be done tonight, right?"

"Yes, if you think that's best."

"I do. Let me do some research while you get some rest."

"But—"

"Really, Allye. I know you got some good news today, but tonight has been rough, and you're probably still running on adrenaline. Rest now so you don't crash later."

It was probably already too late for that, but he was right. "I'll try."

"Please do. I'll see what I can uncover tonight." His pen clicked once again. "Listen, I have to testify in court tomorrow afternoon, and in the morning, there's a meeting I have to attend at the station. But there should be plenty of time in between for us to handle talking to your family. How about I come pick you up after my meeting, and we'll warn Bryce and Corina first? Maybe they'll have some insight on how to best handle telling your mom."

"Okay." She didn't know what else to say.

His voice softened. "We're going to figure this out. Trust me on that."

"I hope so."

"We will. I'll call before I head your way, but it'll probably be about nine or so."

"Okay. 'Night."

"Goodnight."

She sat quietly with her phone in her hand after they hung up. Eric sounded so sure they'd get to the bottom of things, but what was it going to cost? The good guys didn't always win. Not on earth anyway. Sometimes good people died. *Please, God, don't let that be the case for us. Keep the people I love safe. Help us make the right decisions, and help Eric catch these guys before anyone else gets hurt.*

While Eric had given her good advice about trying to rest, she doubted there'd be much, if any, sleep for her tonight.

29

ALLYE HAD BEEN RIGHT about not being able to sleep last night. She'd dozed off once or twice, but each time she'd jerked awake before logging more than a few minutes. Around 4:00 a.m., she'd finally given up and decided to at least attempt to get some work done instead.

Now it was nearing seven, and the exhaustion had caught up to her. Her eyes felt scratchy, and her head . . . Well, she imagined it felt about the same as if she'd just listened to a concert from the middle of the trombone section—and got thunked with the slides every other stanza.

She massaged her forehead. Even with her screen set at minimum brightness, she couldn't ignore the building misery any longer. Better take a dose of her migraine meds before her concert hit a crescendo.

Setting the laptop aside, she lowered the recliner's footrest and stood. A prickle of nausea came with the motion. She may have waited too long already.

Halfway to the kitchen, she stopped. A groan escaped her. She couldn't take her meds—the bottle was empty, as she'd discovered last night. Why hadn't she paid more attention and gotten it re-filled before she ran out? Maybe she could hold out long enough to call it in and wait for the pharmacy to fill it, but she'd have to drive feeling like this.

Nothing to do for it. She pushed on into the kitchen and found the bottle where she'd left it last night. The tiny print on the label blurred in and out of focus. She closed her eyes and counted to thirty. When she opened them again, things were slightly clearer. Clear enough for her to read the "No refills" notation. This was not good.

She slumped into a chair and dialed the prescriber's number. After navigating the automated system—she hated those things—and leaving a message, she lowered her head into her hands. The nausea was hitting harder now. She didn't have time to wait for a callback.

As usual, dizziness hit as she rose, but she held on to the edge of the table until it eased. "Gotta move," she mumbled. She made a beeline to the bathroom and rummaged through her medicine cabinet, looking for something stronger than ibuprofen. Her eye landed on a bottle of prescription pain pills hiding behind the cough syrup. Desperate, she pulled it out, then popped the lid and shook a tablet into her hand.

She stared at it, debating whether taking it was worth the aftereffects. These things tended to knock her out—one of the reasons she had so many pills left. Even with the broken wrist they'd been prescribed for several months ago, she'd preferred the residual ache after an ibuprofen to being painless but out of commission for hours on end and groggy afterward. She could half it, but taking it at all was still a risk.

Did she have a choice? The tablet swam in her hand, and she leaned against the counter as dizziness washed over her again. She'd had enough migraines lately to know that ibuprofen wasn't going to touch this one, and acetaminophen wouldn't be any better. If she didn't get this thing under control, she'd be in bed for two or three days minimum, and she didn't have time for that—especially not with the festival starting tomorrow.

It would be a while until Eric came by to pick her up. He'd

texted a bit ago to let her know he'd been called out to a scene and might be delayed. But even if he made it back by his original estimate, that gave her almost two hours to get past the drowsiness. That should be enough, right?

Before she could talk herself out of it, she split the tablet and dropped half back into the bottle. She popped the other into her mouth and quickly washed it down with water from the sink. On her way back to the living room, she dropped the bottle on the kitchen table and grabbed a sleeve of saltines. Inviting a whole other type of nausea by taking hydrocodone on an empty stomach wasn't on her to-do list. She'd eat a few crackers, then try to sleep until Eric called.

BANG! BANG! BANG!

Allye forced heavy eyelids open. What in the world?

The pounding came again. Her door shook with the force of the blows.

"Allye? Allye, open up." Eric?

Grabbing her glasses, she lurched to her feet and stumbled to the door. She flipped the locks and pulled the door open. Instantly, his strong arms enveloped her.

"Eric? What's wrong?"

"Are you okay?"

"I'm fine. What's going on?"

He pulled back enough to look into her face. "No one could get ahold of you."

"I was asleep."

"I've been calling for thirty minutes. Bryce and Corina too. He's probably on the way here."

"Sorry. I really didn't hear anything." And her mouth felt like cotton. Much as she liked the feel of his arms around her, she tugged away. "I need something to drink." She motioned him to follow her to the kitchen. She opened the refrigerator and stared blankly at the contents.

Eric's voice sounded behind her. "Are you sure you're okay?"

"Yeah." She shook her head. The movement didn't clear her mind. Why was her brain so foggy? She pulled out a pitcher of iced tea that she'd made yesterday. She removed two glasses from the cabinet. "Do you want some?"

"No, thanks."

She poured herself a full glass and took a healthy gulp. She didn't have the energy to press him. Or to return the extra glass to the cabinet.

"What are these?"

She turned to see what he was talking about. "What?"

He waved an orange vial at her. "Why do you have narcotics sitting on your table?" Accusation dripped from his words.

She blinked, the fog still hovering over her. What was his problem?

"How many did you take?"

Heat rushed to her face as the implication sank in. She reached for the bottle, but he held it away from her.

"Is that why you were so hard to wake up? You took too many pills?"

"Would you just stop?"

He shut his mouth, but his eyes shot daggers.

She tried to come up with an explanation that would calm him down. "They were prescribed when I broke my wrist back in the spring."

He looked pointedly at her wrist. "It isn't broken now."

"Obviously, but—"

"Then why did you keep them?"

She threw her hands up. "I don't know. I guess I forgot they were in my cabinet."

He stepped back, lowering the bottle. "They're clearly not in your cabinet, and you're clearly under the influence of something."

Her head started to hurt again. "It isn't like that. I—"

"Are you taking them?"

She held up a finger. "I took one, okay? No," she corrected herself. "I took half of one."

He huffed. Clearly that wasn't good enough for him. And that irritated her. It wasn't any of his business anyway.

"I took it because I was having another migraine, and I'm out of my normal prescription. That's the only thing I could find that might cut it."

"These things are dangerous. You know how many people get hooked on painkillers every year?"

"Eric, I'm not—"

"You aren't untouchable."

The tea was helping, but her brain still struggled to keep up with his accusations. She slipped into a chair. "Eric, you need to calm down."

His voice rose. "I need to calm down? You're basically taking drugs!"

"I. Am. Not."

"Then what do you call these?" He shook the bottle again.

He wasn't listening, and she didn't have the energy or brain clarity to make him. She put her head in her hands, squeezing her eyes shut. She would *not* cry in front of him.

"What's going on?"

Allye turned to see Bryce in the doorway between the living room and kitchen. How much had he heard?

"Ask her." Eric threw the bottle of pills onto the table and stalked out.

Bryce strode to her side and placed a hand on her shoulder. "Allye?"

"I don't know. I took half a hydrocodone to try to knock out a migraine, and Eric—" She opened her mouth to explain further, but nothing came out. She pushed up from the table and fled to her room, hot tears tracking down her cheeks.

What had just happened?

30

ERIC STOOD WITH ONE HAND on the roof of his car, head lowered. Everything inside him quivered. He had to get himself under control before he got behind the wheel. Could he trust no one anymore? Allye was the last person he'd expected to see with narcs.

Allye's front door slammed. Eric lifted his head to see Bryce barreling toward him.

"Dude, what is wrong with you?" His friend's normally easygoing manner was nowhere to be seen.

"She's taking narcotics."

"She took *part* of one hydrocodone. That's not the same thing."

"She took enough to knock her out. I called her five times on the way over here and again while I stood at the door. That's not counting however many times you and Corina tried."

"Maybe her phone was on silent."

"I could hear it from outside. And I banged on that door for a good thirty seconds before she stirred." He shook away the memory of her lying unresponsive in her chair. "She was out cold, and half a pill doesn't usually knock someone out." His parents could down a handful before even getting a buzz.

"It can when you aren't used to taking them."

"She shouldn't be taking them at all. They were prescribed for her *broken wrist*."

"And the fact she still has almost a full bottle should let you know she's not been taking them and never took enough to build any tolerance to them."

"Not buying it."

Bryce crossed his arms. "She said that's all she took, and it was for her migraine. I believe her."

"Really?" He shook his head. How many times had he heard an addict or a desperate family member say that? It was just one joint. Just one pill. One last high before they got clean.

"Yes, really. She's not a liar, and she does get migraines. If she took *one*, it was because she had a good reason."

"So did my parents. They liked a high, and that was a good enough reason for them."

Bryce's voice dropped to an intimidatingly low pitch. "You know Allye better than that."

"Do I?"

"I can't believe you. A few days ago, you were making eyes at her and escorting her to the park—yes, I know you followed her out there after you left our place. She let it slip when I installed her new locks the other day."

Eric opened his mouth, but Bryce didn't give him a chance to talk.

"And now you're accusing her of being a druggie because she took something for a migraine?"

"That's what she *says*. But she also says she's sick—maybe her symptoms have more to do with drug dependence than a mystery disease."

Bryce went still. "What do you mean, mystery disease?"

Even as hot as he was, he immediately realized what he'd done. Regret yanked his temper back into line, and he waved a hand. "Forget I said that."

Bryce stepped closer. "What's wrong with her?"

"I don't know. She doesn't even know, and she didn't want you worrying." Or did she not want her family to suspect a different sort of problem? His anger started to rise again, but he fought to keep it in check.

"Look. I don't know what's going on with her, but I can guarantee you she isn't on drugs."

"You didn't see—"

"I don't have to. I know my sister, and she doesn't deserve your accusations." He started to walk off, then turned and pointed a finger in Eric's face. "If you're half the man I thought you were, you'll make this right. Otherwise, stay away from her."

Eric stared after him for a second, then jumped in his car and pulled out, narrowly missing a passing minivan. He didn't know how long he drove, but eventually he found himself parked in a gravel driveway leading to one of the many abandoned barns in the area.

He threw the door open and launched himself down the driveway. Overgrown fields flanked him on either side. Not much chance anyone would interrupt him here. He needed to blow off steam, needed to get his head straight.

He hadn't told Bryce or Allye that he'd glimpsed her through a slit in the curtains. Seeing her unresponsive in her chair while he banged on the door had terrified him. He'd feared the worst. For a moment, he'd felt like he was reliving one of the worst days of his life. Then when he'd realized her stupor had been drug-induced . . .

"Gah!" The exclamation startled a flock of birds into flight. He ignored them and kept going. Although he hadn't verbally acknowledged it, he'd begun to have feelings for Allye. Begun? Yeah, right. His heart was totally involved already.

But he absolutely would not—could not—pursue a relationship with someone who abused drugs. His career aside, he couldn't handle the heartbreak it would eventually cause. The shattered trust. The pain for her and everyone around her.

He reached the end of the driveway. A log sat near the barn's door, and he plopped down onto it. Leaning his head back against the side of the barn, he let out another exasperated yell. Silence answered him. He let it engulf him. As he sat there, his anger began to ebb.

"God, why?" he finally croaked out. His hopes for a relationship had been tempered with the knowledge of Allye's health issues, but they'd still been stronger than he'd realized. No, she wasn't a picture of health, but if he were the type of guy to make a list of qualities he wanted in a woman, she'd have checked all the boxes—she was a fellow Christian, great with kids, cared deeply about others, witty and sassy, and she didn't look down on him for his family background. The fact she was a great cook and beautiful too were bonuses.

How had he missed the warning signs? He thought back over their encounters, especially from the last few days. But other than the green glow, there was nothing. Nothing that couldn't be explained just as well or better by the illness she claimed. And while he couldn't explain the green glow, he'd been present for last night's events—they most certainly hadn't been imagined. Neither had the body found in the woods. None of that proved her innocence, but it sure made a good case for giving her the benefit of the doubt. At the very least, he could have listened to her.

And he would have known if she lied. Though addicts were often good liars, Allye couldn't believably lie if her life depended on it. Her face broadcasted her thoughts and feelings like an old-fashioned blue light special.

Bryce was right. He did know her better.

Unless he'd lost every bit of intuition and skill he'd ever had, she had been telling the truth about her illness and fears. And about what she'd taken this morning and why.

He groaned and dropped his head in his hands. He'd been a jerk. A royal jerk. Perhaps worse, he'd betrayed her confidence.

Maybe she would have told her family about her health issues today anyway, but that should have been her call and done in her way. He was supposed to be her moral support. Instead, he'd not only jumped to conclusions and lost his temper, he'd also refused to listen to her and then left her to deal with a serious situation alone.

Not for the first time in the last year, he wished he could call his mentor and ask for advice. Losing Officer Mike last November was one of the hardest things Eric had ever gone through. Even now, the loss still burned in his gut.

Gramps had done his best once he gained custody of Eric, but he'd struggled to keep up with an angry teen. Still, he'd been a stable force in Eric's life, and he'd taken Eric to church, quietly shared his deep faith. Officer Mike had done that too. Both men had seen more than an angry teen destined to follow in his drug-addicted parents' footsteps. And once Gramps was gone, Mike had taken on even more of a father role to Eric. Somehow, between the influence of both men, Eric had turned out all right.

At least, he thought he had. Today, he wasn't so sure. Yeah, he could come up with plenty of reasons why he'd jumped to the conclusions he had—the fact he'd just come from the scene of yet another overdose, the drug-induced stupors he'd witnessed his parents fall into time and again. He shook his head. None of that excused his actions.

If he'd learned one thing from his father, it was that anything could be justified if you wanted to badly enough. The man had been a master of excuses. Right up until he—

With the memory, something else clicked into place, and he knew the real reason for his overblown reaction. He groaned.

How he wished he could take it all back. But that wasn't possible.

And he didn't know how to fix it.

31

AFTER GETTING HER EMOTIONS UNDER CONTROL, Allye slipped into the bathroom. She wet a washcloth and held it to her face. The cold soothed her burning eyes and cheeks.

What happened in there? she asked herself again. Her head had begun to clear, but she was still reeling from Eric's angry accusations. She'd never seen him like that. He was always cool and collected—levelheaded even in the most charged of situations. What flipped that switch in him?

A light tap sounded on the bathroom door, then Corina's voice filtered through. "Allye? You okay?" Her sister-in-law was here too? She should have expected that.

She pulled the cloth away from her face. "I'm fine," she croaked. Oh, that sounded awful. She swallowed and tried again. "I'm fine. I'll be out in a minute."

A board creaked in the hallway floor, then she heard Corina's light footsteps retreating back toward the kitchen. She let out a breath and dabbed at her face with the cloth. Not much could be done about the redness, but she needed to get a move on before they came to check on her again.

When she emerged from the back of her house a few minutes later, she found both Bryce and Corina camped at her kitchen table.

She rested her hand on the back of a chair and focused on Bryce. "What are you two doing here? Aren't you supposed to be at work?"

"Eric called me when he couldn't get ahold of you," he said. "He was just outside the far end of town and hoped I could get here faster, but I was checking an engine and missed his first couple calls. I headed right over when I couldn't reach you either, but he'd beat me here by that point."

She didn't want to talk about Eric right now. Shifting her attention to Corina, she asked, "What about Western Outfitters?" She was pretty sure her sister-in-law ran the shop by herself on Thursdays.

Corina shrugged, but the movement was anything but nonchalant. "I closed up for a few hours. It'll be fine. Making sure you were okay was more important."

"Why wouldn't I be okay?"

Bryce leveled his gaze on her. "You tell me. What have you not been telling us?"

Was he parroting Eric's accusations? "I'm not hooked on pills, if that's what you mean." She lowered herself into the chair, feeling like her strength had suddenly bottomed out again.

Bryce's gaze softened. "It's not. But Eric wouldn't have called me frantic if something weren't going on."

Eric had been frantic when she didn't answer her phone? With everything going on, she supposed she couldn't blame him for that.

"And he said you're sick."

Her stomach dropped with the addendum. She felt a flicker of anger that Eric had betrayed her secret, but she didn't have the energy for it to ignite into full flame. And Bryce and Corina were waiting for her response. She massaged her forehead. Where did she even start?

She decided to go with the most important matter. "First of all, I need to warn you guys to watch your backs. Eric and I were supposed to warn you together today, but I guess that's my responsibility now."

Bryce placed a hand on his wife's arm, but they both waited quietly for her to continue.

"I, uh . . ." It was harder getting the words out than she'd anticipated. She moistened her lips and took a deep breath. "I witnessed a murder."

"You what?"

"Why didn't you tell us?" Corina asked.

She grimaced. "I know I probably should have, but it was . . . complicated." As succinctly as she could, she explained what had been going on over the last week. "And I have been sick. For several months." She averted her eyes and traced an invisible line on the table. "Based on my symptoms, I suspected MS, and I didn't want to burden anyone with that until I knew for sure."

"Oh, Allye."

She held up her hand to halt Corina's sympathetic words. "It's not MS though—at least, the tests so far seem to be ruling that out. But we don't know what it is yet." She shook her head. "I wasn't ready to share about my illness, and so much of the confusion about what I did or didn't see was intertwined with the possibility that I was losing it. I was overwhelmed and didn't know how to explain one without the other, so I just didn't say anything. But last night, I got a text threatening you two and Mom if I didn't tell the police I was mistaken about everything."

"I see," Bryce said slowly. "Have you warned Mom yet?"

"Not yet. We were going to tell you two first, but telling Mom is a little more complicated." She reiterated the pertinent part of last night's conversation with Eric, along with her suspicions of the mayor's involvement.

They both looked stunned. Again. Corina found her voice first. "Mayor Jennings? Are you sure?"

Allye raised her shoulders in a helpless shrug. "I'm not sure of much right now, but he's acting weird, and he knows things he shouldn't. While I have no intention of throwing false accusations around, I don't trust him. And I don't know what to tell Mom. She needs to know to be careful, but I don't want to hinder the investigation or, worse, put her in more danger by telling her."

"Come on, Allye. Give Mom a little credit. She might not like it, but I think she'll agree not to say anything while the investigation is going on."

Would she? Allye wasn't sure, but the critical-thinking part of her brain felt like it had been operating on fumes for weeks. At this point, she wasn't sure she could trust herself. She rolled Bryce's words around in her mind. He was probably right.

Her body slouched further in her chair, whether from relief or the weight of helplessness, she wasn't sure. Perhaps a combination of the two.

"I wish you'd told us what you were dealing with." Corina's soft voice held concern and maybe a bit of hurt too.

"I'm sorry. I didn't want to worry everyone, and I guess maybe I didn't want to admit how bad things were getting. It would have felt so . . . final." But it hadn't felt that way when she'd spilled her guts to Eric and Hailey. And while the weight of her illness hung heavy with every word, she realized it was no more real now than it was a few minutes ago.

"What can we do to help?" Corina asked.

"I don't know. I don't have any idea what I actually have if it's not MS." And she didn't want them to feel obligated to step up. They were still newly married and had their own lives to tend to.

As if he'd read her thoughts, Bryce got up from his seat and gathered her into a bear hug. "We're here for you, sis. And we want to be. You're not an obligation."

She squeezed him back, but she couldn't speak past the lump in her throat. Hailey had said basically the same thing, but did they really get what kind of toll that could take on them if she ended up needing more than occasional support? She'd heard so many stories of burnt-out caregivers.

After Bryce retook his seat, he and Corina gently pressed her for details about her symptoms and then about the attacks she'd experienced. The more she shared about the latter, the harder his expression grew.

"You really shouldn't be staying here alone. Why don't you stay with us for a couple days?"

"Absolutely not."

Corina touched her arm. "You and Bryce stayed with me through all my danger last year."

Allye shook her head, determined to hold her ground on this point. "That was different. These threats aren't aimed at me, they're aimed at you guys to intimidate me into keeping my mouth shut. Plus, you have the baby to think about."

"There's a lot less chance someone will come after any of us if we're all together." But Corina's hand slipped to her stomach and hovered protectively over the tiny bump.

"They used my camera for target practice when I was with Eric last night. If they're not afraid of a cop, I doubt they'll be scared off by you two." She shot her brother a look. "And don't even think about offering to protect me by yourself—leaving Corina alone would be like putting a bullseye on her back."

"What about a bodyguard?" Corina suggested. "I could look up the info for Peter's agency."

Allye thought about the British bodyguard who had nearly lost his life trying to help protect Corina last year. Those had been unusual circumstances, but she still shuddered to think how close he'd come to dying. She wasn't sure she'd be okay with someone putting himself in that kind of danger for her.

A sigh escaped her. It was irrelevant anyway. She had no idea what hiring a bodyguard cost, but it had to be far more than she could afford. She was already going to be making payments on the copay for her MRI.

She shook her head. "I'll figure something out." A bodyguard was out of the question, but she was not going to endanger the people she loved—at least, not any more than she already had.

32

TELLING HER MOM WAS EASIER than Allye anticipated. She'd opted to go it alone, despite both Bryce and Corina offering to accompany her. As it turned out, she'd had to settle for a phone call anyway because her mom was doing a showing out of town and wouldn't be home until late afternoon. She supposed she could have waited, but she'd been afraid to take any chances.

Like Bryce and Corina, Mom had been more concerned about Allye than about herself. And while she hadn't been at all convinced that Mayor Jennings was somehow involved, she'd agreed not to say anything that might impede an investigation.

It felt like a huge weight had lifted with that phone call. Her problems hadn't gone away, but the burden of secrecy was gone. She hadn't realized how heavy it had been.

Now she had to figure out what to do with herself for the rest of the day. While a fresh pot of tea steeped on her counter, she evaluated her options.

She should go to her studio and get some work done. Maybe print off those extra postcards to add to her festival booth. Although she'd lost a lot of her recent photos when her primary camera was destroyed, the ones from the Spicebush Trail were on a different memory card.

She should have printed them earlier this week, but she'd been too preoccupied with everything going on to make it to her studio. As she removed the infuser basket from her teapot, a touch of panic settled on her at the thought of returning alone to where this whole mess had started. Was she even safe there? Being alone at home with her new locks was one thing. But at the studio, she'd be exposed both on the stairwell and in the alley.

A knock at her door interrupted her thoughts. She groaned and set the tea leaves aside. As much as she loved people, it felt like her house had a revolving door today.

She nudged back the curtain blocking the window. Her neighbor smiled and held up a container. Allye quickly disengaged the locks and opened the door. "Shannon! Come on in."

"Hi, Allye. I've been in a baking mood and got a little carried away, considering there's only two of us in the house now that Tyler's away at college. Would you be interested in some cookies?"

"I can always use cookies." She motioned for Shannon to follow her to the kitchen. "You have time to stay a few minutes? I just made a pot of tea, or I can put on coffee if you'd prefer that."

"Tea sounds wonderful."

Allye selected two rose-patterned teacups and matching dessert plates for the cookies. When she turned back to her guest, she paused at sight of the frown on her face. "What's wrong?"

"Don't take this the wrong way, but do you have a mold problem?"

Allye blinked. "Mold?"

"It smells the tiniest bit musty in here. There's been a similar odor at our place, and we haven't been able to pin down exactly where it's coming from."

"I haven't seen anything." Or smelled it either.

Shannon quirked her lips to the side and tapped her nose as if she'd heard Allye's silent addendum. "I have a strong smeller. My husband sometimes calls me the bloodhound."

"I'll keep my eye out."

"Thanks. I asked Cornell to pick up a test kit on his way home from work this morning, but he forgot. I plan to run to the drugstore later and see if they have any in stock, but if not, it'll be back on his to-do list for tomorrow." She set the container on the table and popped the lid. "I wouldn't worry about it, but my allergies have been on overdrive almost since we moved in. Mold is one of my triggers."

"Let me know what you find out, if you don't mind. Maybe it would help explain my migraines." Finding an answer to even one of her symptoms would be a win.

As she poured the steaming amber liquid into their cups, a classical waltz blared from her phone. Eric. She flushed and sent the call to voice mail. She needed to change his ringtone to something less enjoyable. Maybe an old-fashioned funeral dirge?

She pushed Shannon's cup toward her and eyed the cookies. "Chocolate chip?"

Her neighbor's eyes sparkled. "Dark chocolate chip."

"Even better." Allye helped herself to one. She bit into the still-warm cookie and allowed a soft moan to escape. "These are *good*."

"They're Cornell's favorite."

"I can see why."

Shannon took a cookie for herself. "Did the cops ever catch the guy who broke into your house the other night?"

How much of the investigation should she divulge? She chewed slowly, then took a sip of tea. "No," she said, deciding to keep it simple. "His identity is still a mystery."

Shannon shivered. "That's freaky."

That was a good word for it. She still hadn't figured out what that break-in had accomplished, but everything else going on had pushed it to the back of her mind.

Eric's ringtone interrupted them again. Again, she rejected the call. "Sorry about that." She shot her guest an apologetic smile, though everything in her wanted to cry.

"No worries. You could have answered it."

"Not someone I wanted to talk to right now anyway."

What had they been discussing? She blinked. Whatever it was, it was gone. She sighed. Hopefully, it wasn't important.

Her phone dinged with a text. A quick glance showed it was from Eric.

Are you okay?

She considered ignoring it, but the last thing she wanted was for him to show up banging on her door again. Her emotions couldn't handle seeing him again right now.

I'm fine.

After sending the text, she snoozed the conversation and tried to focus on her guest, but her concentration was blown. When her phone went off again a few minutes later—this time with her mom's designated ringtone—Shannon stood.

"I'll let you answer that. I need to see about getting that test kit." She set her teacup by the sink. "Thanks for the tea."

"Anytime. Thank *you* for the cookies." Allye waved and snatched her phone. "Hey, Mom."

"Hey. I didn't think I was going to get you."

"Sorry, I was in the middle of something. What's going on?" She heard her front door close behind Shannon.

"Just checking to make sure you're doing all right."

She barely suppressed a sigh. It had only been a couple of hours since they talked. This was one of the reasons she'd been hesitant to admit her health issues.

"Everything's fine." She wrinkled her nose. "But I think my neighbor just told me my house stinks."

Throaty laughter filtered through the line. "What does that mean?"

"She asked me if I have a mold problem."

Her mom's voice turned serious. "Do you?"

"I'm not aware of one."

"You should check. I know you don't own your place, but it's something you should be proactive about."

"My neighbor said they're running some sort of test for it."

"Good."

They chatted about other things for a few minutes, but then her mom turned the conversation back to her home.

"When Corina's side of the duplex flooded last year, did you have your side inspected?"

"No need to. Nothing got in." The way the ground slanted in front of the duplex, Corina's door was practically even with the ground while Allye's required a few steps to get inside. Her half had stayed dry, and Corina's ended up with three inches of water, requiring the landlord to repaint several walls and replace the carpet. Or at least, that had been the plan before her stalker trashed it, requiring a more extensive remodel.

"How long was it between the flood and when Mr. Bright did the repairs? I seem to remember him dragging his feet."

Allye massaged her forehead. "I can't remember. Why?"

Her mom was quiet for a few seconds, and Allye could picture her pursing her lips. "I'm just wondering if mold might have gotten into the walls between your units or into your basement."

"It's possible I guess, but that was over a year ago."

"Exactly."

"And your point is . . . ?" She let her words trail off, hoping her mom would elaborate. Whatever she was getting at should be obvious, but Allye wasn't following. She hated this brain fog.

"Mold spreads. Untreated, the problem gets worse, not better. If you've been breathing in increasing quantities of mold spores for the past year, that could be a factor in your illness."

Allye propped the phone between her ear and shoulder and began prerinsing her dishes. "Mom, I don't have allergies. I'm having MS-like symptoms." Except it wasn't MS.

"I've dealt with mold-infested homes," her mom insisted. "Mold doesn't devalue properties just because it's ugly or irritates allergies. It can lead to serious health issues. Just consider it, okay? Maybe do a little research when you have time."

She sighed. "Okay. I can do that."

"Good. Listen, I expect to finish work early today. Is there anything I can bring you? I don't mind swinging by the grocery or grabbing takeout."

"I have everything I need, but thanks."

"Anything I can help with on the festival prep?"

"The only thing left to do is load everything into my car and do the actual setup tomorrow morning. I can handle that."

"If you're sure. But let me know if you change your mind or think of anything I can do, okay?"

"Okay."

"Well, I'll let you go, then." She sounded reluctant to hang up. "Love you."

"Love you too, Mom. Talk to you later."

She set her phone aside. Exhaustion pummeled her again. She could probably head to bed right now and take another nap, but she was afraid she wouldn't sleep tonight if she did. And she had to sleep tonight—the festival started tomorrow.

Going to her studio wasn't going to happen either though, at least not right now. She sighed again. Since she'd promised her mom to research mold issues, she could run a quick internet search while she was thinking about it. Might as well get it over with.

Grabbing another of Shannon's cookies, she moved to the living room and powered up her laptop. As soon as the search browser loaded, she typed in *mold illness* and hit enter. Her screen filled with results. She scrolled down and saw that more pages were available.

Oof. She wasn't expecting that. Where to even start? She scrolled back up and clicked on one that looked promising.

Forty-five minutes later, she emerged from research into mold allergies and toxicity. Maybe the possibility wasn't as far a reach as she'd assumed. While not all of her symptoms fit neatly within the mold-toxicity box and there were a few common ones she didn't have, the similarity between what she read and her experience was striking.

Were they grasping at straws? Maybe. But it was worth looking into—if for nothing else than to rule it out. Still, she quashed the hope attempting to rise inside her. She'd wait for the results from whatever test her neighbors were running. If it came back negative, maybe she'd test her studio. But if it was positive? She eyed the screen. If it was positive, she'd need to look further into this.

33

AFTER TESTIFYING ABOUT HIS INVESTIGATION into a string of local robberies, Eric returned to the police station and beelined for his desk. He needed to sort his thoughts and come up with a strategy to put a stop to the drug flow in this town before anyone else died. And at some point, he'd have to figure out what to do about Allye. She was still in danger . . . and still ignoring his calls. He couldn't blame her for not wanting to talk to him, but he needed to apologize and, perhaps more importantly, make sure she wasn't throwing caution to the wind because she'd lost faith in him.

The two problems were intertwined. Unless Allye was totally mistaken about the things she'd seen and heard, they had to be. Which meant Dion's continued disappearance was likely related as well. If he could just figure out how, maybe, just maybe, things would break wide open.

As he passed through the receptionist area, the door to Chief McHenry's office opened. The chief stuck his head out and spotted him. "Thornton, I need to talk to you."

Eric redirected his steps to join the chief in his office. McHenry didn't immediately offer him a seat. The hair on the back of his neck prickled. That wasn't a good sign.

The chief flipped through a pad of paper bearing his scrawled writing. "I had several personal calls this morning, asking where we are in various investigations. Darla says she's routed inquiries to your office number, but these people don't seem to have received a callback."

"I just returned from court and haven't had a chance to check my messages today."

"It's not just today. It's been all week."

He grimaced. "I have been in the field a lot this week. I suppose I let the calls slip."

The chief gave a noncommittal grunt and set the notepad on top of a stack of files contributing to the clutter of his desk. "Make that a priority this afternoon."

"Yes, sir."

"Speaking of priorities, you've been spending a lot of time on Allye Jessup's situation."

"With several incidents in a week's time, I'm rather concerned about her."

Doubt flickered in the chief's eyes. "Her claims are concerning, but she's always been a bit . . . dramatic." Eric stiffened, and the chief waved his hand. "I'm not calling her a liar. Just making an observation. I'd never want anything to happen to the girl, but we can't waste limited resources on outlandish claims."

He tried to word his response carefully. "With all due respect, sir, there's good reason to believe that at least some of those claims are true. I witnessed one of them myself, though that incident didn't fall under our jurisdiction. I suspect the attacks on her might be connected with a local drug ring. If we can track down her attacker, maybe we can shut his operation down."

Sweat dripped down his back as he watched for a telltale reaction. Making the assertion was a gamble—he knew that. If McHenry told him to stand down on the investigation because he didn't see the value in it, things could become extremely difficult. But if McHenry was in any way involved, he could still tell him to stand down or choose to do away with Allye before anything came of the investigation.

The chief held his gaze, his eyes giving nothing away. Finally, he scrubbed a hand down his face. "All right. If you think it's a valid lead, I'm not going to call you off. Yet. But don't let the important things slide."

"I believe this is important. People are dying because of these drugs. There was a new victim this morning."

"I know this matter is personal to you, Thornton. You're driven. I appreciate that. And I agree, these deaths need to end." He steepled his fingers. "But the hard truth is we're never going to stop the drug flow completely. Addicts are going to find a way to get what they want, and if we cut off one supply, they'll either find a new one or create a new synthetic."

Heat crept up his neck. "Are you suggesting we give up?"

"No, but I'm not going to have you so laser-focused on one issue that you neglect your other cases."

"Sir, I'm not—"

"Have you followed up on last week's vandalism of the strip mall?"

Eric opened his mouth. Shut it. Shook his head.

"How about the break-in at the storage units?"

"No, sir."

"And the gas pump card skimmers?" Chief McHenry waited until Eric again shook his head. "I have a responsibility to the citizens of this town. All of them. I get it—we're shorthanded, and lives are more important than buildings or finances. But that doesn't mean those things don't affect people too." He held up a hand as Eric started to protest. "Before you say it, I also know not every case can be closed quickly, and some are never solved, but I'll be hanged if I allow lazy investigating to be the cause of it. If you have a hot lead on the drug front, by all means, follow it. But do not spend all your time chasing rabbits."

The chief's reprimand stung. Perhaps he'd be a bit more lenient if he knew all the facts about the cases Eric was focused on. Or he'd double down because of his relation to Mayor Jennings. Since he didn't know for sure where McHenry stood, he kept his mouth shut.

The chief leaned back in his office chair. "Another thing. Where are your reports from the last few days?"

He had known that question would come sooner or later. He'd hoped for later. "I haven't typed them up yet. It's been a hectic week, sir."

"I thought you of all people would know better than to use that excuse. I expect to have them up to date and on my desk by Monday morning."

"Yes, sir."

"You're dismissed."

Eric returned to his desk on stiff legs. That could have gone much worse. Didn't make it easy to swallow though, especially since he still believed his focus was in the right place. But the chief wasn't wrong about the need for follow-up on his older, but still recent, cases.

Not for the first time since his promotion, he wished the city had approved funding to open two detective positions instead of one. He was thankful for the job, but having a colleague to share responsibilities with would be extremely helpful at times like this.

Instead of digging into the cases pressing on his mind, he called up the voice mail on his work phone. McHenry had given him a direct order to prioritize them. Might as well get it over with. But when the automated voice stated the number of new messages, he winced. This would take a while.

By the time he wrapped up the last of the calls, Darla had waved her good-byes and headed out for the day. The chief was still in his office, door closed. It wasn't unusual for the man to stay late. He expected a lot from their small police force, but he gave a lot too. It was part of the reason Eric respected him so much and struggled with the thought of him being dirty. Was it even possible?

But he knew it was possible for anyone to be corrupted, no matter how highly he thought of them. Still, he wouldn't assume it without proof. His spectacular failure at Allye's only highlighted the need to carefully weigh the evidence before coming to a conclusion. If only he had remembered that before losing his temper this morning.

He sighed and jotted down the time and pertinent info regarding the call he'd just made. The owners of the storage units broken into a week and a half ago weren't happy about the lack of progress on the case. But the thieves had been smart and hadn't tried to hock anything yet—at least, not to any of the local pawnshops or neighborhood social media pages that Eric was watching. But they could have easily driven to a larger city or posted it somewhere else online. Unfortunately, he didn't have the time to monitor every possible sales avenue.

That task finally done, he allowed his mind to fully return to the bigger issues Kincaid was facing. He had plenty of official notes on the investigation already, but he flipped to a blank section of his notebook. He needed to look at this from a fresh angle.

Priority number one was to identify and arrest Allye's attacker before the man struck again. The man was almost definitely a murderer and likely more than a low-level drug dealer. They needed him off the streets.

He scratched *1. Allye's Attacker* onto the page and underlined the words. Beneath them, he noted the meager description Allye had given, then wrote *Sketch Artist* under that. *Click.* Once Allye worked with the forensic artist and they got even a preliminary sketch, they'd have a lot better chance of finding the guy, but he hated that they had to wait that long.

There wasn't much else they knew about her attacker. The guy seemed to have vaporized. But then again, Allye and possibly Dion were the only ones who would recognize him on the street. For all Eric knew, he could have passed the guy walking into Zhan's or nodded to him at a gas station. His jaw tightened. The situation was maddening.

But frustration wouldn't get him anywhere. Making a conscious effort to relax, he continued on, adding the few connections he did have, each on its own line.

Kincaid Lake?
John Doe's murderer?
Drugs?
Dion?

When he could think of nothing else pertinent, he moved to the next item on his list: Mayor Jennings. He turned to a new page and stared at it, clicking his pen as he thought. He still didn't quite understand what the mayor's connection was to all this. Jennings was there the first night Allye was attacked. He claimed he'd heard her scream from his office and found her unconscious and alone in the alleyway. Truth? Lie? Eric wasn't sure.

If Jennings wasn't involved and had unknowingly scared the attacker away, then how did he know about the green glow from the break-in? But if he was involved, then why show up and help her? Neither scenario made sense, but it had to be one or the other, right? There was no doubt anymore that the attack had happened.

As he touched his pen to the paper, the inner office door opened and McHenry strode out. He stopped in front of Eric's desk.

"Heard anything yet on the missing kid?"

Eric straightened and set his pen aside, glad he hadn't written anything yet regarding the mayor. "No. I've followed up with his friends and teachers. They all insist they haven't seen him since before his mom OD'd. And no one has called in any tips. He seems to have vanished." How was he staying hidden so well? He had to eat. Had to have somewhere to sleep. Did he have a friend covering for him?

The chief shook his head. "The whole situation's unfortunate. At least we know he's alive and missing of his own volition—or was as of Sunday night."

Eric suppressed a grimace. McHenry's tone didn't imply he blamed him for Dion's second disappearance, but it didn't have to. He blamed himself. If he'd been more attuned to the situation or taken better precautions, Dion might be safe right now.

McHenry tapped the desk. "Keep me posted on the situation."

"Yes, sir."

With that, the chief headed for the door, leaving Eric alone in the building.

Since Dion's situation was fresh in his mind, he jotted his thoughts and questions on that subject before turning his attention back to Mayor Jennings. To be safe, he headed the page *MJ*. Not wildly imaginative, but if someone happened to glimpse his notes, it wouldn't garner as much attention as it would if he used the man's name.

After transcribing a shorthand version of his questions, he sighed. There wasn't much to go on. What he really needed was to dig into the mayor's background, associates, and financials, but he could only go so far without a warrant. And there was the risk of tipping him off—or tipping the chief off, which might have the same result.

A buzzing from his personal phone interrupted that line of thought. He tugged it from his belt and checked the screen. Bryce. He was surprised his friend was still talking to him. Blowing out a breath, he swiped the screen to answer.

"Hello."

Bryce cut right to the chase. "I need to know what you know about Allye's situation. She gave us the basics, but I want to hear it from you. How much danger is she in?"

"To be honest, I don't know." He glanced at his notebook. "At the very least, she's on the bad side of a man who has no qualms about murder. But this whole situation is bizarre. He could have killed her multiple times over and didn't."

"And yet he's resorted to threats against the family."

"Yes."

"It doesn't make sense."

"Not at all. We're missing something—probably several somethings—and I don't know what they are."

"Now that we know, Corina and I will both be keeping an eye on our surroundings. I don't like leaving Allye alone, but she's stubbornly refusing to stay with us or let us stay with her. If the threat hadn't included Corina, I think I could have talked her into letting me camp at her place for a few nights, but that's a no-go now."

He could see that. It fit Allye's desire to protect everyone else, even if it meant putting herself in greater danger. And leaving Corina alone could be just as dangerous a scenario as what they were currently facing. At least Corina was armed. As far as he knew, Allye wasn't.

"I'll see if whoever's on nights will make a point to drive by, and I'll swing by there as often as I can. I know I'm the last person she wants to see right now, but perhaps the frequent police presence will be a deterrent to anyone watching." It was the least he could do.

"I'd appreciate it." A pause stretched across the line. When Bryce cleared his throat, Eric braced himself for the redirection. "By the way, Allye isn't your parents. They chose their path and defied anyone who tried to help them off it. Allye didn't choose to get sick, and I can guarantee you she's going to fight whatever it is with all she has."

He rubbed the back of his neck. "I know."

"Then tell her that."

"It'd be a lot easier if she'd answer my calls."

Bryce huffed a humorless laugh. "If that's what you're waiting for, you're going to be waiting awhile. You hurt her, and she's probably afraid that either you're going to bite her head off again or that she's going to take *your* head off if she picks up."

He shifted the phone to his other ear. "So are you telling me to back off and let her cool down?"

"No. You deserve to have your head bitten off."

"Thanks."

"Anytime. Seriously, you need to apologize before she makes up her mind you aren't trustworthy. Once Allye gets that in her head, it's game over for any chance of a relationship between you two. But you're going to have to get her to listen, and it probably isn't going to happen by phone."

He knew Bryce was right. Somehow, he'd find a way to apologize. This was all his fault, and he refused to follow in his dad's footsteps. He'd take responsibility for his actions, make his apology. Whether Allye accepted it or not was her call.

"By the way? Pull a stunt like that again, and *I'll* take your head off."

34

ALLYE DROVE TOWARD THE PHARMACY on autopilot. Her doctor's office had finally returned her call and let her know they'd sent in her new prescription, but she only had a short window to reach the pharmacy before it closed. She'd wanted to ask them about the research that had been dominating her thoughts the past couple of hours, but she knew the office staff wouldn't give her any advice. She'd need to send her doctor a message or book another appointment.

She was still reeling from the possibility that her home could be basically poisoning her. Could her issues of the past months be something so simple? Of course, *simple* might not be the right word for it. Though medical opinion seemed to be split on the matter, there seemed to be at least a decent possibility that prolonged mold exposure could cause all sorts of long-term problems, including triggering autoimmune issues in some people. The possibility that permanent damage could have been done was frightening. Still, if they could determine the cause, they could better treat it.

Red and blue lights flicked on in the car behind her. She groaned and glanced at her speedometer. Five over. Not too bad, but bad enough to get ticketed if the officer was in the mood to hand one out.

She pulled to the side of the road and turned off the engine. A ticket was the last thing she needed right now. She checked the clock. If this stretched out, she might not make it to the pharmacy in time, and she really didn't want to have to decide between a migraine and risking another dose of hydrocodone if the pounding in her head ratcheted up again.

Movement caught her eye, and she returned her attention to her mirror. The door to the unmarked car opened, and a man stepped out. Allye stiffened. Why was Eric making traffic stops? He wasn't a patrol officer anymore. And why had he pulled *her* over? No way he wouldn't have recognized her car with the huge Allye's Photography logo on the rear windshield. He knew it was her.

She lowered her window as he approached but kept her eyes straight ahead.

"Everything all right?"

"Everything is fine, Detective."

He hesitated as if her use of his title had thrown him. "You haven't answered my calls."

"Is that why you pulled me over?" She wasn't in the mood for this.

"You were speeding."

"I'm aware."

"Allye, I need to—"

She finally met his gaze. "Are you going to give me a ticket?"

He stared at her a long moment, regret in his eyes. "No."

"Then may I go?"

"We need to talk."

"I need to get to the pharmacy before they close and pick up my *migraine* medication."

He winced and stepped back. "Later?"

"Later." Sometime. Maybe.

She waited until he was almost to his car before screeching back onto the road. Tears filled her eyes, but she refused to look in her rearview. She felt a little bad for being so short with him, but his accusations from this morning still stung.

She punched the radio on and turned the volume as high as she dared to drown out his voice. It silenced her mental replay of the encounter but did little to lift her spirits. Despite her long break from dating, she'd never let go of the hope of one day finding someone to spend the rest of her life with. Until she'd gotten sick, anyway.

But despite her reluctance to pursue anything when her health hung in the balance, Eric had made her hope that a relationship might be possible. Then today he'd shown her a side she didn't know he possessed. And she wasn't about to let herself get drawn into a relationship with someone who couldn't trust her or felt he had to control her.

She made it to the pharmacy with minutes to spare. "Thank you, Lord," she murmured, throwing her seat belt off. She hurried inside and to the back. Thankfully, the line was short. Only two people waited ahead of her, and she recognized the tech behind the counter. Michelle would get them through quickly.

When her turn arrived, she mustered a smile and approached the counter.

"Hey, girl!" Michelle's grin was wide. "It's been a bit. We missed you at Bible study this week."

She felt her smile slip. "I totally forgot. This week has been so hectic, it didn't even cross my mind."

"Oh right! You're prepping for the festival, aren't you? I'm looking forward to visiting your booth. Hold on and I'll grab your prescription." She rushed off before Allye could respond.

Maybe it was better that way. Wool Fest, as much as she loved it, was the least of her concerns at the moment. But she had no desire to go into the details of the last week and especially not in a public place.

"Here you go." Michelle set a paper bag on the counter and stated the copay amount.

Allye paid, trying not to wince at the price. "Thanks, Michelle. I'll look for you at the festival."

"Can't wait! See you there!"

Bag in hand, she headed for the front of the store. Her steps slowed as she passed through the candy aisle. She eyed the Ghirardelli squares. She really shouldn't . . . but she could use a bit of chocolate tonight. Grabbing a variety pack, she rushed to the checkout counter. The cashier waved off her apology for the late purchase.

"No worries, hon. It's only five past." She counted the change back to her and stuck the receipt in the bag. As she pushed it across the counter, she nodded toward someone behind Allye. "You're not the only one still here anyway."

Allye took the offered bag and slipped her prescription into it before turning in the direction the woman indicated. A young man, his face obscured by a baseball hat, lingered by an endcap featuring an assortment of protein bars. At that moment, he glanced up. Their eyes met, and his widened.

"Dion."

Before his name left her mouth, he was darting for the exit. She ran after him, but he had a few seconds' lead, and he was fast. By the time she cleared the doors, he was nowhere in sight. Had he circled the building? She jogged to the nearest corner and poked her head around.

Nothing.

She spent several minutes searching, even combing the lot to see if he'd taken cover behind a parked car, but it was no use. The teen had given her the slip.

Exhausted, she slumped against the building, chest heaving. She needed to call someone. Dion couldn't have gone far. Maybe there was still hope of finding him if help arrived quickly. She fished her phone from her purse. For the briefest of moments, she wished Eric were here. He'd know what to do.

Should she call him directly? He'd probably come himself.

But part of her shrank at the thought. She still wasn't ready to face him. But that was selfish, wasn't it? Dion was more important.

Steeling herself, she entered his number and held the phone to her ear. It rang. And rang. Finally, it dumped her to voice mail. She didn't bother to identify herself. "I just saw Dion at the pharmacy. He ran when he saw me. Not sure which way he went, but he was on foot, so he has to be close by somewhere. Uh, that's it." She hung up.

Now what? Should she call 911? She glanced around to make sure the teen hadn't come back into view. He hadn't, of course. Wait. Wasn't there a tip line? She pulled up a browser and searched for the alert she'd seen the other day. There it was. The instructions said to call the PD's nonemergency line.

Should have thought of that first. She entered the number and identified herself. Her phone signaled an incoming call, and she pulled it from her ear long enough to glance at the screen. Eric. He could wait. Forever, for all she cared.

She gave the little information she had and was assured an officer would be dispatched. After the call ended, she dropped her phone into her purse. She could go now, but she hated to leave before an officer arrived. If Dion was merely hiding out, she didn't want to risk him slipping away in the interim.

But she needed to get off her feet before her legs decided not to hold her any longer. She eyed her car. She could wait inside. Forcing herself to take the first step, she trudged across the lot and climbed in.

Please, Jesus. Help them find him this time. Her energy might be too depleted to continue searching, but she could pray while she kept watch.

Dion still hadn't reappeared when Eric's car turned into the lot several minutes later, but that was her cue. Time to go.

DION CROUCHED BEHIND A DUMPSTER that smelled like something was rotting in it. He wanted to kick himself. He'd known it was a bad idea to show up in the pharmacy right before closing when people were picking up last-minute meds.

But he'd taken the risk because he was hungry and didn't want to walk the extra half mile to the gas station. Stupid decision.

He glared at the protein bar in his hand. He hadn't meant to steal it. But when Allye recognized him, he'd panicked and taken off. Too bad he hadn't had time to pay for it—and a few more. It would have to last him until tomorrow at least.

He shoved the bar into his pocket, then peeked around the dumpster. Looked like the coast was clear. He needed to get out of here before someone decided to look a little closer.

Pulling his cap low, he emerged from his hiding place. He glanced around. A car that looked like Eric's was parked in the pharmacy lot. No one inside. Maybe he was in the pharmacy asking questions. If so, Dion needed to be gone before he came back out.

He forced himself to walk casually until he was out of sight of the store and its parking lot. Then he broke into a sprint and didn't slow until he reached a wooded area bordering the road out of town.

Once he caught his breath, he pulled out the protein bar and savored a few bites as he headed for his new home. The abandoned barn he'd found to stay in didn't look like much, but it was a roof over his head and provided some protection from the wind. Too bad there were no vending machines like when he was camping at Kincaid Lake.

Soon, he'd have to find someplace else to stay. Winter was coming, and he wouldn't survive without better shelter. Maybe he'd migrate south for the winter—once he figured out how to settle things with Bernie.

BACK HOME, Allye made a fresh pot of chamomile tea, then settled into her office with the takeout she'd picked up as a consolation prize on her way back from the pharmacy. Hopefully, she could lose herself in work and not spend any more time wallowing in disappointment—either over Eric or over losing Dion again.

She needed to work on Jayden's senior pictures anyway. With everything going on, she hadn't made it back to the light edits she'd begun on Monday, and she'd really like to finish and get them off to his mom. There would be more work to do once the family chose which poses they wanted, but at least she would have one step complete.

While the program loaded, she reached for her remote and turned the small office TV to a classic movies station. She smiled as she recognized the film. It was one of her favorites, but she'd seen it enough times it shouldn't distract her from her work.

Chopsticks in hand, she sent up another prayer on Dion's behalf, then she popped the lid off her pad thai and got started.

An hour later, she clicked send on the email to Mrs. Alexander and pushed back from the computer. She'd been further along in the process than she thought. Removing one thing from her plate was a relief. But staring at the screen for an hour had amplified the pain in her head, despite the tinted glasses she'd remembered to put on halfway through. Still, she'd done it, and she decided to take that for the win it was.

She powered off the computer and TV and headed for the kitchen with her leftovers. After stowing the container in the fridge, she slipped into a chair and folded her arms on the table, then lowered her head to rest on them.

It was too early to go to sleep, even though that's all she really wanted to do at this point. Maybe she should head to bed anyway. There wouldn't be much time to recuperate over the next few days. Starting fresh tomorrow—hopefully, minus a migraine—would be preferable to navigating the entire three-day festival in misery.

Before she could convince herself to make the trek down the hallway, knocking sounded at the front door.

Seriously, what was it with people today?

"Allye, I know you're home." Eric's voice filtered through the window she'd left open. *Knock, knock, knock.* "You said we could talk later."

She stifled a sigh. Ignoring him wasn't accomplishing anything. She pushed to her feet and walked to the door. She snapped the dead bolt back, did an about-face, then plopped into her recliner, leaning her head back against the headrest. Eric could let himself in.

After a moment, the door slowly swung open. "Can I come in?"

She'd prefer he didn't. "Yes."

He crossed the room to her couch and perched on the edge. "How are you feeling?"

"Fine."

"Why the tinted glasses, then?"

"Because I like them." An awkward silence filled the space between them. That hadn't been entirely true, and her conscience wouldn't allow the falsehood. She closed her eyes. "I'm trying to ward off another migraine."

"I'm sorry." He lowered his voice. "We couldn't find Dion."

Her heart panged, but she only nodded.

"Thank you for calling me though. It's a relief to at least know he's still okay." He paused, but when she offered no response, he asked, "Any new incidents or messages?"

"Nope."

"Good." He went quiet again. She waited him out, hoping he'd get the hint and leave. But apparently he wasn't finished yet. He cleared his throat. "Allye, I'm really sorry. I was a total jerk this morning."

"Yes. You were."

Despite her curt response, he continued. "I was wrong to assume the worst about you, and I had no business telling Bryce about your illness. I just want to say I'm sorry."

Tears sprang to her eyes at the sincere humility in his words. No excuses. No projecting the blame elsewhere. She squeezed her lids more tightly shut.

The couch squeaked as he stood. "I'd better let you get some rest." His not-so-confident footsteps trailed across the floor. "Let me know if you need anything."

The door squeaked open.

"Eric?"

"Yeah?"

"I forgive you." She didn't dare look at him if she wanted any chance of holding back her tears, but she heard his breath of relief.

"Thank you." The door shut softly, and a moment later, his engine roared to life.

She'd have to spend some time thinking about whether a relationship with him would be wise—assuming he even wanted one. Forgiving him didn't mean his words didn't still hurt or that she could easily trust him again. She had enough on her plate without subjecting herself to the emotional upheaval of a relationship characterized by simmering rage and angry outbursts.

Then again, she'd never known him to lose his temper. Most of the time, he was almost exasperatingly calm. Maybe that's why this morning's incident had shocked her so much.

She sent up a prayer for wisdom. Her muddled brain wasn't in any state to make further decisions tonight. But one thing was certain.

A man who owned his mistakes and took steps to make things right was the real deal.

35

AFTER LEAVING ALLYE'S, Eric headed for home. It had been a long, draining day, and he was over it. He just wanted to get something to eat, veg a little, and hit the sack. Tomorrow he'd launch into the investigations with a fresh mind.

If only he could say the same about his relationship with Allye. But he'd dug himself into that hole. And though he'd apologized, it was up to Allye if she wanted to fill it with water and drown him or offer a hand up instead.

He wouldn't blame her if she chose the former.

He pulled into the driveway but didn't immediately exit his car. Arriving home to a dark house didn't usually bother him, but tonight the emptiness screamed across the space between it and him.

Sighing, he went inside and straight to the freezer. Too tired to come up with something more appealing, he pulled out a frozen dinner. He stuck it in the microwave and stared at the digital display as the numbers counted down.

When it beeped, he removed the plastic tray and carried it to the living room. He dropped onto the couch. It was Thursday. Should be a football game on. He had no idea which teams were scheduled, but he didn't really care. He just needed noise and distraction.

Three bites into the meal, his work phone went off. He muted the TV and swallowed his mouthful of mediocre chicken before answering.

"Thornton."

"It's Richards. I'm on my way to the station with a backseat passenger. Guy had a nice stash of drugs in his vehicle—too much to just be a user. You interested?"

"Definitely." This might be just the break he needed. "I'll be there in ten." He scarfed down the rest of his dinner in less than two minutes and rushed out the door.

When he arrived at the station, Richards met him in the reception area.

"Thanks for calling me in. What've you got on this guy?"

"His name's Samuel Phillips. I clocked him doing fifty-five in a thirty-five. When I pulled him over, he was clearly under the influence."

"Drunk or high?"

"High as a comet. Tried to tell me the drugs sitting in the passenger seat were preportioned baggies of baby powder for his girlfriend's kid." Richards scrunched his face into an absurd expression.

"Ooookay, then. You said it was quite the stash. How much we talking?"

"A dozen or so bags. Haven't logged them yet, but I'd guess they're about five G's apiece."

Eric let out a low whistle. That would fetch a pretty penny on the streets. "He say anything on the way over?"

The officer chuckled. "He hardly shut up, but most of it was unintelligible mumbling mixed with bouts of singing. Guy's got a decent voice. Too bad I'm not a classic country fan."

"Pity." He glanced toward the back of the building. "He in the interrogation room?"

"Yeah, Vernon figured there wasn't much sense hauling him in and out of the holding cell if you were only gonna be a few minutes."

"I'd better get back there, then. If Mr. Phillips is that much of a chatterbox, Vernon's probably getting tired of babysitting."

"Probably." He slapped Eric on the back. "Good luck."

He could use some right about now. Stopping by his desk to grab a voice recorder, he sent up a quick prayer for help. Then he cut through to the small room at the back of the building. The words to "Take Me Home, Country Roads" greeted him before he reached the closed door. Richards was right. The guy wasn't half bad.

He rapped on the door and opened it. Vernon's half-glazed expression morphed into relief so fast, Eric almost laughed. Stifling his smile, he took a quick visual inventory of Samuel Phillips.

The man was young—twenty-two, maybe twenty-four, max. Dark hair. Average height and build, maybe a bit on the thin side. Dressed in baggy cargo pants and a wrinkled T-shirt, he looked and smelled like he hadn't showered in days. The condition of his teeth gave a pretty good indication of his drug of choice.

A full three seconds later, Phillips noticed him and broke off his song in the middle of the chorus. "Hey. Who're you?" There was no defensiveness or demand in his tone, only curiosity.

"I'm Detective Thornton. You can call me Eric if you'd like." He could already tell this guy would respond better to friendliness than intimidation.

Vernon slipped out quietly, and Eric lowered himself into the vacated chair. He pulled out his notepad, then started the recorder and stated the necessary information. Phillips watched as if totally intrigued.

"So, Samuel—do you go by Samuel, or can I call you Sam?"

"Everybody calls me Sam." He scratched his arm, and his left leg jiggled like he had a spring attached to his heel. "Well, except for my mom. She always calls me Samuel. But everybody else says Sam."

"Great. Sam, then." Eric glanced at his paper as if referencing a notation, though nothing was written yet. "How long you been dealing?"

The man swiped at his nose. "I dunno what you're talking about."

"Oh, really? I heard you had a lot of product in your car."

"Whoever said that made a mistake. I didn't have anything illegal in my car. I was just on my way to . . . to . . ." His eyes roamed as he thought. "To hit a drive-through. Yeah. I was just going for something to eat. No crime in that."

"But what about all those bags you had?" Eric leaned forward and lowered his voice conspiratorially. "They made up quite the stash. Looked like a couple grand worth."

"I still don't . . . know." Sam's eyes continued to skitter around the room, and he scratched at his arm again. "I mean, I need to clean it out. Yeah. There's probably lots of burger wrappers and fast-food bags."

Eric shook his head but kept his tone conversational. "I'm not talking about those. I'm talking about the little plastic bags with powder in them. Remember those? The officer you came in with collected about a dozen of them from your passenger seat."

"Oh. Those bags. That wasn't anything. Just sugar."

Eric cocked his head. "Sugar?"

"Yeah. I got a sweet tooth."

"Why all the separate bags?"

"I, uh . . ." He scratched harder. A dot of blood appeared on his forearm. "It's not as messy as carrying around the big bag. You know, the five pound one."

"Makes sense, I suppose. So why'd you tell the officer it was baby powder?"

The man blinked. "Oh, uh, some of them are baby powder."

"Sounds like it'd be a nasty mistake if you happened to grab the wrong one."

"Yeah." He attempted a disgusted look, but the effect was more comical than believable. "I did that once. Tasted awful. Had to wash my mouth out and everything."

This had gone far enough. The guy was too high to realize how ridiculous he sounded. Eric was going to have to add a little pressure if he wanted to get anything useful from him.

"I'm going to level with you, Sam. We know the bags aren't sugar—or baby powder." He leaned back and clicked his pen. "Fact is, you had a serious amount of drugs in your possession."

Sam's leg started bouncing faster and harder. "No, I don't sell drugs. Don't do 'em either. Just say no, right? That's what my mom always said."

"But see, here's the problem. We found them in your car. You could serve some serious time. Worse—" he paused for effect— "people around here have been dying from fentanyl-laced meth. If your bags come back from the lab showing fentanyl content, you might go down for homicide."

His leg stopped bouncing for the first time since the interrogation started. "No! These are clean. Marco's the one who did the lacing, and the big guy said anyone else caught doing that would pay like he did. I don't wanna die."

Gotcha.

Eric kept his face placid, but his mind raced with the new information. The lacing hadn't been sanctioned. Somebody had stepped out of line to pad his own pockets, and the "big guy" hadn't been happy about the deaths—probably because it called too much attention to their operation. Who was this Marco? Was that the name of their John Doe? He stuck that question in his pocket for later. He had a more pressing one first.

"So who's the big guy?"

Sam's eyes widened, and sweat broke out on his forehead. The jiggle returned with renewed vigor. "I dunno."

"You don't know who the big guy is?"

He shook his head vigorously. "No clue. I ain't never heard his name. Never saw him either. Don't want to."

That wasn't surprising. Sam Phillips was a low-level dealer and a user. The head of this ring likely guarded his identity with all but his most trusted. It had been worth asking though.

Eric clicked his pen. "Who's your supplier?"

"I can't talk about that, man. Not for you or anybody else."

"Come on, you've gotta give me something." When Sam didn't respond to that, he decided to try another tack. "Okay, don't worry about that for now. I wouldn't want to cause you trouble with these guys."

Sam relaxed, but only a fraction. Eric needed to get him comfortable and talking again. Maybe he'd let something else slip.

"Hey, you want a drink? We've got water, Coke, Sprite."

"I'd take a Coke. Those are my favorite."

Eric leaned out the door and signaled Vernon. "Can you get him a Coke?"

The officer gave him a two-finger salute, and Eric retook his seat.

"We'll have that to you in just a minute, all right?"

His head bobbed. "No problem. I'm a patient guy. No problem at all."

Vernon opened the door and handed in the bottled soft drink. Eric gave Sam a moment with his distraction. The man hummed as he struggled to break the seal, then after he finally got it, he took a long drink and grinned.

"Good?"

"Perfect. You want a drink?" He tilted the bottle toward Eric.

"Nah, I'm good. You enjoy it."

"It's just right—bubbly and ice cold." With hardly a breath's pause, he launched into another topic, the words popping out like he couldn't hold them back if he tried. "You know, you're a nice guy. I always thought if I ever got arrested that the cops would be a bunch of mean guys with a superiority complex. You're all right."

Eric smiled. "Most of us aren't so bad."

"Good to know. I'm glad to hear that, really. Especially since I'm here in the middle of the station, surrounded by cops, you know?"

"Sure. That's gotta be a relief." He tilted back in his chair. "I'm curious about something though. This Marco—what's his last name?"

"Hmm?" Sam stared at him blankly.

"Marco, the guy who laced the drugs? You know his last name?"

"Uh, maybe Stevens? Stevenson? Something like that. I don't pay too much attention to names unless they're weird." He shimmied his shoulders and hummed like he didn't have a care in the world.

"So what happened to him?"

Sam took another drink of his Coke and continued humming.

Eric snapped his fingers but kept his posture relaxed. "Hey, Sam, you hear me?"

The humming stopped. "Oh, sorry. The music's really loud in here. What'd you say?" He squinted as if focusing was a difficult task.

"I asked what happened to Marco."

Sam's lip trembled. "They killed him. He didn't mean it though—didn't want anyone to die. He told me. He just put too much in, and then it was too late. But the big guy didn't care. He had Bernie call him in, and then—" His voice cut off in a sob.

"And then what?" Eric made a mental note of the new name, but he didn't write it down. If Sam realized he'd slipped up, he might stop talking.

"I don't wanna talk about it." Head swaying back and forth, Sam attempted to screw the cap back on his bottle, but it spun off and skipped across the table.

Eric snatched it before it hit the floor and returned it to the man. "Sounds bad. How'd you find out about him?"

"They videoed it." The words escaped in a hoarse whisper. "Sent it to us all as warning."

That was a surprise. There was a video of this murder floating around? Allye hadn't mentioned anything to that effect. Did that mean this was a different murder after all? Or had she just not noticed the camera or phone? She had seen another man in the shadows, so it was a possibility he could have been filming.

"When did this all happen?"

Sam touched his thumb to his index finger, the middle, then the ring finger as if counting. He repeated the motions, then shrugged. "Couple days ago? I dunno. Time's just a blur sometimes." He launched into a ballad about quickly passing time.

Eric didn't recognize the song, but that didn't matter. He was done here. He used his phone to snap Sam's photo, then stopped the recording and passed the man back to Vernon's care. It was late enough, Sam would spend the night in the holding cell. Tomorrow he'd be transferred to a neighboring county since theirs didn't have a jail.

After settling at his own desk, he texted Allye the photo with the words "Recognize him?" He was pretty confident Sam was not her attacker, but it would be foolish not to at least confirm.

While he waited for her response, he ran a search for a Marco Stevens or Stevenson in the area. He got a couple of hits in the driver's license database, but only one fell within the age range of their John Doe. He pulled that one up first. Despite the condition of the body they'd found, he could see the resemblance.

His phone buzzed with a text from Allye.

Sorry, no

That was the answer he'd expected. He sent her a thanks, then returned his attention to the screen. He pulled up a picture of the victim and compared them side by side. They'd have to do comparisons, maybe call in family to see if they could identify him, but Eric would bet this was the same guy.

With that done, he put in an electronic request for a warrant to search Sam's phone and computer, if the man had one. He hit send, then moved on to transcribing his thoughts from the interrogation while it was still fresh in his mind. Sam hadn't given him as much information as he'd hoped for, but he had a few leads and some names. It had been well worth coming in.

He leaned back in his chair. He needed a plan for tomorrow. If nothing happened to disrupt his morning, he'd start by listening to the recording with fresh ears and make sure he hadn't missed anything. Then he'd see about finalizing their victim's identity. Hopefully by then, he'd have the warrant to search Sam's devices. Finding that video—and the sender—would be gold. He just might be able to solve this case before anyone else got hurt.

36

FRIDAY MORNING AT WOOL FEST, Allye straightened a few of the photos she'd spread across the front table of her booth. She frowned, then tilted some of them. Better.

She grabbed her backup camera and took a picture, then stood back and surveyed the finished setup. Despite how far behind she'd felt over the last several months, she'd managed to put together a good display. She smiled. No, she hadn't made it back to her studio to print the extra postcards from her new photos, but there were still plenty to choose from.

The larger prints and canvases depicting local nature and places of interest would be the big draw—along with the hand-knitted projects scattered tastefully among the artwork. For now, each knitted piece was carefully placed where its color scheme would best complement the surrounding photos. That would be short-lived once festivalgoers began picking through her offerings, but she didn't mind.

She checked the time. The festival didn't officially open for another hour, but anticipation was high among the vendors. Shows like this could be hit or miss on immediate profitability, but they didn't do it just to make a buck. They did it because they loved their craft and the excitement and camaraderie of the festivals.

Allye shared that sentiment, although this was the only area festival that she regularly participated in. She'd probably still set up regardless of whether she recouped her costs, but she always made at least that much. And she usually booked a few photo shoots that resulted in repeat customers. All in all, it was worth her time and effort.

She moved behind the table and lowered herself into the lawn chair she'd brought. Normally, she'd take this extra pre-festival time to greet the other vendors in her tent and admire their handiwork, but her own setup had drained her. Perhaps if she rested for a bit, she'd find the energy to make her rounds before the first festivalgoers arrived.

And if not? She frowned as she reached for the extra-large knitting bag she'd packed for today. She didn't like not knowing her limits and abilities anymore. But she wasn't going to let anything ruin her day—not her health, not the danger stalking her, not the emotional baggage from yesterday. She was going to enjoy this festival if it killed her.

She pulled out her current project. The fingerless glove, second of the pair, was nearly finished, but she'd come prepared. Before leaving this morning, she'd stocked her bag with several sets of needles and a variety of yarn so she'd have options to choose from after completing the gloves. She hoped to make it to the Wool Tent later and browse the selection of naturally dyed yarns too.

The first couple of hours of the festival passed in a blur, and Allye was glad she'd taken the time to rest. By midafternoon, she was ready for a nap. But she was enjoying herself enough that she didn't mind.

After placing another handful of postcards on the table to replace the last dozen sold, she took a few moments to stretch before returning to her seat. Her phone vibrated, and she glanced at it. There was a missed call and a text, both from Eric. She frowned. She still wasn't sure what she ought to feel toward him since his apology, but she hadn't intentionally ignored him this time. The phone just hadn't rung. Reception was always spotty out here near the state park. She checked the text.

> Forensic artist coming back early. Can you meet with him Sunday?

Before she could answer, a second text came through.

> *After the festival, of course.

The festival did end earlier on Sunday than on the first two days—6:00 p.m. instead of ten, but that didn't mean she could leave at six. The takedown process would require quite a bit of work on her part, and she wasn't sure how late it would be by the time she made it back to Kincaid.

> I'll have to pack up and load my car before I'm free.

> I can help

Her finger hovered over the screen. Should she accept the offer? No doubt she'd be more than exhausted by that point, and she had no idea how long a session with a forensic artist would take. No matter how much she might prefer space from Eric right now, she'd be foolish to refuse his help.

She sent him a simple *Okay*, then reached for her insulated mug of iced tea. But she misjudged the distance. The container tipped, and in her attempt to right it, she dropped her phone. It tumbled to the ground and bounced under the table and out of reach.

Someone from the opposite side of the booth stooped to pick it up. "Whoops." The man rose, her phone in hand, and offered it to her. "Here you go."

"Thank you." She hit the power button to black the screen and set it aside. "Good to see you, Thomas. Enjoying the festival?"

"Always." The reporter flashed her a toothy grin and held up his camera. "Mind if I take some photos?"

"Of course not." She'd gladly take the free publicity if he chose to include a photo of her booth in the paper. She smiled for a wide-angle shot, then scooted her chair back to give him extra room as he focused in on her collection of offerings.

Once he'd taken several shots, Thomas let the camera rest against his chest as he looked more closely at her postcards. He picked up one featuring the outside of the historic newspaper office. "You really have an eye for this stuff, Allye."

"Thank you." She felt herself blush.

"I mean it. These are good. If you ever want to freelance for the paper, let me know." He selected a few more and paid for them. "I'll see you around. Keep up the good work."

"Thanks," she said again as he continued to the next booth.

37

ALLYE PULLED INTO THE DRIVEWAY of her duplex and tried to summon the energy to go inside. She shouldn't be this tired at 11:00 p.m., even after such a busy day. She'd always been a night owl. At least until developing whatever illness this was. But over the last couple of months, she'd found herself slipping into bed exhausted at eight or nine and still managing to sleep until nine in the morning. Of course, since the craziness of the last week started, she hadn't had that luxury, and she was feeling it now.

Better get moving or you'll end up sleeping here.

She blew out a breath and grabbed her purse and everything bag. She thought about locking the Jetta's door and decided not to bother. Maybe it was lazy, but it would save her a step in the morning. No one seemed interested in her things anyway—unless it was to send her a message. If they wanted to use her car to do that, they'd just bash out a window or something, right?

The glow of a nearby streetlamp assured her no one lurked too close to her house, but it also left her feeling exposed as she stood on the porch trying to fit her key into the new dead bolt. Something rustled in the yard, and she spun, palming her keys to use as a weapon if need be. Nothing. She was being paranoid. The recent incidents and threats had spooked her. She forced herself to turn back around and slow down. The key slid easily into place. She pushed inside and nearly slammed the door shut behind her. She threw the dead bolt, then leaned her back against the door while she caught her breath.

Her vision started to blur, and she squeezed her eyes shut before dizziness could hit. After a moment, she opened them a fraction to test her vision. A little better. She needed to get off her feet. Now.

She made it to her recliner and collapsed into it, letting her bags slide to the floor. After engaging the footrest, she toed off her flats and grabbed her cell.

While she'd gotten intermittent texts throughout the day, her phone had started dinging in earnest once she crossed back into an area with good reception. She should probably check those now. She turned her screen to the lowest possible brightness before checking the half dozen messages and squinting through blurriness to respond to the ones from family. Begrudgingly, she did the same with the message from Eric. He was only making sure she'd made it home safely. She could give him that peace of mind. But as soon as that was sent, she set her phone aside and tried to do the same with thoughts of the detective.

She blinked away the blur. It had been a long day. The festival had been as enjoyable as ever, and her symptoms had been manageable overall. Her head still hurt, but it wasn't anywhere near migraine level.

Sales had been decent too. And with tomorrow beginning the true weekend, chances were good they'd be even better going forward. She reached for her purse and pulled her sales log from it.

She'd sold very few of the big items, but the fingerless gloves had been quite popular. The postcards had been the real show-stopper though. She looked at the bundled tick marks indicating the number sold. *Five, ten, fifteen . . .* Her vision started to blur again. She placed a finger on the page and squinted, determined to finish her calculations.

Forty-seven. She'd sold forty-seven postcards. Not bad at all. If tomorrow went this well, she might sell out of them before Sunday. She hoped her family arrived in time to see her booth before it looked too picked over.

Would Eric come to the festival tomorrow too? After the amount of time they'd spent together this week, it felt odd to go a day without seeing him. But he was probably busy with the investigation, and, really, did she want to see him anyway? She wasn't sure.

And she didn't want to think about that tonight, she reminded herself. She replaced the sales log in her purse so she wouldn't forget it tomorrow, then allowed her eyes the relief of closing. She really should go to bed. Every bit of rest she got could only help her make it through the weekend.

Problem was, her brain felt like it was stuck on a spinning wheel. The commotion of the festival had allowed her to keep her mind off her troubles for much of the day, but now that she was in the quiet of home, everything was vying for her attention. She might as well try to get something done. But what?

Editing photos was out of the question. If her vision couldn't handle a moment of staring at a page, she certainly wouldn't be able to spend any time staring at a screen.

Knitting, however, might be doable. After finishing the gloves earlier, she'd selected another pattern that she'd used several times before. The cabled scarf was just complicated enough to require her to keep mental tabs on which row she was on, but not so complicated she would need to keep her eyes focused. Might not even have to look at it much at all. And while her hands were tired from the cumulative hours with her needles today, they were better off than her eyes.

Worth a try. And maybe the familiar motions would help her brain settle.

Much as she would prefer to stay in her seat, the overhead

light needed to go. The lamp would be much easier on her eyes. She stood, waited until her equilibrium caught up, then made those adjustments. Might as well retrieve a drink while she was up. Did she want tea?

Yes. But she didn't want to be on her feet long enough to prepare it properly, and microwaved tea wasn't an option. She grabbed a bottled water instead and returned to the living room.

Her knitting bag already sat next to the recliner where she'd dropped everything when she arrived, so she settled in, then lifted the bag to her lap. She pulled her needles out, leaving the skein inside, and surveyed her progress. Scarves felt like they took absolutely forever, but she'd made decent headway in between customers.

Once she figured out which row of the cable pattern she should be on, she scooched down in her seat and closed her eyes as she worked. Her needles clicked in a quiet rhythm. Her brain, however, continued to spin.

Using her backup camera today had reminded her that she needed to order a new camera to replace the one that was destroyed Wednesday. Should she order the same model, or should she upgrade? She hadn't had hers that long—only about six months. Though she didn't need to add to everything already on her plate, she would have to take time to do that research sometime next week.

A stitch felt off, and she cracked one eyelid open to assess the issue. Easy fix. She repositioned the needle and shut her eyes again.

Her mind strayed to Dion. Was he still okay? She prayed again for his safety. Then she prayed protection over her family. Heaven knew they needed it until this situation was resolved. She was less sure what to pray about the situation with Eric. Might as well just be honest with God.

I'm so confused about yesterday. Is Eric that angry beneath the surface? Or was yesterday just a fluke? I know everyone makes mistakes. I sure do, and you know that better than anyone.

Her prayer trailed off, her mind finally beginning to quiet. Apparently, God wasn't going to give her a direct answer tonight. But she was okay with that. She just needed to know he had it in hand and remind herself not to make snap decisions based on her emotions.

Her fingers slowed, and her head began to droop. She caught herself with a jerk that sent a lightning bolt of pain shooting down her neck and into her shoulder.

This wasn't working.

She set her knitting aside. As tired as she was, she'd start dropping stitches if she tried to keep going. She should go to bed.

Or she could just stay here.

Drowsiness won. She placed her glasses beside the knitting, then flipped the lamp off and snuggled back down in her chair.

A little while later, she awoke with a start. Had she heard something? She lay still. There it was. A scratching sound as if a key was being inserted in a lock. She reached for her phone. Felt yarn. A knitting needle.

The front door opened a crack. She froze, heart in her throat.

After a slight pause, the door swung inward. The hinges let out a low squeak.

The sound kick-started her brain. She launched from the chair, fingers closing around the knitting needle, and ran for the kitchen.

Heavy footsteps sounded behind her. She screamed. Her shoulder caught the doorframe. Before she could right herself, a hard hand landed on her other shoulder and spun her around.

Allowing the momentum to carry her, she grasped the knitting needle like a dagger and swung.

It sank in. The man yelled and released her. She lost her grip on the makeshift weapon. No time to worry about that. As his curses filled her ears, she turned and sprinted toward her bedroom, vaguely registering the clang of thin steel striking a solid object and bouncing to the floor.

She made it to her bedroom ahead of him, but not by much.

She threw the door shut and turned the lock. It wouldn't hold long. She tried to shove her dresser in front of the door even as the knob rattled. Too heavy. What would work as a weapon?

Moonlight illuminated the room just enough for her to make out shadows. Derryck's bat. She grabbed it. Lifted it to her shoulder as the door splintered inward.

She put all her strength into the swing. The blow glanced off the man's forehead. Something heavy clattered to the floor. He staggered back, hand held to his head. He growled.

"Get out!" She almost didn't recognize her own voice.

The man hesitated, and she shouldered the bat again.

"What's going on in here?" A voice sounded from the hallway. Cornell from next door. "My wife's on the phone with the cops."

The intruder hesitated only a second longer before he turned and fled, shouldering past the neighbor who'd come to her rescue.

"Hey!"

She couldn't move. "Please let him catch him," she whispered as two sets of feet pounded away from the bedroom. Something crashed. An engine roared. Tires squealed.

Someone headed back down the hall, and Allye lifted the bat.

"He got away." Cornell's voice again. He returned, rubbing his left shoulder.

She dropped the bat. Tried to catch her breath.

"Allye, you okay?"

"Yeah, I'm fine." But her legs turned to water, and she slid to the floor.

38

ERIC PARKED BEHIND ALLYE'S JETTA and dashed up the porch steps to her house. He'd gotten a brief rundown from the dispatcher, who said Allye was unharmed, but he needed to see for himself.

Another break-in spelled trouble. Something had changed, and not for the better.

Allye met him at the door, a teacup cradled in her hands. Those rose-tinted glasses were perched on her nose again, and her face was paler than he'd ever seen it—a stark contrast to her fiery red hair. But she was whole and standing on her own two feet.

Relief washed over him at the assurance she really was okay, and he nearly gave in to the impulse to take her into his arms. But he restrained himself. He had no right to even a friendly hug, not after yesterday. Instead, he said the first words that popped out. "Another migraine?"

"Yeah." She waved him inside. "Can't seem to totally kick it, and now it's flared again. But I figured we'd prefer not to have our conversation in the dark. Can I get you something to drink?"

"No. Thanks though." He followed her in, noting her overturned coffee table and a shattered glass a few feet from it.

They entered the kitchen, and he stopped short. He hadn't

realized she wasn't alone, but a man nursing a cup of coffee leaned against the counter, and a woman sat at the table, phone in hand.

"The detective is here," the woman said into the phone. "We're good now."

Allye turned to face him. "Eric, these are my neighbors, Cornell and Shannon Howard. She called 911 while he came over here to check on me. He scared the intruder off." Her voice cracked. "Once the coast was clear, they offered to stay until someone arrived. Cornell, Shannon, have you met Detective Eric Thornton?"

Eric shook Cornell's offered hand. "I appreciate you coming to help. We need more people who care enough to jump in when needed."

The man rolled one shoulder as if uncomfortable with the praise. "Couldn't live with myself if a tragedy happened because I refused to be bothered."

Eric nodded. He felt the same. "I'll need to get your statement."

"Sure thing. Didn't see much though." He rinsed out his coffee mug and set it in the sink. "Mind if I use your restroom first, Allye?"

"No, go ahead. First door on the . . . left." She paused almost imperceptibly, but Eric caught it. And if he wasn't mistaken, it was on the right, not the left.

After Cornell disappeared down the hall, she returned her attention to Eric. "You sure I can't pour you some coffee or something?"

"If it'll make you feel better."

"It would." She set her teacup aside and retrieved the half-empty coffeepot and a mug from the counter. "Cream or sugar?"

"Just sugar, please."

She handed him the mug, and he noted the pronounced tremble in her hands as the liquid sloshed dangerously close to the rim. She was shaken. More than any of the times before.

"You should sit." He kept his tone low, for her ears only. Without argument, she grabbed the nearest chair. Eric took the one closest to her and readied his notebook and pen. After taking a sip of the coffee, he addressed the woman across the table. "Shannon, is it?" She nodded. "Mind telling me what you witnessed?"

"Less than Cornell, unfortunately. We were in bed, but I was still awake, reading. We heard a scream, then a shout, and with what happened last week, we didn't want to wait to see if anything else caught our attention. We ran outside, and when Cornell saw the door was open, he yelled for me to call the police and stay put." She shivered. Her husband reappeared and placed a hand on her shoulder. She reached up and held it. "A minute later, I saw a big man run out. He took off in the opposite direction, and I heard an engine roar to life right after he disappeared around the curve."

Eric caught his notes up, then asked, "Did you get a good look at him?"

Shannon shook her head. "No. Just that he was tall and well-built. He never faced my direction."

"But you saw him?" He lifted his gaze to Cornell.

The man pursed his lips. "Not very well. Too dark, and it happened too fast. When he realized I was there, he knocked me over and took off. I think he was wearing a ski mask too. I'd peg him around six foot though. Allye might have gotten a better look."

"I think you're right about the mask. Regardless, I didn't get a good look either." She glanced between the two of them, then addressed Eric. "Can you go ahead and take their full statements first? It's late. I hate for them to have to stay here longer than necessary."

Shannon gaped at her. "Your home was just broken into again, Allye. Don't worry about us."

She twisted a napkin in her hand. "But I'd feel better if you were able to get to bed. Didn't Cornell just finish a week of night shift?"

"Yes, but I'm used to it. We're okay," Cornell answered.

But Allye didn't let up. "Still. It just makes more sense for some of us to get rest." She turned to Eric. "You don't mind, do you?"

Sensing she really would feel better if her neighbors were released soon, he nodded. "Fine by me." He focused on Cornell, who began his account without further prompting. But he didn't have much to tell either. Eric thought he managed to control his expression when Cornell described coming upon the intruder in Allye's bedroom, but inside, he was fuming. This was the second time they'd come after her in her home.

Cornell's experience only took a few minutes to relate, and Eric's follow-up questions only took a handful more.

Once the neighbors had left for their own home, he turned back to Allye. She was staring into her empty teacup with the blank look of someone who could go into shock at any second. He took her hand. She lifted her gaze to him, and her eyes cleared, but he still didn't like her pallor or the chill to her fingers.

"Hold on." He remembered there being a blanket draped over the arm of her couch. After retrieving it, he draped it over her shoulders, then refilled her cup from the teapot on the counter.

She wrapped her fingers around her cup. "Thank you."

He sat back down and looked her in the eyes. "Are you sure you're okay? He really didn't hurt you?"

She shook her head. "Might have wrenched my shoulder a bit when he grabbed me, but that hardly counts."

It counted to him. He was absolutely not okay with the fact the guy had laid a hand on her. Fisting his hand, he counted to ten, then relaxed it and shifted his mind to investigation mode. "Was it the same guy as before?" He'd wanted to ask that earlier but had held the question back for when they were alone. He had no reason to distrust her neighbors, but the fewer people who knew details about the investigation, the better.

"I've been thinking about that." She slowly lifted her teacup to her lips, took a sip, then set it back on the saucer. "Honestly, I don't think it was my attacker. He seemed taller, and his voice was wrong—too deep. He carried himself differently too. At least, that's the impression I got. It really did happen fast."

That complicated things, but he kept the thought to himself. "Okay. Can you tell me anything else about those mannerisms or what he looked like?"

"I don't know how to describe it. The attacker from before was so in control, cocky really. This guy wasn't. He was big, and came after me when I ran, but he just had a different . . . vibe, I guess. But then again, I'd fallen asleep in the living room, and he probably expected me to be in bed, so that might have thrown his plan off."

He made note of that. "How about his physical description? You said he was big. What else did you notice?"

Her shoulders slumped. "Not much. It was dark, and I didn't have my glasses on."

"What kind of big, then?" he encouraged. "Are you talking overweight, muscular, or just tall?" Her neighbors had already described him as tall and well-built, but he needed Allye's perspective as well. She'd probably been closer to him for longer.

"Tall. But muscular too."

"How tall do you think?"

"I don't know." Frustration crept into her voice. "I'm not a good judge of size even when I can see clearly."

"It's okay," he said. Fear and adrenaline often skewed a victim's perspective anyway. And he needed to think of Allye as a victim right now, not as the woman he was fast falling in love with. He stood. "What about compared to me? Was he a similar height? Taller?"

She worried her lip and looked up at him. "I don't know. Maybe a little taller? I had to reach with the bat. Not that I've ever swung one at your head."

Her answer was so unexpected he wasn't able to completely stifle his laugh as he retook his seat. "Thank heaven for that."

Some of the color returned to her cheeks. "Sorry. I'm . . . still rattled."

Understandably so. "So you hit him? With a bat?" Anyone who knew Allye knew she was feisty, but he had trouble wrapping his mind around her taking a bat to someone.

Allye cringed. "Yes, but it didn't take him down. I think he would have come at me again if Cornell hadn't shown up."

"Was he armed?"

"I don't know. I didn't see a weapon, but like I said, I'd just woken up and didn't have my glasses. Besides, it was dark, and I was more focused on trying to get away."

"All right." He clicked his pen. "How about you run through what happened from the beginning?" He should have just started with that.

She told him about falling asleep in the living room, being awakened, running, and the intruder grabbing her shoulder. For her sake, he struggled to keep his face expressionless, but he wanted to pummel the guy.

Her eyes widened, and her mouth formed an O.

"What?"

She'd obviously remembered something.

39

"I STABBED HIM."

Eric blinked. "You what?" Not much surprised him, but Allye was doing a good job of it tonight.

"With my knitting needle. I had it beside me and grabbed it when I heard him coming in. I didn't exactly plan to, but when he came after me . . ." She swallowed.

What would a knitting needle wound look like? He pictured the sticks he'd seen her pull out on multiple occasions. Sometimes he'd seen her work with short wooden ones, other times with a long metal version that he'd estimate at about a foot long. Neither was an ideal weapon, but they could inflict some damage—especially the long ones.

"Where did you stab him?"

The color drained from her face again. "His chest or maybe his shoulder? It happened too fast, and like I said, I didn't plan it."

"What did he do then? How did he react?"

"He yelled. But he let go of me, so I ran."

"Did you keep hold of the needle?"

"No, I just ran. I think it stuck there, but I heard it hit the floor after I took off, so he must have pulled it out." Her pale cheeks took on a greenish tinge.

"Allye, you were protecting yourself. It's okay." He didn't mind pressing a criminal, but a victim was a different story—especially Allye. But he needed to wrap this case up fast. Before she really got hurt. He cleared his throat. "Where were you when that happened? I'll need to take the needle as evidence if he left it behind."

"Near the doorway between the living room and kitchen. Can you—can you get DNA from it?"

"We'll try, but no guarantee it'll go anywhere. DNA often doesn't." If it penetrated or even scraped the skin, they might have enough for a DNA test. He wouldn't hold his breath on the results, but there was always a chance their guy would be in the system. The wait time was a serious pain though. And if the guy wasn't in the system, it would be a dead end anyway.

Her hopeful expression faded, and he hated that he'd dampened that hope. "Maybe we'll get lucky though. If we can get a good sample and he's in the system, it'll show." Regardless, he'd do his best to have her intruder behind bars long before DNA results could come back. "All right." He stood and pulled on gloves. Time to see what evidence was left behind. "Walk me through."

She led him back to the living room and leaned against a bookshelf while he surveyed the space. He found the knitting needle and slipped it into an evidence bag.

He eyed the coffee table and shattered glass. "This happen when he came after you?"

"I don't think so. Maybe he ran into it when he was running from Cornell?"

Or he'd flipped it in hopes of slowing Cornell down.

He moved on to the door. "He entered by the front?"

"Yes."

Interesting. The back door would have provided more protection from passersby. But then again, it was well after midnight. He examined the locks. Neither the dead bolt nor the doorknob showed obvious signs of tampering.

"Did you have the dead bolt locked?"

"I think so?" Her face screwed up in thought.

"Especially until this is resolved, you're going to have to make sure to keep the dead bolt thrown."

"I know. And I've been trying to remember, but I've been so tired and off my game with this . . ." She spread her hands and waved them in a helpless gesture. "With everything."

"I understand, but do your best. Maybe you could look into getting an alarm system installed too."

"Not sure I can afford one right now."

He got that. Didn't like it, but it was reality for a lot of people.

They moved on to the rest of the house. He followed her through the kitchen and down the hallway toward her bedroom. The light was already on when they entered, and he took in the rumpled bedspread and the clothes tossed over a chair.

"Sorry about the mess."

"No problem." He continued to scan the room. When he turned to face the door, a dark object caught his eye. "What's this?" He knelt to get a better look. A full-size handgun rested next to a pair of discarded shoes. He looked up at Allye. "I'm assuming this isn't yours."

She shook her head, wide-eyed. "No. I did hear something fall after I hit him with the bat, but I'd forgotten."

He turned his attention to the baseball bat lying on the floor nearby. "That bat?"

"Yes."

"I'd like to take it as well. We might find trace evidence on it."

She twisted a lock of her hair. "Will I get it back? It was Derryck's." Her voice softened as she mentioned the younger brother she'd lost.

"Yes."

She gave him permission, and he collected both it and the gun. He wouldn't hold out hope the firearm was registered to the intruder, but it might give them something to go on—fingerprints if they were fortunate.

They returned to the kitchen, and he placed the evidence bags on the table while she propped herself against the counter.

"Do you need anything else from me?" Allye asked.

"Not at the moment." He studied her. She looked ready to drop. "Have you called your family yet?"

She shook her head. "It's so late. I'll tell them tomorrow."

"You need to call someone. You can't stay here alone anymore." Not without better precautions in place.

"I don't have much choice. I'm not going to carry the danger to my family, and this is my home."

"Then let me stay with you."

She stared at him.

He held up his hands. "No strings attached, and it's just for tonight or until we come up with a better option. I'll keep watch from the living room, and you can go to bed."

"I won't be sleeping anymore tonight," she said quietly.

"Fair enough. But you still shouldn't be alone. He could come back."

She opened her mouth. She was going to argue, he could see it.

"Please, Allye. Let me keep you safe."

She turned her back to him and braced her hands on the countertop, tilting her head to stare at the ceiling. Finally, she released a sigh and glanced at him over her shoulder. "Okay."

AFTER ERIC RIGHTED HER COFFEE TABLE and she'd swept up the broken glass, they settled into the living room—him on the couch and her in the recliner. She thought about starting a movie, but if they were going to spend hours together, she might as well get some answers first.

"I want to know something."

"Shoot."

"Why did you get so angry at me yesterday?"

His gaze dropped to the fresh cup of coffee she'd insisted on pouring for him. "I shouldn't have. It was totally uncalled for."

She agreed, but—"That's not what I asked." She wished he would look at her.

"You scared me."

She'd figured that much. When he didn't elaborate, she sighed. Looked like she was going to have to drag it out of him. She tapped a nail against the side of her teacup. "How?"

His Adam's apple bobbed, and he looked like he was debating whether to share. She waited. She knew his apology had been sincere, but she needed to get to the root of why he'd blown up in the first place. If he wasn't willing to do that—to be honest with himself and her—she wouldn't be able to trust him with more than a surface friendship.

Finally, his expression changed. He'd come to a decision. When he spoke, his tone was clinical. "My dad died when I was fourteen. Overdose. I found him in his favorite chair. Thought he was passed out."

Allye's chest ached. "But he was . . ."

"Dead." Eric finally met her gaze. The pain shimmering in his eyes didn't match his detached narration. "He played around one too many times, and it took him." His fingers flexed. "Mom said he died doing what he loved."

Allye couldn't stop her gasp.

He gave her a weak smile. "Yeah. She was high when she gave his eulogy." He pursed his lips. "But she wasn't lying."

"Oh, Eric. I'm sorry."

"You didn't do anything wrong. I'm the one who overreacted. *I'm* sorry." He took a deep breath. "I saw you lying there unresponsive, and I thought whoever's been breaking into your house may have hurt you. Then when I found the pills before I had time to wrap my brain around the fact you were fine . . ." He shook his head. "I didn't realize until long after I drove off that it was more a PTSD reaction than a logical one." He stared across the room at the darkened TV.

Time stretched like the space between them. Eventually, Allye couldn't take it anymore. She grabbed her teacup and moved to the couch, leaving a little room between them. But not too much. "Tell me about that day."

His jaw tightened. Would he clam up? Or would he risk letting her in? Seconds ticked by. Just as she was about to give up hope, he drew in a sharp breath and started talking.

"He'd promised he was clean, that he was going to make up for lost time. We were supposed to head to the gym that morning, get a membership, and start a workout routine. Together." His voice cracked on the last word. "Apparently, he decided he needed one last hit first."

Allye couldn't help herself. She slipped her hand over his and felt relief when he intertwined his fingers with hers. "Where was your mom?"

"Jail." No mistaking his disgust. "Minor charge. She was out in time for the funeral, but my grandpa took me in. Told my mom to get her act together or he'd sue for permanent custody."

She was almost afraid to ask, but she did anyway. "Did she?"

"Only around tax time."

"Ouch."

"Yeah. Gramps told her to take a hike."

"Where is she now?"

"No idea."

"You haven't forgiven them, have you?"

He blinked slowly. "The best I can do is not think about them."

She squeezed his hand. "But it still eats at you. And it will until you forgive them."

"Easy for you to say." He withdrew his hand.

She flinched. Maybe not the best time to tackle this subject. *Too late.* She lifted her teacup and cradled it between her hands.

"Not really." She took a sip. The cooled liquid slid soothingly down her throat. "I had to forgive the guy who caused the car accident that killed Derryck. The terrorist who blew up my dad in Afghanistan."

Eric's expression softened. "Point taken." Not exactly an apology, but she hadn't been fishing for one. His jaw worked. "I'm a little broken, Allye. Maybe a lot broken. I've got a lot of baggage, and I'm jaded when it comes to trusting people."

"I'm broken too. I think everyone is to some extent." And she wasn't just talking about her health. "Maybe the more important thing is that we do the hard work and let God mend those broken places."

"Maybe you're right." He gave a slow nod and finally turned to face her again. "So where does that leave us?"

"Is there an us?" She realized that's what she really wanted, but she needed to know they were on the same page.

"I'd like there to be. Can you give me another chance?"

"Yes."

40

ALLYE REPLENISHED HER DISPLAY YET AGAIN. The temp had dropped overnight, and her fingerless gloves, hats, and mittens were selling like hotcakes.

She'd been worried that the few hours' sleep she'd managed with her head resting on Eric's shoulder wouldn't be enough to get her through another busy day, but so far, she was doing surprisingly well. They'd gotten moving early so Eric could log last night's evidence, then follow her out to the festival. She would have preferred to have just come together, but though he was off duty today, there was always a chance he could get called in if a major crime occurred, and she didn't want to risk getting stranded here without her car.

Eric smiled as she sank back into her lawn chair. He'd brought an extra chair for himself, and they'd spent the last few hours enjoying each other's company in between customers. They'd kept their conversation light, and it had been nice not to talk about attackers and intruders for a while.

Someone with a brisket sundae passed near the booth, and Allye's stomach gave a loud rumble as the scent of rich layers of mashed potatoes, gravy, and smoky brisket wafted by. Her cheeks warmed, but Eric chuckled.

"I'm hungry too. Want to get lunch?"

She glanced at the crowded tent and the woman browsing her wares. "It's not a great time to leave my booth."

"I could grab food and bring it back." He surveyed the area. "I really don't like leaving you alone though."

"I didn't have any issues here yesterday. I'll be fine."

He frowned but stood. "Still . . ."

"Seriously, I won't wander off by myself." She gave him a teasing grin.

"All right. What do you want?"

She gave him her food order and watched as he walked away. She appreciated his concern, but there were too many people around for the men after her to try anything.

A woman who'd spent several minutes eyeing her canvases asked about where one of the photos was taken. Happy to share, Allye chatted with her for several minutes about the nearby farm and the couple who had given her permission to photograph their property. The woman ended up purchasing the canvas, and Allye wrapped it for her before tucking the payment into her cashbox.

When she looked up, she caught sight of Wesley rushing toward her. His expression made her stomach drop. Something was wrong.

He reached her a few seconds later and braced his hands on the table. His breaths came in pants. "Hailey just got a call from your mom. Bryce and Corina are on the way to the hospital. Something's wrong with the baby."

"Oh no. Why didn't anyone call me?" She checked her phone as she asked the question, then blew out a breath. "Never mind." No signal again.

She looked for Eric. People filtered into the tent entrance, but he wasn't among them. She glanced at her screen again. One fifteen. Prime time for the food vendors, meaning extra long lines. How long had he been gone already?

Wesley shifted. "Your mom wants you to come as soon as possible. Hailey sent me ahead to find you."

"I promised Eric I wouldn't go anywhere alone." But she hadn't expected something like this.

He puffed his cheeks. "I can take you."

"What about Hailey and Jenna?"

"We just got here. They'll be okay long enough for me to get you there and get back. I know Hailey will want to be at the hospital with you guys, but she won't want to take Jenna."

Allye hesitated a second longer before nodding. Eric would understand. She jotted him a note and slipped it under a paperweight before grabbing her cashbox. A wave of dizziness hit her as she stood. *Not now.* She closed her eyes and leaned against the table for a moment.

"You okay?" Wesley asked.

"Yeah, just stood up too fast." She shouldered her bags and tucked the cashbox under her arm. "I'm good now. Let's go." She started toward the parking area, Wesley close behind.

DION BIT INTO HIS HAMBURGER. First thing he'd eaten today. His mom would have told him he was wasting his money coming here, and maybe he was. But it wasn't like she hadn't wasted all hers on drugs.

He'd hoped Lucky's foster parents might choose to come today, but although he'd gotten here early, he hadn't spotted his brother.

An ache formed in the pit of his stomach. Lucky shouldn't have to be in a stupid foster home. It would be almost four years before Dion could legally get him out of that system.

A large group with several children entered the festival area. Dion scanned each face. No Lucky. His shoulders sagged.

Two men split off at the tail end of the group and headed for an uncrowded area along the fence line. Dion straightened. What were Bernie and Lenny doing here?

Things were never good when they showed up.

Dion tugged his ball cap lower and sidestepped into a narrow opening between two tents, keeping his eyes on the men. Bernie leaned casually with his back against the fence as if enjoying the view. Or waiting for someone. A crowded family-friendly festival wasn't his usual stomping ground.

He turned his attention to the other man. About the same size and build as Bernie, Lenny's attempt to give off a carefree vibe fell a bit short. The average festivalgoer might not notice, but there was a subtle tightness in his shoulders and a hardness in his eyes that belied his easy grin. The man didn't talk much and had a reputation for being willing to do anything for a price. Dion would bet he was in Bernie's pocket.

Dion ate his burger slowly, as if savoring it, but he'd stopped tasting it the moment he caught sight of the two men. They were trouble.

After a few minutes, Bernie shifted, his eyes locking onto something. He nudged Lenny with his elbow.

Dion followed his gaze.

That redheaded chick who'd been with Eric at the park was heading for the exit with someone he didn't recognize. The two men waited until they passed before falling into step behind them.

Dion shoved the rest of the burger into his mouth.

This wasn't good.

He looked around for Eric. He knew Detective Thornton was here. He'd had to dodge him a few minutes ago to avoid being spotted.

Eric was nowhere in sight.

The small entourage passed through the exit. He didn't have time to find Eric. Not if he wanted to warn Allye of the danger she was obviously in.

He knew he shouldn't get involved. Bernie would kill him if he caused him trouble. But Allye had been kind to him the other day, and she obviously meant something to Eric. She didn't deserve whatever Bernie had in mind. He could at least see where they were going and pass on the information.

He jogged after them, dodging oblivious festival attendees on his way to the exit.

JUST OUTSIDE THE EXIT, Wesley stopped and slapped his forehead. "Hailey has the car keys."

"That's okay. I can drive." She'd planned to follow him in her car anyway.

"Do you mind? It'll take more time than we have to track her down in this crowd."

"No problem." She fished her keys from her purse and searched for her Jetta. "Did my mom say what exactly is going on?" All the things that could go wrong in a pregnancy shot through her mind.

"No, but she sounded panicked."

She cringed. Her mother's calm and collected demeanor flew out the window when danger threatened one of her kids. Allye couldn't blame her. None of them were prepared to lose another family member, even one they hadn't met yet. She finally spotted her car—three rows from where she thought she'd left it. She redirected them. As they walked, she looked toward the lane leading to a side road. Traffic was backed up as far as she could see on the way into the festival area, but the road out was clear.

"Are you sure you want to go with me? I'm probably okay in my car, and I can call Mom to meet me when I get to the hospital."

Wesley shook his head. "No guarantee of that. You know what happened to Corina when that stalker was after her."

A shiver ran through her. He was right, but she couldn't help another protest. "I hate to pull you away from time with your family. I know Hailey's been looking forward to today."

"She'll understand."

Yeah, she would, but that didn't mean she wouldn't be disappointed.

"She'd rather you be safe than have our afternoon uninterrupted," he said as if reading her mind. "I'll get an Uber back to Kincaid after you're settled and take Hailey out to dinner. We'll be okay."

Accept help. She pulled in a breath as they reached her Jetta. "Okay. Thank you." She stashed her cashbox under the driver's seat and climbed in.

Wesley checked his phone.

"Anything new?"

He shook his head. "No. Just letting Hailey know what's going on. Signal's low, so it probably won't go through until we hit the main roads." He tapped out a message as she started the car.

"Tell her I'm sorry."

"It's fine, Allye. Really."

"Thank you."

She retrieved her phone from her purse. Had Eric found her note yet? No notifications had come through, but she still had only one bar flickering in and out. She opened her text messages.

The phone was snatched from her hands.

"Hey!" She looked up as Wesley tossed her phone out the window. "What are you—"

The back passenger door popped open, interrupting her. A man slid inside. Her stomach bottomed out as she recognized the attacker from outside her studio.

He smirked at her. "Hello."

She plunged her hand toward her seat belt release, but Wesley caught her wrist. She stilled at sight of the gun in his other hand.

41

ERIC BALANCED A BOTTLE of Snapple peach tea and two brisket sundaes on top of a take-out style box from the food vendors. The lines had been long, as usual. But brisket sundaes and homestyle french fries were totally worth it.

Weaving his way through the crowds, he was headed back toward Tent B when a booming voice called his name. He turned to see Chief McHenry approaching him.

"I hear there was another disturbance at Allye Jessup's. What happened?"

Eric gave him the short version.

"Not good. Any evidence?"

He blew out a breath. "Not enough. A possible DNA specimen or two, and he left his gun behind."

"Description?"

"Suspect is tall and muscular, with a possible puncture wound in his upper torso or shoulder and a splitting headache."

The chief rubbed his mustache. "Interesting injuries."

"Allye stabbed him with a knitting needle, then took a baseball bat to his head."

Chief McHenry actually laughed. "Somebody picked a fight with the wrong gal."

Eric allowed himself a smile. He wouldn't have expected anything of the sort from petite Allye Jessup, but her quick thinking probably saved her life. He sobered. She could easily have been killed last night. He doubted she could have held out much longer on her own.

At least she was all right. And there were witnesses this time —and physical evidence. Whoever was after her had messed up.

McHenry's wife joined him. She offered a hello to Eric, then looked up at her husband. "The band is about to start."

The chief offered Eric a rueful smile. "Guess that means I need to get a move on. Keep me posted about the situation."

"Yes, sir." He'd have to figure out whether it was safe to share the details or if he'd need to keep things vague. But as the chief and his wife disappeared into the crowd and Eric continued on to the tent where Allye's booth was set up, he considered all he knew about the man. He just couldn't see him being involved. He'd have to think more on that later.

As soon as Eric stepped inside, he noticed Allye's empty booth. She was supposed to stay right there. He glanced around but didn't see her with any of the nearby vendors. Maybe she'd run to the restroom. He walked to the edge of the tent and looked toward the nearest restrooms. No line outside, so if she was in there, she should be out shortly. He waited a few minutes, but she didn't emerge. An uneasy feeling started prickling his gut as he returned to her booth.

The booth next to hers was unoccupied as well, so he crossed the aisle to the wood-carver.

"You happen to notice the photographer leaving?" He pointed with his thumb over his shoulder.

The guy nodded. "Yep." He peeled a layer of bark from a thick stick.

"Did you happen to hear where she was going?"

"Nope." Another strip of bark fell to the ground.

"Can you tell me what happened?"

"Some guy came up and talked to her for a minute, then she grabbed her cashbox and left with him."

"Did she seem upset?" Had someone forced her to leave?

He shrugged. "Dunno. They did seem to be in a hurry." He swiped at some wood shavings on the table. "The guy was acting kind of nervous."

"Nervous how?"

"Out of breath, glancing over his shoulder like he was afraid someone was watching him. Grabbed something off the table before he followed her out."

Not good. "When was this?"

"'Bout ten minutes ago, I guess."

"Which exit did they take?"

"The front." Wood-carver gestured with his knife toward the northeast opening Eric had just come back through.

"Thanks." Eric pulled out his phone and dialed Allye's number as he strode that direction. Immediately, her perky recording greeted him. Either her phone was off or she didn't have signal. He hung up and dialed again. Same thing.

"Hey."

He barely stopped in time to avoid plowing into Bryce as he and Corina rounded the corner to the entrance.

"Have you seen Allye?"

The couple's grins disappeared.

"She isn't here?" Bryce asked.

"No."

"We were on the way to check out her booth," Corina added.

"She was supposed to wait there while I grabbed lunch." Why had she left without telling him?

"Oh, Corina!" A woman Eric only vaguely recognized engulfed Corina in a hug. "What are you doing here?"

"Is there a reason I shouldn't be?" Lines formed between her brows.

"No, no, of course not. I just—well, I must have misheard."

"Misheard what?"

"I thought Wesley told Allye you were at the hospital. She left with him right after that."

"Are you sure?" Eric asked.

"They walked out together, yes. But obviously Corina is here, so I'm not sure who he was talking about."

"Did Allye say anything to you?" he pressed.

The woman shook her head. "I wasn't quite to her booth, and I don't think she noticed me."

"Bryce—" But Bryce already had his phone out. A moment later, he shook his head. "He's not answering." He dialed again, then growled. "Lost signal."

"Keep trying. I'm going to look for her."

Eric rushed from the tent and scanned the people milling about. Too many people. He glanced at his phone. Nothing from Allye.

"Eric!"

He stopped and searched for the voice. Male, not Allye. But with the crowd he couldn't quite place who . . . His gaze landed on Dion. "Where have you been?"

"Come on. Bernie took Allye." The teen started back toward the exit.

Eric jogged after him. "Dion, wait."

Dion glanced over his shoulder. "No time."

The words sliced at him. But he needed details. Needed to know where they were. How they'd gotten her. How many suspects they were up against. And what was Wesley's part in all this?

He broke even with the teen as they passed through the exit. "Who is Bernie?"

"Trouble."

"You know him?"

Determination slipped over his features. "Yeah."

"How?"

Dion didn't answer him, just kept running. Eric grabbed his shoulder. "How?"

Dion shrugged him off. "That's not what's important right now, man. You wanna save her or not?"

42

ALLYE STARED AT THE WEAPON in Wesley's hand. What was going on? She finally found her voice. "What are you doing?"

"What I have to." He didn't look as confident as he sounded, but the gun aiming her direction held steady. He released her hand. "Let's go."

She hesitated a moment longer. Would Eric realize what was happening? Could he get here in time? And would it do any good? She was sure they were both armed. It would be two to one.

Wesley waved the gun. "I said let's go."

Her attacker spoke up from the back seat. "Get going or I might have to start shooting. I can start with that family over there."

She looked at the couple who'd just exited their car with two little kids. Her attacker might be bluffing, but she couldn't risk it. She put the car in drive and prayed for help as she pulled from her parking spot.

As she turned onto the main road, pieces started falling into place. Wesley worked with Mayor Jennings. Mayor Jennings was involved somehow. And for some reason, they'd decided to eliminate her as a threat.

She was dead if she didn't come up with a way out of this. Could she wreck the car and run? She glanced at Wesley's gun. It was pointed directly at her side, and his finger rested on the trigger. If they wrecked, she'd almost definitely get shot. Even if she didn't, the only way she could outrun the men was if the collision knocked them both out. She had no way of guaranteeing that.

"Watch the road."

Allye tore her gaze from the weapon and yanked the car back into her lane. She tried to keep her voice calm. "What's going on?"

No one answered her.

"Does Hailey know about this?" She couldn't believe her cousin would be part of anything illegal. Much less part of a plot to hurt her.

"No. She doesn't know anything."

"What's she going to think once this all comes out? Because it will eventually."

Wesley didn't answer. He glanced in the mirror, and she followed his gaze. The man in the back seemed to be enjoying the show.

She couldn't do anything about that right now, but if she could get Wesley distracted, maybe she'd have a chance to try something.

"Hailey thinks you're her hero."

He refused to look at her.

"And what about Jenna? You really want her growing up knowing her dad is a killer?"

"Shut up."

"That's what you'll be if you pull the trigger."

"Do what I say, and I won't have to pull it."

"Then what do you plan to do with me once we get wherever we're going?" Because he sure wasn't planning to let her go.

"*I* don't plan to do anything with you."

"Who will then? Him?" She tilted her head to indicate the man in the back.

Wesley's lips compressed into a tight line.

"Why, Wes?"

He blew out a breath. "You're starting to get on my nerves. Just drive."

"This may be the last time I get to talk to someone in my family." She glanced at him from the corner of her eye. He flinched slightly at the last word. Maybe she could get through to him. "I still don't understand why you're involved with any of this. You're a great guy. You didn't kill that man behind my studio. Why are you risking everything to silence me?"

"Take a right here."

Allye slowed at the intersection, then turned.

"What are you doing?" Wesley yelled.

Allye jerked. "What you said."

"I told you to go right."

She blinked. Reimagined the intersection. She'd gone left. "I'm sorry. I got confused."

"Turn around. Now."

She pulled into a driveway and made a U-turn.

"Do not pull a stunt like that again."

"It wasn't a stunt. I'm not good with directions, and you holding that gun on me isn't helping."

He shifted the barrel slightly away from her. Not far enough.

A cop pulled off a side road and fell in behind her. Could she get his attention somehow?

"Don't even think about it."

She glanced in the rearview at her attacker.

"You get pulled over, I'll shoot the cop. You don't want blood on your hands."

"Do what Bernie says, Allye."

She looked at Wesley. Sweat dripped from his temple. He wasn't as okay with this as he was pretending to be. *Bernie.* She filed the name away.

The patrol car turned off at the next intersection. They continued on for another mile before Wesley indicated a gravel drive barely visible among the trees and overgrown weeds. "Turn here."

Allye took the turn and started down the drive. She tried not to panic as Wesley's gun bounced with every bump.

What appeared to be a hunting cabin came into view, and Wesley directed her to pull up in front of it. As soon as she put the car in park, Bernie got out. She watched him head for the cabin door and enter a code. Should she take her chances with Wesley and try to make a run for it?

As soon as the thought entered her head, another vehicle barreled down the lane and pulled behind her, blocking her in. A man she didn't recognize stepped out and lit a cigarette. Without sparing them a glance, he ambled toward a nearby shed and disappeared around the side.

She turned to Wesley, but before she could ask who the man was, her door flew open. Bernie grabbed her arm.

Allye yelped. "Let me get my seat belt off first." She slowly reached for the buckle, sending a quick glance around for some type of weapon. The only thing she saw was her keys. She started to reach for them as the seat belt released, but she wasn't fast enough. The man grabbed her arm again and hauled her out of the car and inside the cabin.

Once inside, he shoved her into a chair. "Don't move."

She rubbed her arm where he'd gripped it. She'd have a major bruise if she lived long enough for it to form.

Wesley dropped into a nearby chair and lowered his head into his hands. Should she try to get through to him? Though he seemed a willing participant in all this, he also didn't appear to like it. Maybe there was a chance she could convince him to escape with her.

She glanced at Bernie. The tastefully decorated cabin was small, but he'd gone to a kitchenette at the opposite side of the room, pouring himself a tumbler of some type of alcohol. If she kept her voice low, she should be able to communicate with Wesley without being overheard. But she needed to get on it. She didn't know what was going on, but she doubted she had much time.

Keeping her eyes on Bernie, she whispered, "Wesley." He didn't respond, so she tried again a little louder. "Wes."

He shook his head. At least that let her know he could hear her.

"Wes, I don't know how you got mixed up in all this or what's going on, but it's not too late to change your mind. We could use your gun to escape."

He finally looked at her. Grief filled his eyes. "I can't. I'm sorry, Allye, I really am. But I made some bad choices, and these guys have me over a barrel."

Allye tried to track what he was saying. Blackmail? Was that it? "Whatever they're holding over your head, we can figure it out. Even if you've done something illegal, it can't be as bad as being an accomplice to murder."

His jaw worked. "Believe me, if it were only that, I'd take my chances. But they—they threatened to kill Hailey and Jenna if I refused to bring you."

She gasped.

He broke eye contact and gave a pitiful shrug. "It's you or them."

She struggled to pull air into her lungs. Were Hailey and Jenna actually at risk? If so, she couldn't blame Wesley for choosing his wife and baby. She'd take their safety over her own any day. But would they ever be safe as long as these guys—whoever they were—had Wesley under their thumb? How long until they leveraged that threat again to force him to do something? Or harmed one of them to make a point?

"Those aren't your only options, Wes." She had to make him see that. "If we get out of here, we can work together to bring these guys down and make sure they can't hurt anyone." She let the words hang between them and sent up a silent prayer that he would listen.

Precious seconds ticked by. Finally, he took a deep breath and glanced at Bernie then back to her. "Maybe—"

The sound of tires on gravel interrupted him. Wesley's gaze shot to the front window. He stood and took a few steps toward it. His body went rigid as a car door slammed. Less than a moment later, the cabin door opened. A shadow fell into the room, but Wesley blocked her line of sight.

"Took you long enough to get here," Bernie said from the kitchenette.

"I had business to attend to."

Allye recognized the voice as the newcomer stepped into view.

"You?"

43

ERIC'S MIND RACED AS HE DROVE AWAY from the festival and farther into the country. He was following Dion's directions, and he prayed the teen knew what he was talking about.

"You're sure this is where they're taking her?" he asked again.

"Yes. Right before he got in her car, Bernie told one of his guys to meet him at location five."

He hoped he was right. As Dion directed him down another road, he radioed backup with the update. He'd be first on scene, but help would be close behind.

"What kind of place is this?" He needed to know what they were heading into.

"It's a cabin, like for hunting. It's right on the edge of the woods."

Most of the properties around here were on the edge of the woods, but not all of them had hunting cabins.

"Is there a house nearby?"

"Not within sight."

"Okay. How many rooms does this cabin have?"

"I dunno. I've never been inside. One of the other guys brought me out here once to pick up . . . stuff." Even though they'd already established that Eric knew he'd been involved in dealing, Dion still hedged around actually saying the word *drugs*. "I stayed in the car."

Eric glanced at him. The boy was risking everything to help save Allye. Eric didn't like taking him with him into danger, but he had little choice. Dion's knowledge of the drug ring's locations was their only hope of finding Allye quickly. And while Dion was confident he could get them there, he didn't know the address or street names.

Their only other recourse was to get a warrant to track Wesley's phone—and that would only help if Allye was still with him and they were in range. Eric knew in his gut that they didn't have time for that.

"Turn here."

Eric slammed on his brakes to avoid missing the turn. He noted the street name and called it in.

"We're close. Don't go too fast. The turn in is hard to see."

Please keep Allye safe. Let us reach her in time.

THOMAS MARSHALL grinned at Allye. "Surprise."

She gaped at the reporter. "You're involved with this? People have been overdosing—dying."

"Unfortunate, but not my fault." He shrugged. "I've taken reasonable steps to avoid unnecessary deaths. Dead druggies don't make good customers."

His callous dismissal turned her stomach.

"Oh, don't look so shocked."

She glanced at Wesley. He looked sick too, but when she caught his eye, he turned and strode to what she guessed was the bathroom. Her hope of enlisting his help crashed to the floor. She was on her own, and she needed to get her wits together. *God, please help me think—and send help!*

"Whad'ya want, Thomas?" Bernie called.

The reporter kept his eyes on her, an unsettling smile playing about his lips. "Bourbon."

"Coming right up."

"What about the man Bernie killed? Was he not profitable enough for you?"

Thomas didn't seem bothered by her question. "Now, *he* got what he deserved. As will you. I should have just let Bernie kill you then. Would have been much simpler."

"You were there?"

"Of course."

Realization dawned. "You were the man in the shadows."

"Bingo. I knew you couldn't have seen me well enough to identify me. But you saw Bernie, and I couldn't let my brother go down."

So they were brothers. Strange she'd never seen Bernie around before. Maybe he didn't live in Kincaid.

"So why didn't he kill me then?" The information might not matter at this point, but as long as he was still talking, he wasn't giving the order to kill her.

"Jennings heard you scream and interfered. He argued that killing you would draw too much attention. He had a point. You're too well-known and liked for no one to care if you disappeared or turned up dead." Thomas narrowed his eyes. "But you wouldn't let things go."

"Why the break-ins at my house?"

He waved a hand in the direction Wesley had disappeared. "The illustrious mayor and councilman orchestrated the first one. Fools thought if no one believed you, your testimony would be worthless. Insisted there was no reason to kill you." He sneered.

So they'd tried to save her. In their own messed-up way. She swallowed. "What about last night?"

His expression darkened. "You were going to meet with the forensic artist tomorrow. I couldn't let that happen, but Bernie sent an incompetent fool to snatch you last night instead of going himself like he should have."

Allye suppressed a shudder. "How do you know I'm supposed to meet with the artist tomorrow?"

"I saw your texts when you dropped your phone yesterday. Knew then that you had to go."

A toilet flushed, and Wesley returned to the main room. He didn't look her direction.

"People are still going to notice that I'm gone. They'll look for me—look for you when they find my body. You'll eventually be caught."

Allye jumped as Bernie plunked a glass down on the island that separated the sitting area from the kitchenette.

"Order up, Tom."

Thomas sauntered over and retrieved the drink, then returned his attention to Allye. "I'm touched by your concern, but that isn't an issue anymore. We've had a bit of time to plan over the last week. Bernie scouted out the perfect place to dispose of the evidence, and there's nothing connecting either of us to you."

"Thomas, we need to talk about this," Wesley said. "There's got to be another solution that doesn't involve murder."

Thomas turned on him. "Yeah, why don't we just have a tea party and discuss it? I'm sure she'll keep her mouth shut once she realizes we're a friendly lot."

"I'm being serious." He lowered his voice and took a step closer to Thomas.

Allye strained to hear his argument, but she couldn't make out the words. There was no mistaking the disdain on Thomas's face though. Wesley might be buying her a few extra minutes, but he wasn't going to convince this man of anything. *Please, God, send help.*

Wesley's voice rose slightly. "She's not stupid—she'll back off."

Thomas thrust his finger at Wesley's chest. "You're more of

an idiot than I thought. She knows too much." He swiveled to fully face Allye again. "And she has no intention of backing off."

"I—"

"Save your breath." He sliced a hand toward Wesley. The liquid in his glass sloshed over the rim. "She knows you're involved now. Knows *I'm* involved. You think for one minute she won't turn us all in?"

"Why *are* you here?" She couldn't figure out why he'd risk showing himself to her instead of just ordering a hit.

Thomas looked at her and grinned. The evil expression looked so like Bernie's that her stomach constricted even more than it already was. He lifted his glass to her in a toast. "No sense in wasting a good show."

Wesley paled, and Allye felt horror fill her. She remembered the victim behind her studio. Bernie had beaten him to death. While Thomas watched.

They weren't planning to shoot her.

44

BANGING ON THE DOOR pulled Allye from her shock. Thomas spun away from her and sidled up next to the window. He lifted an edge of the heavy plaid curtain, then yanked it back and cursed. He strode to the door and flung it open.

"What's he doing here?"

"Caught him poking around outside."

He cursed again. "Get him in here."

Allye half rose as Eric stepped inside, hands raised. The man who'd blocked her car in earlier was close behind him and held a gun to his back. *No.* Eric's eyes met hers, and she saw relief mixed with concern there.

Thomas pulled his own gun, which appeared to be equipped with a suppressor, and pointed it at Allye. "You, sit." She sank back into the leather wingback. He glared at the newcomers. "Was he alone?"

"Yes." The man's low voice was slightly familiar, but Allye couldn't place it.

Thomas's face smoothed somewhat, but he still looked massively irritated. He trained his gun on Eric. "Tie him up, Lenny."

The man produced zip ties from his pocket and quickly secured Eric's wrists behind his back, then shoved him to the floor.

Thomas lowered the gun and took a sip of the bourbon he still held. "Well, Allye. Looks like you don't have to die alone."

Bernie came up beside his brother. He cracked his knuckles. "I'm ready. Which one you want me to take first?"

"Take me," Eric said, struggling to his feet. His hands were still bound behind his back, but he squared his shoulders. "Or are you chicken?"

Eric, no! But she couldn't get the words past her throat. She watched in horror as Bernie's eyes darkened and he started toward him.

"No." Wesley's determined tone drew all eyes to him. He'd backed into the kitchenette and drawn his gun, which was now pointed at the ringleader. "This has gone far enough. Drop your gun, Thomas. Rest of you keep your hands where I can see them."

"Your family is dead," Bernie hissed. He took a step in Wesley's direction, which also brought him closer to Allye.

"Stop right there. I'm not afraid to pull the trigger." But the weapon trembled in Wesley's hands. Even from halfway across the room, Allye could see the sheen of sweat on his forehead.

"Don't be an idiot," Thomas said, his voice level. "We don't want your family dead, but you know as well as I do that these two have to go. They don't die, we're all going down—you included."

"Then I'm going down. I should have taken responsibility for my wrongs a long time ago. Now drop your gun. Now!"

"If you're sure that's what you want." Thomas started to lower his weapon. Then everything happened at once.

Bernie's hand shot out. Before Allye could move or even blink, he'd yanked her up in front of him and snaked his arm around her neck in one fluid motion.

She caught her breath as the barrel of Wesley's gun swung their direction.

A shot rang out.

Wesley went to his knees. Allye couldn't hold back her scream. Black specks intruded on her vision as dizziness kicked in, but not before she saw the blood beginning to spread across his shirt. Another shot, and Wesley crumpled.

A scuffle sounded behind her, and Bernie whipped them both around. Nausea joined the dizziness. Her vision darkened. *No!* She had to stay conscious and alert. She gripped the arm around her neck and blinked hard, fighting the urge to vomit.

Eric was on top of Lenny. He must have charged when the gunshots went off. But with his hands still bound behind him, he was no match for the other man.

Lenny slammed a fist against the side of Eric's head and shimmied out from under him. He stood, whipping out his gun. "Try that again, and I'll—"

The window near the door shattered. Bernie released Allye and shoved her away from him. She landed half on top of Eric.

"Watch them." Bernie raced to the window.

She shifted so she was beside Eric instead of practically in his lap. "What was that?" she whispered.

"Rock." He inclined his head toward a fist-size stone lying among the glass shards.

Thomas edged along the wall until he was standing next to his brother. "Who's out there?" he demanded.

"I don't see anyone," Bernie said.

The reporter cursed. "Well, get out there and look. That rock didn't throw itself. Lenny, you too. I'll watch them." He leveled his gun at Allye and Eric.

Bernie scowled but headed for the door, Lenny at his heels.

As the two men exited, Thomas moved closer to the window, angling his body to allow him to monitor the situation outside while keeping an eye on his hostages.

Allye exchanged a look with Eric. She was painfully aware that any attempt to escape could turn out very badly. The reporter had proven he had no issue with pulling the trigger. But this might be their last opportunity. She saw her own thoughts reflected in Eric's gaze.

He mouthed something. She couldn't make it out, but he glanced toward his side and mouthed the last word again. *Pocket.*

A quick glance confirmed Thomas was paying more attention to whatever was going on outside than to them. Feeling like every cell in her body was vibrating, she slipped her hand into the pocket Eric had indicated. Her fingers brushed a pocketknife. Quickly, she drew it out and hid it under a fold of her skirt. She thumbed it open. The blade locked into place with a soft click.

Her gaze shot to Thomas, but the man didn't seem to have heard. *It's okay. Deep breath.* Repeating the words silently to herself, she began inching backward until she could reach Eric's bound hands. He leaned forward slightly, and she tried to insert the tip of the blade between his wrists and the zip tie.

"Over there—he's behind the shed!"

Allye startled at Thomas's shout. Eric winced. She'd nicked him. Though he couldn't see her face, she still mouthed, *Sorry.* Willing her hands to stop trembling, she tried again.

The tie snapped just as a gunshot sounded. She almost dropped the knife but somehow managed to keep hold of it. Eric flexed his hands, then took it from her.

"You get him?" the reporter called to the men outside.

Bernie's curse floated through the broken window. "Yeah. It was that stupid kid."

"Dion," Eric breathed.

A sob rose in her throat. What was he even doing here?

"Make sure he's dead and get back in—" Sirens cut off Thomas's words. Gravel crunched as vehicles hit the driveway.

Gunfire erupted outside. Thomas took aim out the window.

"Take cover," Eric whispered. The next instant, he launched forward and tackled the reporter. They rolled, fighting for possession of the gun.

Allye scrambled to her feet and grabbed onto the back of the chair to steady herself. She had to help somehow. The gun went off, and she screamed. But the shot had gone wild.

More shots sounded from outside. Then everything went quiet—everything except Eric's grunting and Thomas's curses as they continued to wrestle for the gun.

The door burst open, and two county deputies rushed inside. They aimed their weapons at the men on the floor. "Stop! Police!" Thomas let out a feral scream and threw Eric off. He swung the gun toward the deputies as Eric rolled out of the way.

Allye dropped behind the chair and slapped her hands over her ears as several more shots filled the air. Deathly silence followed. When she dared to peek around the edge of the makeshift barrier, Thomas lay unmoving on the ground. Eric knelt beside him, checking for a pulse. He shook his head.

"This one's still alive!" The shout came from the other side of the room. "Get a stretcher in here!"

Not trusting her legs to hold her, Allye crawled around the chair and looked for the owner of the voice. One of the deputies was bent over Wesley, applying pressure to his chest. How was he still alive?

Eric rose, wiping blood from his busted lip. His gaze found her. "Are you okay?"

She nodded, unable to speak.

"I have to check on Dion."

"Go," she whispered to his retreating back. Her gaze fell on Wesley again. *Lord, please let them both be okay.*

45

ERIC DID NOT HAVE HIS REPORTS SUBMITTED by Monday morning.

After spending most of yesterday serving warrants to search the devices, homes, and offices of the men involved in Allye's kidnapping, he and Chief McHenry were holed up in the police station conference room, combing through the evidence.

Eric flipped another page on his notepad and clicked his pen before finishing his sentence. If he kept going at this rate, his reports were going to be backlogged for a month. He stifled a sigh. Fat chance McHenry would allow that.

Considering the events of the weekend and their current priorities, the chief had been understanding of his tardiness so far, though he nearly took Eric's head off for allowing a minor to accompany him into a hostage situation. He'd cooled down somewhat once Eric explained that Dion had been instructed to remain in the car, which Eric had left parked in the weeds at the far end of the long drive so he could safely approach on foot.

Unfortunately, Dion had ignored him and followed anyway. When he saw Eric get jumped and then heard the gunshots, he'd attempted to distract the men by throwing a rock through the window. And he'd taken a bullet to the shoulder for it. Eric and

Allye had spent the evening in the hospital waiting room while the teen underwent surgery. He'd lost a lot of blood, but he'd come out of surgery all right and was expected to fully recover with a little TLC.

Bernie had also undergone surgery to treat the gunshot wounds he'd received during the shoot-out. Barring some unforeseen complication, he should survive to stand trial, and Eric couldn't wait to see him behind bars.

Thomas had been pronounced dead at the scene, as had Lenny. And Wesley? He was hanging on by a thread. His prognosis wasn't hopeful, and the doctors had warned Hailey that he probably wouldn't make it another night.

By all indications, Thomas Marshall had been the brains of the local drug ring. Bernie had served as manager and primary enforcer while Thomas orchestrated everything behind the scenes. Despite everything they'd discovered so far, Eric hadn't quite pinpointed what Wesley's part had been or how many other players there were, but he hoped to find an answer to that somewhere in these files.

Mayor Jennings's role also puzzled him. As it turned out, the hunting cabin belonged to him. But so far, nothing indicated that he'd given permission for its use or that he'd been aware of Saturday's activities. According to Allye's statement though, Thomas had claimed the mayor and Wesley had both been involved in trying to gaslight her. But why? And could it be proven? Without further evidence, it was just hearsay.

Eric clicked his pen as he skimmed through more of the reporter's computer files. If they hadn't already suspected the mayor, he might be inclined to agree with McHenry's opinion that Thomas had been blowing smoke. But from where he sat, something smelled fishy.

"If you click that pen one more time, I'm going to confiscate it," Chief growled from the other side of the conference room table.

"Sorry." Eric put the pen in his pocket. He stood and stretched. They'd been at it for hours and still had a ton of work to do. He poured himself another cup of coffee from the ten-cup pot he'd made an hour ago. Looked like he'd need to brew another soon.

Sipping the steaming liquid, he returned to his seat and clicked on another file folder. He straightened. This was interesting. He read the contents of the folder more carefully, then clicked on the accompanying photos. This might just be the proof he was looking for.

He glanced at the chief. Did he trust him? He decided that he did. McHenry had always been a by-the-book guy. Until he had reason to believe otherwise, Eric would give him the benefit of the doubt.

He drew in a breath. "Chief, I think you need to see this."

McHenry circled the table to read over Eric's shoulder. A minute later, he hung his head. Eric hated this for him.

The chief straightened. "You know what you have to do. Do your research, make sure this is real."

Eric nodded. "Yes, sir." He'd do the double-checking, but he was pretty sure they both knew this was real.

THREE DAYS LATER, Eric watched a squad car pull away from Mayor Jennings's house with the mayor cuffed in the back seat.

After a lot of digging and double-checking, Eric had built quite a case against him. Though Mayor Jennings had maintained his innocence when first confronted, Eric had done his homework—or rather, Thomas Marshall had.

The man had caught Jennings and Wesley in a shady business deal several years ago. He'd blackmailed the mayor into letting them use his cabin as a drop point while separately blackmailing Wesley into manipulating certain of the city funds. Each time they acquiesced to his demands, he added the new action to his blackmail files. He'd eventually begun extorting them both as well.

When confronted with the mound of evidence, Jennings finally cracked. His confession filled in most of the blanks they were missing.

He admitted to gaslighting Allye to destroy her credibility in hopes that would satisfy the Marshalls. It had started as a spur-of-the-moment solution when he'd saved her from Bernie that first night. And then when Wesley overheard her conversation with Hailey and how she was afraid she might be starting to hallucinate, the two men had concocted the scheme to break into her house with the green glow.

Because of the high risk of Allye recognizing Wesley's voice, they'd hired Lenny, already a part of the Marshall brothers' ring, to pose as Bernie. Wesley had let him in with her spare key, orchestrated the lighting, then locked Allye out—retreating through the back door and replacing her key where it belonged when they were finished.

They thought they'd found the perfect solution to the problem. Until Marco's body was found, and things quickly began spiraling out of Jennings's control.

Under pressure from Thomas and Bernie, the mayor was also the one who shot Allye's camera and sent the threats about her family as a last-ditch effort to keep her quiet. He still claimed he hadn't been aware of the attempt on her life at his cabin though. They might never know for sure about that.

Once the squad car disappeared from view, Eric started his engine. He was taking the rest of the afternoon off.

He called Allye and let her know he was on the way to pick her up for Wesley's funeral. Five minutes later, he was opening the passenger door for her to climb in.

"It's done?" she asked when he was back in the driver's seat.

"Yeah." He released a long breath. "He still has to go to trial, but the case against him is solid. Jennings will be going away for a while."

She sniffled, and Eric squeezed her hand. He knew she had mixed feelings about the mayor.

In a way, Eric did too. Jennings had carried a heavy load for a long time, and by all indications, he truly had tried to protect Allye. But when it came down to it, he was responsible for his actions. And those actions nearly cost Allye her life—*had* cost other lives, albeit indirectly.

"I have some other good news. We think we caught the other guy who broke into your house."

"Really?" Her eyes brightened.

"Yep. We asked the nearby hospitals to keep an eye out for someone with his description and injuries. He showed up at the ER last night, trying to get antibiotics for his shoulder. We were able to get there before he disappeared again." The man had apparently tried to take care of the wound himself and ended up with a raging infection—but Allye didn't need to know that detail, and Eric didn't plan to tell her. Instead, he whispered, "You're safe now."

With her hand still clasped in his, he pulled onto the road and headed for the church.

ONLY A FEW CARS WERE IN THE LOT when they arrived at the church. Blindsided not only by her husband's death but by what he'd been involved in, Hailey had requested a semiprivate funeral. Family were gathered here, but few others had been informed of the arrangements.

Allye blinked back tears through the service. Wesley had been friend as much as family, and like with Mayor Jennings, she found her feelings toward him now were a jumbled mess. In the end, he'd tried to do what was right. That didn't excuse his prior actions—not by a long shot—but it helped ease the sting a little. She could choose to focus on that.

After the service, they joined the procession to a cemetery just outside of town. As Eric pulled into a parking space and got out to get her door, Allye eyed the small group beginning to take their seats under an awning. Hailey was already in the front row, sitting with shoulders rigid just as she had during the funeral. Allye's heart broke again for her cousin.

Eric opened her door, and she allowed him to help her out of the car. She wobbled.

"You okay?" He wrapped an arm around her waist to help steady her.

She blew out a frustrated breath. "Yeah, I just need a second."

"We've got time." He held her until she felt stable, and she relished his nearness. She almost hated to tell him she was ready. But they needed to join the others. He seemed to feel the same, and instead of releasing her, he took her hand in his for the short walk.

Just as the minister began speaking, they slipped into the seats next to her mom. Mom's gaze fell on their clasped hands. Allye didn't miss the hint of satisfaction that flickered through the grief clouding her eyes.

After the brief service ended, Eric leaned toward her. "Do you two need some time?"

"Maybe just a few minutes?"

"I'll be back." He pressed a light kiss to her temple and then slipped away.

She watched him join a group of men that included Bryce, their uncle, and Corina's dad. Then she turned to her mom again.

"You doing okay?" Mom asked before she could say anything.

"Going to need some ibuprofen when I leave," she admitted.

"Migraine?"

"Not quite to that level yet. I took something before we left." She'd known the tears would set her back. She glanced at the tissue balled in her mom's hand. "Are *you* okay?" She didn't mean about Wesley—well, partly, but more about everything.

She had hoped to break the news about Jennings to her mom privately at home, but Kincaid's grapevine was alive and strong. One of the mayor's neighbors had witnessed his arrest and called her right after it happened. Mom had asked Eric for confirmation when he and Allye arrived at the church, but there hadn't been time for anything more.

Mom didn't immediately respond to her query, and Allye could hardly bear the sadness in her expression.

"You don't have to answer," she whispered.

A tear escaped her mom's lashes, but she managed a smile. She drew in a long, ragged breath, then gave Allye's hand a quick squeeze. When she started to pull away, Allye held on.

Mom looked at their hands. "I really have been trying not to be clingy since . . ." Since finding out Allye was almost killed. She didn't need to finish the sentence.

"It's okay. And maybe . . . maybe I could use a bit of clinginess for a while too."

Her mom chuckled, then sobered again. "I know you're wondering how the news about Raymond affected me. On top of almost losing you. On top of Wesley's death."

"And on top of old grief," she said quietly.

"I won't lie and say it doesn't hurt. All of it. I really thought our relationship was heading somewhere, and his betrayal is hard to swallow. But"—she squeezed Allye's hand again—"I still have you and Bryce and Corina, and we still have the Lord. Our family will be all right. But please don't keep any more secrets from me— even if you think you're protecting me. We need each other."

"You're right. And I'm done with secrets."

"Good." After a long moment, her mom nodded toward where Hailey stood alone at her husband's casket, saying her good-byes. "She's going to need us too—and that is not permission for you to overdo things."

"I promise to pay attention to my limits," Allye conceded. "Or at least try to."

Mom just shook her head. "I think someone else needs you right now though."

Allye followed her gaze. Eric had wandered away to a grave nearer the center of the cemetery. His posture looked . . . vulnerable. She stood.

"You okay to walk it on your own?"

"I'm okay. It's just the first couple seconds that get me sometimes. See you at Bryce's for dinner?"

"I'll be there."

Allye made her way to Eric and slipped her arm through his. She read the small granite grave marker. "I didn't realize your dad was buried here," she said softly.

When he spoke, his voice was rough. "I haven't been here since his funeral fifteen years ago. Even when I came to visit Gramps or Officer Mike, I refused to even look this direction."

"Then you're making progress."

He shrugged. "I still don't understand why he chose his addictions over me. Guess I never will."

Allye leaned into him, and he put his arm around her. She didn't say anything, just let him work through his emotions.

Finally, he said, "I know I need to forgive him, but I don't know if I can. I'm still angry at him—at both my parents."

"You don't have to do it alone. Someone smart told me that once."

"I don't think he was talking about forgiveness."

She shrugged one shoulder. "Still applies. Sometimes being willing to ask for help goes a long way. And I doubt God will tell you no about that."

After a long pause, he cleared his throat. "You're good for me, Allye Jessup."

"Feeling's mutual."

Epilogue

Six months later

ERIC TOSSED A BASEBALL across his backyard. It plopped into Lucky's outstretched glove and promptly rolled out. He hid a smile as the boy dove after it like he thought it would disappear. Although it had taken Lucky weeks to let his guard down, he'd finally begun emerging from his shell.

"Gotta use your hand to keep it in—like you're putting a lid on," Dion called from another corner of the yard. "Like this." He mimed catching a fly ball.

"I did!" Lucky tossed the ball back to Eric. It landed several feet away and rolled toward him. He scooped it up and launched it toward Dion.

The teen had made a full recovery from the bullet he'd taken to the shoulder, though he'd have a lifelong scar to remind him of his injury. He'd had to appear in court for his part in the drug deals, but because of his age and circumstances, along with Eric's testimony of his assistance in bringing down the higher-ups, the judge had been lenient. There would be a lot of community service hours in his near future, but he wouldn't serve any time, and his record would be sealed once he turned eighteen. In the meantime, he was finally getting the chance to be a kid for a while.

There were still occasional reminders of the trauma they'd experienced, but both brothers were flourishing under Eric's care—with the help of the community that had rallied around them.

After the events of last fall, Eric had realized he had a lot of reevaluating to do. He spent some serious time in prayer and felt a peace about stepping into the world of fostering. And while he still knew he couldn't do it alone, he'd decided to see what kind of help God would provide if he was willing to ask for it. The response had been overwhelming.

Chief McHenry had helped him reevaluate his work schedule and priorities. Bryce and Corina, Allye, and even Mrs. Jessup had insisted on going through the background checks and training required to offer respite care. And as soon as he expressed a renewed interest in fostering, Tracy Ann had thrown her arms around his neck in a quick hug, then immediately started connecting him with all sorts of resources he hadn't had any idea existed.

"Knock, knock." The backyard gate swung inward, and Allye stepped through, bags and pizza boxes in hand.

Lucky raced toward her, the game forgotten. Before Allye had a chance to set her load on Eric's patio table, he'd thrown his arms around her legs.

Grinning, Eric joined them and relieved her of the boxes so she could return Lucky's embrace—which she did wholeheartedly. Then just as quickly as he'd come, the boy released her and dashed back to his position. Allye's eyes sparkled as she watched him wave his glove at Dion, signaling he was ready for another pitch.

"I think someone likes you." Eric snatched a quick kiss before tugging her to a seat at the table. "How are you feeling today?"

She shrugged. "Tired, but not too bad."

After her neighbor's home testing kit had indicated a strong mold presence in their duplex, Allye had undergone lab testing for mold toxicity. The results were overwhelmingly positive. She'd moved in with her mom until she could find a safer place of her own and was currently working with a practitioner to detox her body. Besides the direct symptoms related to her body's reaction to the mycotoxins, there was a strong possibility the exposure had triggered other long-term issues that might or might not subside.

But she was taking everything in stride with a grace Eric admired. And while the experience hadn't been pleasant, she was improving. And she'd kept her word to ask for help when she needed it.

Dion lobbed the ball to his brother, and Lucky finally managed to catch it.

Dion pumped his fist. "Yeah, man!"

Lucky turned to see if they were watching. Eric gave him a thumbs-up and shouted, "Good one!" The kid's face broke into the widest grin he'd seen from him yet.

"Looks like they're having the time of their lives here," Allye murmured.

"Them and me both."

"I'm so glad you were able to take them."

"Me too." They needed to start in on the food before it got cold, but he had something he wanted to discuss with Allye in private first. Keeping his eyes on the boys, he lowered his voice. "I'd like to make things permanent."

She turned to face him, her eyes glowing. "You're considering adoption?" She matched his tone, but there was no mistaking the excitement there.

"What do you think?"

"It's a wonderful idea! Have you mentioned it to them yet?"

He shook his head. "I wanted to get your take on it first."

"I think you should go for it if they're okay with the idea."

"You wouldn't mind dating a guy with two kids?"

She lightly socked his shoulder. "I thought I already was. Seriously, Eric, I love those boys. And they need a good dad like you."

"That's one of the reasons I love you."

She blushed, but before she could respond, the boys were running toward them.

Dion dropped his glove on the table and plopped into a chair. "Time to eat yet? I'm starving."

"I'm starving too!" Lucky echoed.

"Why don't the three of you go wash your hands, and I'll get everything set up," Allye suggested. Eric cocked an eyebrow at her, and she gave him an impish grin. "Yes, you too."

"Yes, ma'am." He rose and winked at the boys. "You heard the lady." They groaned but followed him inside without protest.

When they returned, Allye had pulled paper plates, napkins, and a small container from one of her bags. She offered them each a plate, and the boys dove into the pizza.

"No pizza for you?" Eric asked as she opened the other container and lifted a fork.

"I have to avoid cheese as part of the detox diet. Mold." She wrinkled her nose.

He lowered his slice of pizza. "I'm sorry. I didn't even think about that." When Allye had called with the offer to bring dinner, he'd just chosen what he thought would be easiest for her.

She waved her fork at him. "Don't you dare stop enjoying your pizza because I can't have it right now. My leftovers are more than fine, and picking up pizza for you guys was a lot easier than preparing a meal." She redirected the conversation and soon had Lucky giggling at knock-knock jokes while Dion and Eric groaned appropriately.

As the sun sank lower in the sky, the temperature began to drop. Soon it was uncomfortably cool, and they relocated inside to watch a movie.

Lucky insisted Allye take the middle of the couch so he and Eric could both sit by her, and less than halfway through the film, he'd fallen asleep with his head on her lap. Eric exchanged a grin with her. He loved that the boys were becoming so comfortable here.

When the movie ended, Dion scooped up his brother and carried him to bed, but Allye lingered.

Eric stroked her hair. She fit so well nestled next to him. "You know what we were talking about earlier?"

"Mm-hmm?"

"I had another idea I wanted to run past you."

"Hmm?"

She sounded drowsy. Should he wait for a better time? But it had already taken him a week to get up his nerve.

He took a deep breath and dug in his pocket. "What if, instead of *me* adopting the boys, *we* adopted them?"

Her head spun toward him so fast, he would have laughed if he hadn't been so nervous. When she caught sight of the ring box in his hand, her eyes rounded.

He slipped off the couch and knelt in front of her. "I can't promise you a perfect life or even an easy one, but I can promise to love you with all my heart, to be faithful in sickness and in health, to admit when I'm wrong, and to stand by your side through life's trials if you'll let me. Will you marry me, Allye?"

Tears shimmered in her eyes. "Nothing would make me happier."

"Is that a yes?"

"It's an emphatic, one-thousand-times-over-every-day-for-the-rest-of-our-lives yes."

He placed the ring on her finger and sealed their engagement with a kiss. He held her close, her cheek against his. "I love you, Allye Jessup," he murmured.

"I love you too. So very much." She turned her face for another kiss, and he gladly obliged.

If you enjoyed *Shadowed Witness*,
keep reading for a
sneak peek of the last book in

THE SECRETS OF KINCAID
SERIES

Available summer of 2026

1

SOMETHING WASN'T RIGHT.

Hailey Nieland frowned at the spreadsheet on her left computer monitor. She compared it to the statement on the screen to her right.

The final numbers on both were close, but there appeared to be several more transactions on the second document than on the first.

She blew out a frustrated breath and took a sip from her bottled water. This was the third set of records she'd found anomalies in.

If she'd known how much trouble this account would be, she wouldn't have campaigned so hard to have it added to her client list. But when her coworker Frank Pierce succumbed to a heart attack last week, her boss had been scrambling to divvy up his clients among their remaining CPAs.

In truth, Hailey would prefer a slightly lighter load so she could spend more time with her daughter, but as a new widow and first-time single mom, she needed the extra income. And Eukaria Investments was a major catch.

It had been hard diving back into the workforce. While she'd kept her CPA certification up to date, she'd hoped to remain a stay-at-home mom at least until Jenna entered elementary school. All that had changed with her husband's unexpected death last year.

At the thought of Wesley, her hand clenched, making the water bottle crackle. Would there ever come a time when she'd be able to remember him without instantly feeling the double slap of grief and anger?

She set the bottle on her desk, resisting the urge to take her frustration out on it. If she were home and not in her office cubicle, surrounded by coworkers, the thing would be mangled already. Instead, she took a deep breath, held it, then let it out slowly.

With effort, she refocused on the problem at hand. The sooner she got this done, the sooner she could head to her parents' to pick up Jenna. Her almost-two-year-old had adjusted to their new routine, and Hailey's mom loved the opportunity to spend more time with her granddaughter, but Hailey hated how much she was missing of her little girl's early years.

"Staying late again?"

Hailey started at the caustic voice behind her. She'd been too focused to notice Stefania approach. Her eyes drifted to the corner of the computer screen. Five twenty. It wasn't that late.

"Just finishing up a few things."

Stefania leaned her hip against the edge of Hailey's desk. "Gleason's gone. You can drop the industrious act."

Hailey's cheeks burned, but she kept her eyes on her work. "I've got a full load right now." As soon as the words left her mouth, she regretted them. Stefania had been livid that Eukaria Investments had been added to Hailey's client list. The entire office had witnessed the explosion when she heard the news.

"Eukaria Investments should have been mine." Though she couldn't see Stefania's face, the bite in her tone was unmistakable.

"That was Gleason's call."

"And he shouldn't have made that decision while I was on

vacation. If I'd been here to put my bid in, you know it would have gone to me."

Hailey wasn't convinced of that, but there was no sense arguing. The decision had been made.

She turned to face her coworker. "Is there something I can help you with? I'd really like to finish what I'm doing so I can get home to my daughter."

The woman rose to her full height. "Of course." She took a step away, then called over her shoulder, "I forget you don't have a husband to help with things." Disdain dripped from every word, leaving no doubt of the intent behind them.

Hailey managed to bite back her retort, unwilling to let on how much the barb had stung. Cheeks aflame, she spun her chair back to face the desk and stared determinedly at the screens until the office door swished shut, muting the sound of Stefania's clip-clopping heels.

She forced herself to breathe slowly as she waited to make sure her coworker wasn't coming back. The clock on her monitor tracked one minute. Two. When it hit three, she lowered her still-burning face into her hands. She couldn't cry. Wouldn't give Stefania that victory.

But pointed references to Wesley's betrayal and criminal activity hurt. And while Stefania was the only one in the office who freely tossed those verbal grenades, cloaked as they were in language their boss would view as harmless, Hailey knew Stefania wasn't the only one who disliked, or at least distrusted, her because of her husband's actions. Actions she'd had no knowledge of until it was too late.

Again pushing away thoughts of Wesley, she attempted to make sense of the spreadsheet, but her focus was blown. The numbers weren't adding up, and her frustration grew by the minute. Finally, she closed out the document and logged off the computer. All she was doing was wasting time. Maybe things would make more sense in the morning.

She stood and slipped her purse over her shoulder before heading to the break room to grab her lunch bag. On her way back, she gave the office a quick scan. The place was empty. Apparently, no one else had felt the need to stay late today. That meant she was responsible for turning out the lights.

Lunch bag in hand, she flipped the switch by the door, leaving only the dim overnight lights on, and stepped out into the hallway. She let the door close, then gave it a gentle tug to make sure it had latched properly behind her. The one-way locks engaged at five p.m., shutting out everyone without an access badge, but the door had been known to stop before the latch engaged, leaving the office accessible overnight.

Satisfied she wouldn't be the one in hot water for a preventable security breach, she turned and headed for the elevator. The hallway was deserted, her own footsteps the only sound marring the quiet. The darkened insurance office across the hall seemed empty as well. The whole place felt eerie.

Which was ridiculous. She'd been here after closing plenty of times and never had a problem. She shook off the odd feeling and punched the down button for the elevator.

As the elevator car took its sweet time rising to the third floor, her mind wandered to the spreadsheets she'd left behind. She found it hard to believe Frank had made so many mistakes. The impression she'd had of the man indicated he was almost ridiculously meticulous. But he hadn't been the same after his wife left him. Perhaps the stress had affected his work as well as his health.

The elevator finally dinged, and she entered as soon as the doors were open. She leaned against the wall and closed her eyes for the short ride to the first floor. Stefania's words replayed in her mind, and she fisted her hands. It wasn't fair that she and Jenna had to suffer the repercussions of Wesley's choices. Her little girl was too young to understand the full implications or be bullied over it, but she'd missed her daddy for a long time, and now she'd have to grow up without him.

And there was nothing Hailey could do about it.

The elevator slowed, and she straightened, putting on her game face. If by chance Stefania was still around, Hailey wasn't about to appear the least bit vulnerable. After an interminable moment, the car came to a shuddering stop. Another long moment later, the doors opened. Hailey strode into the lobby, casting a quick glance around.

She needn't have worried about being seen. The lobby was empty, and the darkened business fronts indicated everyone else had closed up shop and gone home on schedule. If she didn't know better, she'd think she was the sole occupant of the building. But the property owner paid for on-site security—a must with the kind of businesses set up here. At minimum, there was one security guard on duty at all times.

She cleared the double doors at the main entrance, again waiting for the confirmatory click, then hurried toward the side lot primarily used by employees. As she rounded the building, two lone vehicles confirmed her suspicions about being essentially alone. Bypassing what she assumed was the security guard's SUV, she headed for the back corner space where she'd left her Explorer.

Once she got inside, she'd call her mom. Let her know she was on the way. If Mom invited them to stay for supper like she usually did, she might take her up on the offer. After today, she didn't want to even think about cooking. And Thursdays were usually spaghetti night at her parents' house. Jenna would be thrilled. While Hailey wouldn't relish the inevitable task of trying to get sauce out of her daughter's clothes, it would be worth it.

Her lips lifted at the thought of Jenna's impish grin shining through a smear of spaghetti sauce, and she picked up her pace. But a few feet from the vehicle, she pulled up short, her smile fading. The Explorer tilted heavily to the left, and she hadn't parked on a hill.

She groaned. The rear driver's side tire was completely flat.

She hadn't noticed any issues this morning. Must have run over a nail or something.

Huffing out a breath, she dug out her key fob and popped the hatch. Thanks to her dad's insistence that she drive prepared, she carried a mini air compressor with her. She'd be able to air up the tire for long enough to get to her parents' so her dad could take a closer look at it.

She exchanged her lunch bag for the compressor and circled to the driver's side to plug it into the cigarette lighter. Again, she stopped in her tracks.

Not one, but both of her driver's side tires had been slashed, and a black-lettered message was scrawled across the windows.

GO AWAY

Author's Note

Dear reader,

Thank you for joining me for another adventure in small-town Kincaid. While Kincaid itself is a fictional town, it is loosely based on Falmouth, Kentucky, and locals will recognize the annual Kentucky Wool Festival located next to the very real Kincaid Lake State Park. I took a few creative liberties to fit the story, but I hope you'll still enjoy a peek at my beloved Pendleton County. And if you're ever in the area during the first weekend in October, I highly recommend you stop by to enjoy the Wool Fest.

During the writing of *Shadowed Witness*, I, like Allye, have been dealing with major health issues, and I know many of you probably are as well. For all of my fellow spoonies, I hope Allye's story is an encouragement to continue to cling to our faithful God no matter how long the journey or severe the symptoms. And may we remember the promise He gave the Apostle Paul: "My grace is sufficient for you, for my power is made perfect in weakness" (2 Corinthians 12:9).

Discussion Questions:

1. For a long time, Allye chose not to tell her family about her struggles because she didn't want to be a burden to them. Do you ever struggle to ask for help?

2. Eric felt called to become a foster parent but was afraid he couldn't do it in his current life season. Can you think of a situation where God called you to step out in faith and do something you felt ill-equipped for?

3. In the midst of serious health concerns, Allye determined she would continue trusting God, no matter what. How do you tend to react when facing major life issues?

4. Eric was reprimanded for neglecting some of his lesser cases in favor of the big ones. Do you think this was fair? What are some ways to deal with an overwhelming list of responsibilities?

5. When Allye finally shared about everything going on in her life, she felt like a weight had lifted from her. Have you ever been burdened by a secret?

6. When Eric was struggling to forgive his parents for the pain their addictions caused him, Allye reminded him that he didn't have to do it alone. How have you dealt with situations where you needed to forgive someone who hurt you deeply?

Angela Carlisle resides in the hills of northern Kentucky and is a member of American Christian Fiction Writers and The Christian PEN. Angela is an editor by day and prefers to spend her free time reading, baking, and drinking ridiculous quantities of hot tea. Her unpublished works have won awards in ACFW's Genesis and First Impressions contests and placed in the Daphne du Maurier contest. Her shorter fiction works, including the prize-winning flash-fiction piece "Mansion Murderer," have appeared in *Splickety* and *Spark* magazines. Learn more at AngelaCarlisle.com.

Sign Up for Angela's Newsletter

Keep up to date with Angela's latest news on book releases and events by signing up for her email list at the link below.

AngelaCarlisle.com

FOLLOW ANGELA ON SOCIAL MEDIA

Angela Carlisle   @AngelaCarlisleWriter

Be the first to hear about new books from Bethany House!

Stay up to date with our authors and books by signing up for our newsletters at

BethanyHouse.com/SignUp

FOLLOW US ON SOCIAL MEDIA

   @BethanyHouseFiction